DARK DESCENT

THE ARONDIGHT CODEX - BOOK ONE

NICOLE R. TAYLOR

1

"Scarlett, you have to hide, okay?"

I stared up at my mummy, my bottom lip trembling.

"It'll be okay, I promise," she said glancing over her shoulder. "Stay very quiet, and I'll be back soon." She smoothed her hand through my hair and smiled. "You're so brave, sweetie."

I whimpered as she closed the lid of the big black metal box I was sitting in. I curled up in the dark, thrust my thumb into my mouth, and started to suck. *Mummy looked scared*, I thought. *But Daddy is with her. Daddy is a hero. Everyone says so.*

The sound of banging and muffled voices echoed from outside the box, and I began to cry as my hiding place shuddered, then lay still.

"Mummy?" I called out, my voice barely a whisper. When she didn't answer, I tried again. "*Mummy?*"

The lid of the box opened, and I cowered in the corner as a man appeared. He stood over me, smiling. I didn't know who he was, but he looked mean.

"Here she is," he said to someone I couldn't see. "C'mon, sweetheart." He reached out and grasped me under my arms, then plucked me from my hiding place.

As I was lifted out of the box, I saw Mummy and Daddy lying on the ground. They were covered in red stuff, and their eyes were open like they were staring at the sky. They didn't blink, not even once.

"*Mummy!*" I shrieked, fear rising in my belly. "*Daddy!*"

"Shut up, you little brat," the man growled, his eyes rolling into the back of his head until only the whites showed. "They're dead, and you will be too if you don't be quiet."

"*No!*" I screamed, not understanding how my four-year-old mind knew dead meant forever.

The man's hands dug painfully into my sides as he shook me. "Shut up, you little shit!"

I screamed in terror and squirmed in his arms, trying to get away from the scary man.

"Stop it," he said, his voice sounding strange. "Don't make me hurt you."

I thrashed harder, and he dropped me, my backside landed painfully on the ground. The man towered over me, his eyes glowing red and his jaw opened wide, exposing rows upon rows of scary, sharp teeth.

"I warned you," he said, reaching out with his clawed hand.

I screamed as a flash of purple light enveloped everything.

I blinked, shaking off the unwanted memory that I'd always assumed was of my parents' death. I don't know what had happened after the man had dropped me—the recollection always stopped there.

Steadying myself against the bar, I took a deep breath and glanced around the pub. Twenty years later, and I still didn't know what any of it meant, let alone whether any of it was real.

It was quiet today, and my shift had been agonisingly slow, which probably accounted for the daydreaming. *More like day-nightmaring*, I thought.

Arcade games were flashing and beeping in the back, retro tabletop games lit up a bank of tables in front of the bar, and the wall behind me was bright with LED pixelated video game characters. A graffiti-style mural of the pub's logo was on the opposite side, surrounded by more characters, though I recognised these—Mario, Yoshi, Donkey Kong, and that mushroom guy, Toad.

8-bit was a gamer pub—a place grownups went to pretend to be adults while really they wanted to relive their days in front of their Commodore 64s. Video games upon video games, alcohol, the entire city's nerd population, and a constant stream of tourists. What could go wrong?

Nestled deep within the markets in Camden Town, London, *8-bit* was a part of the alternative mecca of the city. You could find anything at the markets. Black-lit raver shops with furry day-glo leg warmers, poufy rockabilly dresses with cherries and swallows on them, Asian food by the wok-ful, leather handicrafts, vintage markets, goth and cyberpunk fashion, and punks. *Lots* of punks with scarily big mohawks. With my unnatural purple-tinged locks, scarred mentality, and love for tight black jeans and combat boots, I fit right in.

I slumped against the counter, my chest constricting. Luckily for me, only a few people were in the pub and they were all engrossed in a tabletop game and hadn't seen my mini-meltdown.

I tried to fight it, but I inevitably broke out in a cold sweat. Striding down the bar, I dodged a worried-looking Shannon in my desperation to get outside while not looking like a freak in the process.

"Hey, Shannon," I called out on my way past, "I'm going outside for some air. Can you watch the bar for a sec?"

"Scarlett, are you okay?" she asked. "You look a little sick."

"I just need some air."

Not waiting for her reply, I wove past the kitchen and pushed out the rear door and into the lane. Cool air brushed against my face and I breathed deeply, doing my best to calm the wave of terror that haunted my every step.

I wasn't surprised to find that it'd darkened pretty quickly out here. Winter was like that in this part of the world. Four in the afternoon, and the sun was already well behind the row of buildings across the street, and the lane at the rear of the pub was cast in inky shadow, apart from the orb of light I was standing in.

Pressing my palms against my flushed cheeks, I leaned against the wall inside the little alcove that sheltered the door. I hadn't had an episode like that in a long time. Dreams where I woke up gasping for air, alone in my bed, yes; but while I was awake and at work, in public? Never. Panic attacks were the worst, and once people knew, they always wanted to know why. It was a revolving door of awkward questions I couldn't answer. I never knew what any of the things I saw meant, anyway.

The little bulb above my head flickered, and the hairs on the back of my neck prickled. It was that uncomfortable feeling people get when someone's watching them, or maybe it was just the thought of someone lurking in the shadows. Probably just the after-effects of my panic attack. They got so bad that sometimes I puked. Shit, I hoped I wasn't going to projectile into the gutter.

Glancing up and down the lane, I expected to see someone lingering—because being stalked was way better than throwing up, *not*—but no one was there.

The light bulb flickered again, and I shivered. *Should've picked up my coat on my way out.*

Taking one more look, I hesitated when the shadowy figure of a man appeared halfway between me and the mouth of the lane. *What the…?* He hadn't been there a second ago. The man stepped closer, and my heart twisted. Edging backwards, I peered at him as his boots scraped against the cobblestones.

Another figure appeared on High Street, silhouetted by the streetlights and the over-lit tattoo and body piercing shop across the road. He turned down the lane and approached the other man from behind, his steps purposeful. He was wearing a leather biker jacket and big boots, and the other guy looked normal enough—apart from the ugly blond colour of his hair.

Maybe this was one of those 'wrong place, wrong time' scenarios. Luck had never been my strong suit.

Leather Jacket Guy shook out his right arm as he gained on the other guy. A knife slid down his sleeve and dropped into his hand. Striding forward, he grasped the guy by the shoulder and swung him around.

"*No!*" I shrieked as he plunged his knife into the other guy's chest.

A rush of adrenaline surged through my body, and before I knew what I was doing, I rushed out of the alcove and into the lane. Icy air blew through my hair.

Leather Jacket Guy was startled by my cry, and he let go of the body, rising to his full height with the grace of a predator. Our gazes met, and I almost shit myself. He turned towards me, his lips curving into a grin. He had short-cropped, almost black hair, and a thick coating of stubble on his hard jaw, and his eyes… His eyes almost looked silver.

I swallowed hard and took a step backwards. He'd killed a guy in the middle of the street, and now he was looking at me with a creepy smirk on his face. This was bad. Everyone knew you were supposed to run away from danger, not right at it, but I had to be the irreverent, quirky one, didn't I? *Rush right into the gaping maw of Hell, Scarlett. You'll be just fine. Not!*

I stood transfixed as Leather Jacket Guy grunted at me, and then dragged the body of his victim farther into the lane. No one passing by on High Street was even looking at them—like they weren't even there.

I stared at the two men with my mouth hanging open. The knife was sticking out of the man's chest, buried right to the hilt. When Leather Jacket dumped him, the man groaned, a puff of black smoke trailing from between his parted lips. My eyes widened as the inky cloud continued to whoosh out before it escaped into the darkening sky.

"What. The. *Fu*—"

"Well, this is a predicament," Leather Jacket said, his accent very thick and very northern English, acting like this was an everyday occurrence for him. "What are you supposed to be, Purples?"

"P-purples?" My mouth was flapping uselessly. This was so not happening.

"Yeah, Purples. Your hair *is* purple, right?"

I glanced around and shied away when a group of women who stopped on the street and stared at me like I was mad.

"You'd better come farther into this dark alley where no one can see you, lovely," Leather Jacket said, pulling the knife from the dead body. "You see me, but they don't."

"Y-you… you're invisible?"

He flipped the knife in his hand and smirked. "He marked you, Purples. *You're welcome.*"

"M-marked me?"

"I just saved your life." He mock-bowed with a flourish. "You're welcome."

"No," I said, wishing I'd had the good sense to run back into *8-bit*, "you killed him."

Leather Jacket rolled his eyes and grasped my wrist, then yanked me into the darkness. Oh, God, this was it. I was about to be murdered. *Happy birthday, Scarlett.*

I almost fell on my arse as he grasped my face and tilted my head to the side.

"Get your hands off me!" I shoved him away and stumbled back against the wall.

He curled his lip and grabbed my face again. "Where'd you get that lovely scar?" he asked, rubbing his thumb over the puckered line that split through my hairline, down the side of my face directly in front of my right ear, and ended at my jawline.

"None of your business."

"Oh, I think it is," he said, stepping forward and

trapping me with his sheer size. "You can see through my Light, and if I'm not mistaken, you saw the parasite fleeing that man's body. You're either playing dumb or you're manifesting. I'm going to take a stab at playing dumb, because no one manifests at your age."

"My age?" I exclaimed. "What's that supposed to mean?"

Leather Jacket laughed and tilted his face towards the sky. "She sees me excise a demon, and she's worried that I know about her age? *Women.*"

"I don't understand," I wailed. "Just… just let me go. I won't say anything. I—" *You're rambling.*

He stared at me for a long moment, his eyes shining silver in the darkness, almost like a cat…

"You really don't know anything, do you?" he murmured.

"I… I just… I don't know why I came out here."

Leather Jacket sighed, his gaze lowering. He seemed to silently deliberate for a minute before he raised his head.

"Are you going to kill me?" I blurted.

He laughed, looking more and more like a psychopathic underwear model the longer our encounter dragged on.

"Let's give this a try," he mused, combing his hand through my hair.

I wasn't sure if he was talking to me, or if he was referring to what he planned to do with the blood-stained knife in his hand, but he grasped my face again, locking his gaze with mine. "Go back inside and forget what you saw out here," he murmured, his voice washing over me in soothing waves. "This never happened, got it?"

"Yeah," I whispered, "nothing happened."

"Good girl," Leather Jacket purred, letting me go. "Now, go back inside. It's cold out."

Slightly dazed, I turned and opened the door.

2

———

The sound of electronic beeping filled the air. I was back inside *8-bit*, behind the bar where I started. Wait… That didn't make any sense.

My vision focused on a chocolate cupcake with pink frosting and a single candle stuck in the top. The flame flickered back and forth as I blinked, shaking off the unwanted memory that I'd always assumed was of my parents' death.

"Happy birthday, Scarlett."

A pair of black-rimmed glasses and a messy crop of hair came into focus, and I smiled.

Holding the cake was Jackson, my flatmate, best friend, and professional gamer. He'd competed in tournaments all over the world and won big, too. He didn't need a real world job because the prize money in those things was ridiculous. When I'd first moved to London three years ago, I answered his ad looking for someone to rent a room in his flat, and we'd been friends ever since. He was also the guy who used his gamer geek connections to hook me up with my job at *8-bit*. It was the longest I'd ever stuck around for anything. The job *and* the friendship.

"Thanks," I said, tucking my hair behind my ear.

I felt Jackson's gaze linger on the scar that tore up the right side of my face and I shivered. It was a self-conscious day, then. They came and went, but birthdays were the worst. They reminded me of all the things I'd missed out on growing up.

"Are you okay?" Jackson asked, setting the cupcake onto the counter. "You seem little spaced out."

The flame on the candle flickered back and forth and I smiled. "Yeah. Of course."

"Then make a wish and fill those lungs to capacity."

What did I want to wish for? Bringing my parents back from the dead was an obvious one, but necromancy wasn't a thing, so I had to make do with asking the metaphoric universe for something more within the reach of normalcy. Besides, my tragic past didn't make me a special snowflake—lots of people had problems, most of them bigger than mine.

Sucking in a deep breath, I blew out the candle. Smoke drifted upward from the glowing wick and I smirked. After twenty-something years of blowing out candles, I, more than anyone, knew what everyone else did. Wishes never came true.

"What did you wish for?" Jackson asked, pushing his unkempt crop of hair out of his eyes. It was a pointless manoeuvre because it just fell right back.

"If I tell you, it won't come true," I said playing along.

"C'mon, you can tell me," he complained as the door opened and a customer walked in. Some guy with scary bleached blond tips in his hair. *Very nineties.* "I'm a universal safe zone. I negate the laws of physics."

"Yeah, right," I drawled, as the door opened again, letting in a tall, dark figure behind him, "and I'm Princess Peach."

Jackson laughed as the sound of a dubstep remix of the Mario Odyssey theme song started over the speaker system. "This is more your jam, goth Princess Peach," he quipped.

"Give me a pair of combat boots and a tube of black lipstick any day." I winked and went to serve the new arrivals.

Blond Tips was sitting by himself at the end of the bar.

"What can I get for you?" I asked.

"Gin and tonic." His eyes flashed silver like he was a cat lurking in the darkness.

I blinked and shook my head. "Yeah. Coming right up."

Turning, I plucked a bottle of gin off the wall. Glancing at the guy in the reflection of the glass covering the LED display, our gazes crossed. A cold shiver ran down my spine and I quickly looked away, mixing his drink with a shaking hand. What was wrong with me? He wasn't much to look at, but there was something about him that had me on edge.

Maybe he was just one of those people who exuded a creepy vibe? Working in a bar, I saw all kinds, but in a place like *8-bit*? We only got two kinds in here, and Blond Tips wasn't one of them. My guess was he'd have one drink, realise this place served a niche market he wasn't part of, then leave.

My attention shifted to the guy who'd come in after him. He was sitting in the corner, pretending to watch the LED display rotate while one eye was on the door. Probably waiting for his nerdy girlfriend. He stood out even more in his bad boy leather biker jacket, but at least he was easy on the eyes.

"What is this place?" Blond Tips asked as I set his drink down in front of him.

"We're a gamer bar," I replied, picking up a fluoro orange flyer from behind the counter and slapping it down in front of him. "Drink specials most nights. Arcades are pay as you go, and we can switch out notes for coins. Wednesday is anime screening night. Thursday is shooter co-ops with a fiver entry charge. Friday is theme night, this week it's Horizon Zero Dawn. Saturday is the *8-Bit* dance party—cosplay optional—and Sunday is tournament day, you know, PS4, Xbox One, that kind of thing. This week is the Destiny Two Crucible challenge."

Blond Tips raised his eyebrows and handed me a tenner.

"Enjoy your drink," I said, flipping him his change. I moved down to where the guy who'd been lingering in the corner had approached the bar. "What can I get you?"

The guy looked me over and his eyebrows rose. It was like everyone was in a constant state of surprise tonight. I wondered if I had something between my teeth. It seemed like the club to be part of, so I raised my thin purple-tinged eyebrows as well.

He was the tall, dark, and handsome kind. Cropped brownish-black hair, stubble on a chiseled jaw, black T-shirt, biker jacket, and I bet below the bar I'd find a pair of beat-up jeans and combat boots… among other things. *Calvin Klein called and he wants his runway model back*, I thought sullenly to myself. Guys like that never looked at girls like me. Girls like me being scarred internally and externally.

"What?" I prodded, resisting the urge to add a swear word into the mix.

Partially draping himself over the bar, he asked, "Are you always so… *surly*?"

"I work in a gamer bar full of geeks who've never seen a pair of tits before, what do you think?" I slapped my hand over my mouth, stifling a gasp.

The guy smirked and batted his impossibly long eyelashes.

"I don't… I'm sorry… I don't know where that came from."

"I do," he said mysteriously. "Did you know your hair has a purple tint to it? Did you put that there?"

"Uh…" He wasn't weird at all. "No," I said, playing with a long strand that'd fallen forward over my shoulder. "I've never coloured my hair—"

"Aren't you a curious little thing," he mused, tilting his head from side to side, checking me out. "I can see why it came here of all places. You're like a smorgasbord."

"You're making no sense whatsoever," I declared. "Do you want a drink or not?"

"Do I get a flyer?"

I made a face and slapped down a fluoro blue rectangle of paper. "There. Which is it? The cosplay night or the cosplay night? You'd make a great Lunafreya."

"Now I can *really* see why it liked you."

I narrowed my eyes, not understanding why this guy had my hackles up. I was never this rude to customers. Firm, yes, but outright bitchy? That wasn't my MO. Maybe our auras had triggered an unstable nuclear reaction once they'd rubbed together. *Oh jeez, rubbing together with a guy who looked like that? Happy birthday to me!*

I glanced up as Blond Tips opened the door and left. *Another point for Scarlett's unwavering intuition.*

The guy followed my gaze and straightened up. "Thanks for the chat, lovely, but I've got to go."

"Huh?"

"Go home," he whispered, his eyes shining. "Go home and forget."

Jackson appeared in front of me, a confused expression on his face. He put down his empty beer glass and waved his hand back and forth to get my attention. "Uh, Scarlett?"

"What?" I asked, staring after the guy I dubbed as the Bad Boy.

"Who were you talking to?"

I clucked my tongue and rolled my eyes. "The guy in the leather jacket." I waved in his general direction just as the door opened and closed. "He was just…" I sighed and glanced around the pub. He was gone, but hadn't he just been standing right in front of me?

Jackson scratched his head and gave me a confused look. "Scarlett… No one was there."

Scowling, I stared out the windows where I could see Blond Tips and Bad Boy arguing. "He's right outside," I declared. "He's arguing with the guy with the ugly blond tips in his hair."

"What blond guy? Scarlett, are you sure you're okay?"

My scowl deepened to the point my face began to hurt as I glanced back at Jackson before my attention was drawn outside again.

"Yeah, yeah," I said absently.

"Because I was thinking… Since it's your birthday and all, I thought we could go out for dinner or something. I know it's a tough time for you, what with having no family and all. So I thought we could go all out this year. Fast or fancy, your choice. Your shift ends now, right?"

"Yeah." I wasn't really listening to what he was saying because the argument outside was turning borderline violent. Bad Boy had thrust his hands into Blond Tips' shirt and looked to be threatening him. People were walking right by them, doing nothing to defuse the situation at all. *Maybe I should call the cops.*

"I'd really like to take you out, because… Scarlett,

I really need to tell you something," Jackson said, "and it's kind of important."

I tensed as I saw a flash of metal in Bad Boy's hand. *Was that a knife?*

"We've known each other a long time and sometimes feelings can change," Jackson went on. "It's only natural, right? And I guess what I'm trying to say is—"

"*No!*" I shrieked.

"Scarlett?" Jackson straightened up and glanced outside. "What's wrong?"

But I wasn't listening. Rushing down the bar, I weaved through a bunch of tables by the door and pushed outside. The two men were on the street in full view of everyone this time. Wait… this time?

I shook my head and stared at Blond Tips, who was lying on the ground with the knife sticking out of his chest. This was bad news in capital letters, bold, underline, italic, exclamation point.

"Seriously?" Bad Boy exclaimed, standing over his victim, throwing his hands into the air in exasperation. "*Again?*"

I shivered, part of me slightly horrified and the other majorly confused. This had happened before. Just like that. Blond Tips on the ground and… Whoa, *déjà vu.*

"You're impossible," Bad Boy said, pointing at me.

"Am not!" I cried, causing passersby to stare at me like I was crazy.

"They can't see me," he shot back. "You're impossible *and* batshit crazy, Purples. Everyone knows you're supposed to run away from danger, not run directly at it!"

Standing there, completely stunned, I realised no one was even looking at the bloody scene that was unfolding outside of *8-bit*. In a city that'd seen its fair share of tragedy because of these kinds of attacks, I was shocked. Nobody cared. Nobody cared because… I gasped as a wave of nausea smacked me in the gut. *Nobody could see them.*

"What's happening? Am I going crazy?" I whispered, glancing nervously at a group of people walking past.

"I'm standing over a dead body on the street and you're asking me? Get a grip, Purples."

He was playing with me. He was a manifestation of my inner demons. The memories I'd locked away and refused to deal with were finally pushing me over the edge. Was this what was like to go totally insane?

Bad Boy grasped my wrist and pulled me into the lane beside the pub. This looked familiar, too.

"What are you?" he asked.

"I'm…" I didn't know how to answer his question. I was Scarlett Ravenwood, messed up bartender. It didn't get simpler than that.

"Like I said, *impossible*."

"What are *you* then?" I shot back at him. "Are you a terrorist?"

"Am I a…" He snorted and shook his head. "Looks like you need a stronger dose."

Before I could fight back, he'd grasped my face in his big hands and held me steady. His silver eyes flashed and I squirmed, trying to pull away, but he was far too strong for anything I tried to make a difference. He was going to drug and kidnap me. I'd wake up tomorrow locked in some sick and twisted bunker in the middle of the ghetto where no one would hear me scream as he chopped me into little pieces and mailed them to Jackson.

"Go home," he said firmly. "Go home and forget you ever saw me. Forget everything you saw tonight."

Warmth spread through me and my limbs relaxed. *He was so dreamy…*

3

———

"**M**ummy!"

I sat up in bed, my chest heaving. Glancing around the room, I wiped the sweat off my forehead as my bedroom came into focus. I knew I'd been dreaming, but of what, I wasn't quite sure.

I gasped, drawing in breath after breath, my limbs feeling like they were filled with lead. My head didn't feel much better.

Memories were like icebergs floating in an ocean of darkness. Only a little peeked above the surface, while the core stretched into the depths of the inky black of the unknown. Sometimes they caught me unaware, smashing into my psyche and threatening to tear me apart like the hull of the Titanic. Other times, I was able to swim around them and let them drift off into the blackness until they inevitably floated back into my path. They were always there, and that was the problem.

The room was dark. The blinds were drawn, but

light creeped in around the edges, casting a murky glow over my minimalistic design choices. I hated stuff. Furniture, knick-knacks, more than one pair of shoes. Three years later, and I was still using a suitcase as a makeshift wardrobe and my mattress was on the floor without a base.

Breathing deep, I shook off the confusion of my dream. I was in reality. I was sitting here. I was in my bedroom in Jackson's flat in Camden. *Wait…* I didn't remember coming home. I didn't remember finishing work at *8-bit* last night, either.

Turning, I grasped for my mobile phone. It was on the floor, plugged into the charger like always. I hadn't had anything to drink last night, did I? It'd been my birthday, and I usually preferred to forget those, so it wouldn't have been out of the realm of possibilities. My head throbbed, so maybe I was hung over.

My fingers brushed against my phone and then hit an unknown object. I picked it up and made a face. It was a troll doll dressed in a tiny leather jacket and trousers. I stared at the ugly plastic toy and stroked the purple hair into a point. *Where the hell did this come from?*

Purples…

I shook my head and rubbed the grit from my eyes. Man, I felt like shit warmed over.

Knocking at the door roused me.

"Scarlett?" Jackson called. "Are you in there?"

"Yeah," I replied, leaning back against the wall.

"I'm coming in…" The door opened slowly, then

Jackson's head appeared through the crack. "Is it safe?"

"Of course it's safe," I snapped, my temples throbbing. *Ugh, my brain felt like it was trying to claw its way out of my skull.*

"Just making sure you hadn't brought back any, uh… *conquests.*"

"Puke!" I exclaimed. "I don't believe in one-night stands."

"There's a first for everything," he said sullenly, drawing the blinds.

The room filled with bright morning light and I shielded my eyes. I guess I deserved the rude awakening, even though I couldn't remember what I'd done. The mattress dipped in front of me as Jackson sat, his shoulders hunched forward. He smelt of soap and aftershave—clean Jackson smells. I probably smelt like something dead.

"What happened to you last night?" he asked, his brow creased. "You rushed out of *8-bit* like your arse was on fire, then you didn't come back. *At all.*"

I shrugged, knowing I should get up and drink some water and find something to take for the pain. The troll doll stared up at me, looking impossibly happy with its tiny plastic smile. Even it was mocking me and it was an inanimate object.

"I was worried about you, Scarlett," Jackson went on. "You were acting real strange. Are you—"

"Am I off my meds?" I shot at him with a scowl. "No, I'm not, thank you very much."

He flinched slightly and pushed his glasses up his

nose. "You know I had to ask." Plucking the toy from my hand, he said, "Hey, a troll doll." Holding it up he smirked. "It looks like you."

"Shut up." I snatched it back and let it fall to the floor.

"Like I was saying, I was worried about you, Scar," Jackson said, watching me as I picked up my phone.

"You know I don't like it when people call me that," I murmured, starting to feel terrible when I saw the twenty missed calls and fifteen text messages from the loveable geek in front of me. I groaned and drew my knees up so I could lean my head against them. "I don't know what happened."

"You blacked out? Were you drunk or something?"

"No, I don't… I haven't had a drink in a while," I said, squeezing my eyes shut. Images swirled inside my eyelids, but I couldn't focus on any of them. I raised my head. "Wait, what did you say about me acting weird? What did I do?"

Jackson squirmed and wrung his hands. It was how he occupied himself when he knew some juicy piece of gossip but was trying his hardest not to tell anyone. Usually, it was me he was avoiding because when it came to long-lasting friendships, we were two peas in a pod. Our circles were close in the up-close-and-personal kind of way.

"*Jackson*," I prodded.

"You were talking to yourself," he blurted.

"I was talking to myself?" My eyebrows rose.

"*Nuh-uh.*"

"Scarlett… You were serving customers who weren't even there," he went on. "Then you shouted at something or someone that also wasn't there, then rushed out onto the street. After that, who knows what happened because you didn't come back. I tried to call and text, but you never picked up."

I stared at him blankly, trying to recall my shift, but my head throbbed even worse.

"I was starting to think you'd been kidnapped or something." He gestured wildly. "I almost called the police!"

Kidnapped… Black smoke… Black smoke swirling into the sky. My entire body stiffened as the image appeared in my mind, clear and sharp like a HD television channel. Black and thick… like ink swirling in water.

"Scarlett?"

Jackson was staring at me. His glasses were smudged with fingerprints, which annoyed me no end.

"I, uh… I'm sorry about ditching you," I muttered. "I… I think I need to—"

"It's okay," he said, placing his hand on my knee, "I get it. Birthdays suck for you. Twenty-five is like a milestone, right?"

"Stop trying to make me feel better."

"Of course I'm going to make you feel better," he said with a smile I was sure had tinges of sadness around the edges. *What did he have to be sad about?* "We're best friends, Scarlett. It's what we do."

I combed my fingers through my purple-esque hair and shrugged. "I suppose. I'll still make it up to you."

"Up to me?" He blew a raspberry at me. "It was your birthday."

"Jackson… You know what I mean."

He smiled and glanced out the window. "You want breakfast?"

On cue, my stomach groaned and squelched, signalling there was nothing in it. "I guess that's a yes on my behalf."

"C'mon then. Have a shower and we'll go down to the café. My treat."

"Your treat? I think it better be mine." I crawled out of bed, not worried about the fact that I was only wearing an oversized T-shirt and boy short knickers. I hesitated at the door and turned back. "Jackson?"

His gaze flicked up, but I didn't pay any attention to where he'd been looking.

"I really am sorry about last night."

He nodded. "I know."

I detoured past the kitchen, downing a glass or water and a pair of headache tablets before I locked myself inside the tiny bathroom. The flat wasn't much to look at, and it was tinier than a shoebox, but it was home. The floor was uneven, I was sure the plumbing dated back to medieval times, and the kitchen was a hole in the wall with nowhere to sit and doubled as the laundry area, but that was the norm for semi-affordable flats in Camden.

Stripping, I stood in the tub and turned on the

taps, waiting for the water to go from icy to warm. I pulled the curtain around and studied the vintage Pac-man pattern. Ghosts, cherries, and the man himself repeated over the plastic. It was familiar and very Jackson. The whole place was filled with video game decor. Even the cushions on the couch were printed with the Legend of Zelda characters.

As I let the hot water soak through my hair, I mulled over the one thing neither of us really wanted to acknowledge. Jackson had asked me about my meds, but it hadn't gone any deeper than that. The real question should have been, 'Do you want to go back to the doctor to make sure you haven't reached breaking point?' I snorted and grabbed the soap. The mysterious point of no return psych professionals had always threatened me with as a teenager. Anger had been my mission objective back then, but that was a long time ago. I was put together much better these days. The cracks had been repaired, even though some fragility remained. I was good, right?

Then why couldn't I remember last night? I rubbed the soap over my lady bits. I'd had a flashback that much was clear, but what happened after that? I leaned my head against the tiles and circled the soap around and around. Invisible customers? Black inky smoke… *Silver eyes.*

A man stood before me and grasped my face, his silver eyes burning into mine. *What are you?* I gasped as I came on the bar of soap, my knees trembling. What the fu—

A fist bashed against the wall from the other side and I jumped, almost slipping in the tub.

"*Scarlett!*" Jackson bellowed. "Have you drowned in there?"

I swallowed hard. "*No!*"

"Then hurry up! I'm starving!"

Putting the soap back in the holder, I turned off the water and stepped out onto the bathmat. Dripping, I wiped the condensation off the mirror and stared at my reflection. A pair of brown eyes stared back at me, my wet hair black as ink.

"*Where did you go last night?*" I whispered.

"Did you have to bring that with you?"

Jackson poked the troll doll with a finger, and it edged across the table between the salt and pepper shakers.

"Says the fully grown man wearing a T-shirt that says 'I am not a geek, I'm a level nine wizard'."

"Point."

We'd ordered two English Breakfasts with all the trimmings and were currently inhaling it. Sausage, beans, fried tomato, chips, scrambled eggs, bacon, a side of toast, and a pot of tea. *Each*. It was the best cure for a rough night and went down a treat. Thank goodness for all day breakfast menus.

"So, have you changed your mind about wanting a birthday present?" Jackson asked, mopping up the sauce on his plate with a triangle of toast.

"Nope. You know I don't like the pressure of gift giving… or receiving."

"I thought it was more about your lust for minimalism," he shot back with a grin.

"*Mmmhmm*," I muttered, dabbing my lips with a serviette.

I glanced at a man sitting two tables away and did a double-take when I thought I saw his eyes shine silver. Kind of like the way an animal's eyeballs reflected light in the dark. The second time, he looked like a normal dude out for a normal round of beans on toast from the local café. The man caught me staring and nodded, and I blinked before looking away.

Picking up a chip, I dipped the end into the beans and swirled it around, focusing on the troll doll. *What are you supposed to be, Purples?*

"Huh?" I asked, realising Jackson had been talking to me.

"I asked when you were working again." He turned around in his chair, trying to see what'd caught my attention. "What are you looking at?"

"Nothing," I replied with a shrug. "I'm on Thursday. Shooter co-ops. My favourite night." I rolled my eyes.

"Still can't deal with them, huh?"

"Those games attract a certain kind of geek you and I both know full well doesn't mesh with my sensible capabilities as a female."

"Don't be so prejudiced, Scarlett," he said with a laugh before pinching one of my chips and stuffing it into his mouth. "I made most of my money playing Call of Duty, or have you forgotten?"

"You're an anomaly."

"Says the woman who *liked* Mass Effect Andromeda… the very game that *ruined* a perfectly awesome franchise."

"The main guy in it was hot," I complained.

"He was badly rendered. Like first gen console bad. I traded that game as soon as I could just to get it out of the flat. It was like the whole development team was possessed or something when they coded it —possessed or high, either one."

"*Pfft*," I hissed, shielding my plate from his sticky fingers. "I know what I like."

He fell silent as I polished off the last of my breakfast, even eating the fried tomato I usually leave behind. I glanced at the troll doll again, narrowing my eyes. *Purples…* Where had I heard that before?

Black inky smoke… *She sees me excise a demon and she's worried that I know about her age?*

The lane behind *8-bit*! That's where I saw the guy with silver eyes. The guy no one could see… *Holy sh—*

"So last night, I wanted to talk to you about something," Jackson began, turning his empty tea cup around and around.

"That's it!" I declared, almost falling out of my chair.

"That's what?" His eyebrows knitted together and he shoved his hand through his unruly hair.

"I think I know what happened last night." I

began fossicking through my pocket for some change. I had to follow the clues, and then I'd figure it out.

"What?"

"Here," I said, laying down a tenner and some pound coins on the table. "This ought to cover breakfast. *Mostly…*"

"You're leaving?" Jackson asked, glancing from me to the money and back again.

"It's important," I replied, shrugging into my leather jacket and snatching up the troll doll. "I'll be home later, okay?" Skidding to a halt by the door, I waved at him one last time. "I'm sorry! I'll make it up to you, I promise!"

Not knowing exactly where I was going, I legged it to the bus stop, determined to find the man in the leather jacket. He'd done something to me and that guy he'd knifed, and none of it made any sense.

Spying the red double-decker turning the corner, I fished out my Oyster card. I had enough problems to deal with without some random stranger messing with my memories.

When the bus came to a stop, I jumped on, tapped my card, and climbed up to the upper level. What I didn't want to think about was the fact that the mystery bad boy might not even be real, and all of this might be a hallucination created by my mental instability.

Sliding into an empty seat, I combed my fingers around the troll doll's purple hair. There was only one way to know for sure.

Find the man and I'd find the truth.

4

The city was awash with artificial light, but darkness was never far away.

My boots thudded on the stairs as I exited Tower Hill tube station. The barriers squealed open as I slapped my Oyster card on the reader, and I was outside again. Overhead, the stars were obscured—by light pollution or clouds, I wasn't sure.

Across the street, the Tower of London was lit up, looking ominous and out of place in the modern city. It was easy to forget how old London was with all the progress rushing by. Hints of its origins stuck out all over the place for those whose eyes were keen enough to notice it—a building, a tourist attraction, a sign bolted into a wall, the sudden appearance of a church and a matching graveyard between a Lidl and a Sainsbury's.

The troll doll heated in my hand, drawing me past the castle-like structure that'd seen its fair share of death and drama. A bus zoomed past, lit up and full of passengers, and my hair whipped backwards. Man, it was freezing. Checking my phone, I saw it was almost eleven-thirty. I'd been walking all day, pinging from one side of the city to the other on a wild goose chase, unable to shake the feeling I was being pranked to the extreme. If it wasn't for the magical arsehole detector in my hand, I might have given up ages ago.

I was following the heat signature of a troll doll, I thought to myself. *This is not normal.* But I'd kept going anyway.

Bad Boy had killed the same guy twice for crying out loud. He could have skewered me just as many times, though I wasn't sure how that'd work, but he didn't. He'd seemed curious that I was even talking to him until he'd turned full arsehole. Still, it was probably best I approach the guy in a public place if I could. *The things I did for answers.*

The troll was scalding my hand by the time I realised I was standing outside a pub. Clutching the hair so I didn't burn myself, I sighed. Hopefully this was the end of the line. I stood on the footpath as traffic whizzed back and forth behind me, and stared up at the name, *The Hung, Drawn, and Quartered. That wasn't a bad omen or anything.*

From the outside it looked like any other pub in the city district of London. Red brick façade, old window panes with cottage flowers growing in planter boxes on the sills, black and gold signs, a chalkboard easel with lunch and dinner specials—*every pie individually hand-crafted with the finest short crust pastry!*— and benches outside. It was far too cold for anyone to be standing out here with their pints, so I was alone on the footpath. Inside, I could hear the hubbub of punters enjoying a late run on a Tuesday night.

I peered in the window, scoping the lay of the land. The place looked very stately with chandeliers hanging from the ceiling, marble columns, and intricate gold-framed paintings of old people. Old people meaning historical figures I didn't have any inkling as to who they were or why they were famous.

The troll doll warmed in my hand as my gaze fell onto a man sitting in the corner by the open fireplace. His back was to the room and he was nursing a pint of beer, his shoulders slumped and his head down. He was wearing a leather biker jacket, and his hair was all messy like he hadn't bothered to style it after getting out of bed. It looked good on him, which was just insult to injury. Perfect people always looked perfect, even when they'd just been rolling in a mountain of shit.

Thrusting myself over the mass of plants, I pressed my nose up against the window and scowled. Yeah, it was him all right—sexy, brooding, and an arsehole sticker plastered on his forehead. Remembering that morning when I'd unconsciously masturbated on a bar of soap, my cheeks flushed. *It wasn't about him*, I thought to myself. *It was a psychological need for relief.*

A group of men sitting just inside stared at me and laughed. Pulling back, I tossed my hair over my shoulder and stalked towards the door. *Now or never, Scarlett.*

Warmth hit me in the face as I entered the pub, and I wasted no time weaving between the tables, making a direct beeline for Bad Boy himself. The closer I got, the more certain I was that I was about to meet my untimely end. I was doing the whole run headfirst into danger thing again.

Standing beside him, I slammed the troll doll onto the table.

"What did you do to me?" I demanded.

The man tensed, his gaze fixing on the plastic toy. Up close, he smelled like liquorice, citrus, and something metallic.

"How did you find me?" he asked after a moment. His fingers tightened around his glass, the tips turning white.

"The troll doll."

"*Clever.*"

"That's all you've got to say?" I was boiling over like a volcano. Any second now, I was going to blow my top and things would get messy. *Real messy.* "You messed with me, didn't you? At first I thought you might've slipped me a roofie, but I don't drink, not usually and especially not when I'm working. Then I toyed with the idea that you pricked me with a needle."

The man snorted like I was performing some stand-up comedy routine and angled in his chair so he could stare at me.

"But then I started remembering things," I

murmured, leaning closer, doing my best 'bad cop' impression, "*lots* of things."

"Sit down," he commanded, his eyes narrowing.

"No." I was going to sit anyway, but I didn't want to give him the satisfaction of thinking I'd ask how high when he'd just barked at me to jump.

"Have a seat, Purples," he said, gesturing to the padded bench opposite him. "I'm not going to bite."

"Just stab," I shot back, not missing a beat.

"Surly *and* sassy." His lips quirked into a sly grin. "Looks like I've caught a live one."

Gritting my teeth, I slid onto the bench. "Who are you, and what did you do to me?"

The man picked up the troll doll and wound his finger around the tuft of purple hair. "It looks like you, don't you think?"

"Stop avoiding the question," I snapped.

"The question?" he retorted. "It was more like a two-in-one. I've only got enough change for one of those answers, Purples."

I scoffed, "I'm impossible? I've got nothing on you."

The man leaned forward and rested his elbows on the table. Turning the troll doll around so it faced me, he tapped his finger lightly against the side of its little plastic face. "Look here."

I didn't know if it was just a reflex, but I glanced down.

"See that?" he asked.

"See wh——" I almost choked on my spit as the hair

began to writhe, then flicker as the acrylic tuft turned into flame. It glowed a deep royal purple at its core and turned positively electric around the edges.

The man let out a *humph*, then closed his hand around the flame. When he let go, the troll doll was back to normal.

"What was that?" I asked, snatching at his hand. He leaned back and held up his palm so I could see that he was unharmed. His skin was unbroken, though calloused as hell, but there were no burns at all.

"You have no Light, you're obviously not manifesting, but you keep shaking off my attempts at Alteration," he declared. "Something's wrong with you."

"Huh?" I didn't know what any of those things were, but I was severely offended at the part where he said something was wrong with me. I didn't need the reminder.

"Alteration," he repeated like I should know everything about his state of insanity.

"I don't know what that is," I said with a pout. "And you haven't explained anything to me. Who are you?"

"You're wondering if I'm a figment of your imagination?"

"Jackson said he couldn't see you."

"I was cloaked then because it was necessary," he stated. "I'm not now, because I'm off the clock, Purples. I punch in, I punch out."

"Of what?" I asked, my voice rising. "Do you always answer questions with nonsense?"

The man leaned back and ran his hands through his hair with a groan. "*Impossible.*"

"Who are you?" I demanded, the volcano beginning to break through the surface.

"Wilder," he said, thoroughly exasperated. "I knew you were going to be a problem." He closed his fist around the troll doll and muttered something under his breath.

"Well, I'm so sorry I'm such an annoying thorn in your arse cheek, Mr. Wilder," I drawled. "I remember everything, FYI—the name calling, the sexual harassment, the stabbing, the funky black smoke."

"I did not sexually harass you," Wilder exclaimed. "I saved your life and this is the thanks I get?"

"From a puff of black smoke?"

"A demon," he hissed through his teeth. "A particularly nasty one that would've fed on your soul and damned you to Hell."

I made a face. "Well, that isn't outlandish at all!"

"You weren't supposed to see me," he said, shaking his head. "No one is ever supposed to see."

"Yeah, but I did…"

"I'd hate to say duh, but *duh.*"

I still wasn't sure if I was having a mental breakdown, but I was here now and this Wilder guy was talking. Well, it was mostly in riddles, but he was explaining something at least and people could see him this time. I narrowed my eyes at the woman at the next table who was drooling at the sight of the psycho in front of me. *Ugh.*

"So you excised the black smoke demon thing, then came back for seconds. Theoretically, he wasn't *possessed* anymore, but you killed him anyway," I said, leaning forward. "Why?"

"He was a Vessel," Wilder replied.

"A what?"

"A Vessel." He raised his eyebrows. When my scowl deepened, he added, "A willing participant. He was so far gone, it was the humane thing to do, really. Don't worry, I cleaned up after myself."

"This is just getting worse and worse," I said with a moan. "And I'm not even off my meds."

Wilder perked up. "You're on medication?"

"That's none of your business," I snapped.

He stared at me so long, I was sure I'd grown a second head. "You better not be trying that alteration thing with me again because we've already established that it doesn't work so great."

"C'mon," he said, scraping his chair back and rising. "I'm taking you home."

"You're taking *me* home?"

"Don't argue with me, Purples." He flipped up the collar of his jacket. "Something's not right with you, and it'd be negligent to leave you wandering the streets in the middle of the night, even though I'd rather be doing a million other things."

"Like?"

"Asphyxiating on my own vomit."

"*Charming.*"

He picked up the troll doll and held it out. "Don't forget yourself."

"Are you always like this?" I asked as I followed him out onto the street.

"Like what?" He started to walk in the direction of the tube station and I had to jog to catch up with his impossibly long gait.

"So... *prickly.*"

He glared at me before he looked away. "The less you know about me, the better."

Alrighty then.

Whoever—or *whatever*—Wilder was, he didn't elaborate after that.

We got on a District line train, switched at Monument, and walked through the maze of tunnels and escalators under the city, following the signs for Bank Underground station. Wilder never said a word, he just strode through the trickling stream of passengers, brooding and sulking with me hot on his heels.

Thumping down the stairs and onto the platform where the northbound Northern line trains departed, he guided me to the far end, people hastily stepping out of the way as he approached. *Not invisible then, just scary.*

I glanced at him out the corner of my eye as the train zoomed into the station, the wind whipping my hair into a frenzy. What was he exactly? I got the impression he was some kind of demon hunter, which was a completely absurd job description. Did he work for someone? Was he a loner? Maybe he was both. There wasn't a ring on his finger… like that meant anything.

The doors on the train swished open as the recording on the loudspeaker said, '*Mind the gap between the train and the platform*'. Wilder nudged me with his elbow, and I stepped into the carriage. It was mostly empty, so I sat and he took a seat opposite, slouching and man-spreading like a pro.

"See something you like?" Wilder asked, his eyes shining. They were doing that weird silver thing again, and I made a mental note to ask him about that, too.

"I'm just wondering why you need to open your legs so wide," I said. "It's rude."

"I've got huge balls," he said with an evil smirk.

"You've got a disgusting comeback for everything, don't you?"

"Stop rising to the occasion, Purples."

I rolled my eyes and turned my attention down the carriage. Anywhere was better than the gaping crevasse between his legs. I mean, I didn't know why I was so combative with the guy. Usually, I was an under the radar kind of woman. A coaster on the coffee table of life. I never argued unless confronted. I supposed Wilder was confronting and not in a sexual kind of way. He had predator written all over him, which made this whole excursion stupid to the extreme.

Should've ditched him when I had the chance, I

thought. *The moment the train stops at the next station, I'm making a run for it. Then tomorrow, I'm going to make an appointment to get my meds checked. Demons and magic don't exist.*

A man at the opposite end of the carriage caught my eye and smiled. I was immediately skeptical because tube etiquette stated you don't make direct eye contact while commuting. I looked past him, then back again and tensed. I was sure his eyes had turned completely white, but then again, I also thought I was tripping.

An announcement crackled over the speakers. '*The next station is Moorgate. Alight here for the Metropolitan, Circle, and Hammersmith and City lines.*'

Wilder wasn't looking at me. His head had lolled back and his arms were crossed over his chest, exuding total nonchalance.

The train rocketed into the station, slowing until it came to a stop. The doors opened and I counted. One, two, three… I shot to my feet and bolted, leaping off the train and onto the platform.

"Hey!" Wilder bellowed behind me, causing people to turn.

I didn't look back. I ran down the platform, following the exit signs. I took the stairs two at a time, then bolted up the escalators, brushing past commuters standing on the right. Emerging into the causeway, a hand grasped my arm and I turned. White eyes stared back at me and a mouth full of razor-sharp teeth grinned. I shrieked, causing the few late-night passengers and Underground employees to turn and stare. I tore away and vaulted over the barriers, determined not to look back.

Outside, it was nearing midnight, and although London never really went to sleep, this part of the city was mostly empty. I looked left, then right, and when I heard Wilder calling out behind me, I sprinted to the right, mainly because it was the direction I was facing.

Go away, go away, go away!

I crossed a street, ignoring the red man on the traffic lights, the sound of pounding footsteps spurring me on. My thighs burned and my breath twisted my lungs, giving away how unfit I really was. Adrenalin and a little bit of fear were the only things driving me now.

Darting down a side street, I looked for a place to slip into before Wilder could reach the corner, but I tripped and almost fell when I saw a man standing in the middle of the road, his head at an odd angle. I skidded and barrelled into a tight lane between two buildings, my heart galloping faster than it'd ever gone before.

The sound of my boots hitting uneven cobblestones echoed around me, then I was on another street. Directly in front was a fenced off garden—one of those posh green spaces that was reserved for rich people who lived in equally posh houses around it. A wrought-iron fence circled the entire thing, thick with green shiny paint and topped with narrowly spaced pointy bits. There was no way over, so I went left, slipping between two parked cars and onto the road.

I gasped as a figure appeared in front of me and I skidded. Pivoting, I pushed to the left and legged it down the next side street.

Unfortunately, Wilder was waiting for me.

He held something in his hand, and when he saw me, he flicked his wrist and a blade came to life, twisting and shooting out a shower of white-hot sparks.

"Get down!" he bellowed, striding in my direction.

For a split-second, I thought he was talking to me, but I felt a gust of air from behind and my feet slipped out from underneath me. I landed with a thud, my breath wheezing, and Wilder leapt over me like an Olympic hurdler.

He collided with something and sparks showered down around me. Covering my head with my arms, I shrieked as I saw him fend off a creature straight from the stuff nightmares were made of.

It used to be a man, but its arms and knees were all bent backwards and it was crawling around like a spider, its head twisted at an odd angle and its teeth… I almost puked into the gutter. Its mouth was full of razor sharp points and a black, forked tongue waved about, dripping giant globules of saliva on the asphalt. Its eyes flashed white, its shirt was torn, the paisley tie it'd been wearing was flapping about as it skittered over a parked car, emitting an awful clicking sound as it went.

It seemed too fast for Wilder, who was swiping at it with his sword. The demon hunter was leaping and twisting like a ninja, dodging blows from clawed hands. The air vibrated as the pair collided, and the creature—what I was assuming was a demon at this point—closed its jaws around Wilder's sword and crunched. White sparks burst out of its mouth, and it wailed in pain, but didn't let go.

"*Bastard!*" Wilder shouted. He pushed back against it one more time, then the blade disappeared in a shower of white sparks.

My expression turned into one of dread as what was left of the sword was knocked from his hand and clattered onto the road. The blade skidded across the footpath and what remained of the hilt landed at my feet. Wilder let out a roar and shoved his shoulder into the demon's chest and heaved. It went flying, tumbling down the road over and over, until it sprung back up and launched itself towards him with alarming speed.

Without thinking, I picked up the bladeless sword. Holding it up to the light, I wondered if this was another one of those invisible things until my touch seemed to activate something. The end of the handle erupted as the sword emerged from its sheath, the blade flashing a brilliant purple as it snapped into shape. Links unfurled and scales clicked together in a shower of purple sparks.

"What the…" I whispered, almost dropping the sword on the ground. It was as long as my arm!

"*Purples!*" Wilder shouted, scrambling backwards.

The creature's mouth widened, saliva dripping from its teeth as it darted after Wilder. It leapt and

Wilder rolled to the side, the creature's claws cracking the flagstone where he'd been a moment before.

If it got Wilder, then I was next. In a situation like this, there was only one thing I had the sense to do. Yeah, that run headfirst into danger thing. *Again*.

I grasped the sword and rushed forward with a cry. The demon spun, making a horrid clicking sound and launched towards me. It galloped, its limbs twisting and rolling in its haste to tear apart some tasty human flesh. I let out a squeak, then swiped the blade at it. It dodged and I twisted before it raised its claws.

I swung the sword back in a swift arc, and by some miracle, the steel sliced through the creature's arm. I didn't even feel the moment when it cut, but purple sparks lit up the street as the blade severed flesh and bone. The demon screamed, then went for broke. I ducked low, its hind leg kicking me in the back of the head as it tumbled over me, and I fell to the ground.

Wilder was in front of the demon, sinking his knife into its shoulder.

"Purples!" he cried, his hand outstretched, but I only had eyes for the thing that was trying its best to eat my soul.

I pushed to my feet, my arse throbbing, and I raised the sword. With a cry, I plunged it into the demon's back, aiming for the place I supposed its heart might've been—if it had one. The creature screeched, its head reared back, then it burst into a fireball that emitted a stench so foul it almost made me retch.

Stumbling back a step, I gasped as the flames dissipated and I realised there was nothing left of the demon. The whole thing had just disintegrated in a whoosh, leaving a weird scorch mark on the ground.

"Are you all right?" Wilder asked.

"*No!*" I rubbed the back of my head, my breath still evading capture. "What was that thing?"

"A lesser demon."

"There's more than one kind?" I wiped my forehead with the back of my hand, my skin all clammy despite the icy chill in the air.

"The plot thickens," he drawled, putting his knife back into his boot. "You shouldn't have run, you know."

I let out a frustrated cry and squashed down the urge to skewer him, too.

"The blade shouldn't have worked either," Wilder added, taking it from me. The moment he touched it, it recoiled, disappearing into the hilt.

"Why not? It's just a sword." *That clicked into shape like a Transformer with an angle grinder.*

"It's not *just* a sword. It's an arondight blade."

"Aron-what?" I scratched my head, glancing to where the creature had been a moment before. Was it just me, or was the scorch mark beginning to fade, too?

"Arondight blades are forged with the power to slay demons," he explained. "Arondight was the blade given to… Ah, forget it."

"Wilder," I said, my voice shaking, "you can't…"

"I can't what?"

"That just happened," I exclaimed, pointing to the concrete. "You can't brush me off anymore."

He raised an eyebrow. "I assumed you didn't care after your acrobatic manoeuvre on the tube."

But he'd cared enough to follow me. Why was that?

"This has nothing to do with my meds, does it?" I asked, burrowing into my jacket as I started to tremble. "I'm not tripping or having a psychotic break. This is real, right? You're real?"

"Last time I checked." He snorted and slid the bladeless handle *thingy* into a pocket on the inside of his jacket. "I've never seen anyone leap a barrier at a tube station like that."

"*Wilder.*"

"What? You were the one who ran. My work here is done." He turned and went to stalk away, but I grasped his arm and wrenched him back.

"I'm not going to run away again. Like it or not, this is a problem." I gestured wildly to myself, him, and the empty spot where the demon had been. "The second time in as many days, FYI. A little clarity wouldn't go astray."

He raised an eyebrow. "Are you sure you're not on an acid trip, Purples? It would be easier to up the med dosage than to embark on an annoyingly violet-tinted odyssey."

"*Wilder!*"

"*Fine*. Let's walk." He sighed and gestured for me to follow him. "We need to clear out anyway."

I was forced to trot to catch up to him, but easily fell into step this time. The street was empty apart from a few empty night busses that rolled by.

"We call ourselves Naturals," Wilder said as we passed a row of clothing shops.

"Naturals?" I asked, my stomach doing a little flip. "There's nothing natural about any of this."

Wilder narrowed his eyes. "To you, maybe."

"That… spider demon thing back there… He was on the train with us, wasn't he?"

"It," Wilder corrected. "And yes. *You* provoked it."

"Excuse me?"

"It would've left us alone if you'd stayed put. It knew what I was."

I stopped in front of a H&M and leaned against the wall, my chest constricting. Monsters, invisible people, funky swords that shot out sparks, hot guys stalking people—it was too much. This couldn't be real, which meant I was losing my mind. After all these years dealing with the loss of my parents, acting out, going to shrinks, self-medicating, and dealing with depression, I was finally at my wits' end. I mean, I spaced out a little from time to time, but never like this. One second, I was okay with all this, and the next… Something was definitely wrong.

"Purples," Wilder said, grasping my shoulders.

"I can't… I can't…"

"Breathe, okay? I don't want you throwing up on my boots."

"Scarlett," I wheezed, realising he'd never wanted to know who I was. "My name is Scarlett."

"Red *and* purple, huh?" he mused, glancing up and down the street. "Aren't you a rainbow."

I moaned and slid down the wall until I was crouching. I'd forgotten to take my tablets at dinnertime, which is why I was having a mini-breakdown. Wilder said this was real, but what if he was still screwing with me?

"Shite," he cursed, looking at me like I was a problem he didn't want to deal with. "We're getting a taxi."

"Why do you care?" I asked, shoving my head between my knees, knowing I was exhausted, starving, and having a panic attack that was honestly overdue. "Just leave me alone. I can get back by myself."

"There you go wanting to put your head in the sand again. It's so human of you." He sighed sharply and knelt in front of me. "I can't leave you out here like this."

"Yes, you can."

"No, I can't," he snapped. "You're in this now, Scarlett. As much as I don't need the drama, I'm oath bound. I have to get you home at least."

I glanced up. *He called me Scarlett.*

"C'mon." He offered me his hand.

I stared at him.

"If you hadn't killed that demon…" He grimaced. "Well, let's just say I need to repay the favour."

"You won't…" I glanced at his boot, where I knew he'd stashed his murder knife.

"No," he said, "I won't hurt you. That knife is reserved for actual demons, not she-devils."

I snorted and reluctantly curled my fingers around his, knowing I didn't have anything to fear from the guy. Not when I now knew there were worse things out there.

5
——————

I was exhausted by the time the cab dropped us off in front of my flat.

"This is your house?" Wilder asked, staring up at the terraced house that looked like all the other terraced houses on the street—bland and unremarkable.

"It's the top flat," I said with a grimace.

"You don't even have the whole thing?"

"No, and it's Jackson's flat. I just live there."

Wilder snorted.

I sighed and fished in my pocket for my keys.

"You've got a little…" He waved his hand at me.

Looking down, I realised the front of my jumper was splattered with something dark. *Demon blood*. Or the tears of my internal frustration leaking out of every pore on my body.

"I've had enough," I whispered, holding out the front of my jumper so I could inspect the damage.

"You'll have to speak up, I might be a Natural, but I don't have super hearing."

"I said, I've had enough!" I shouted at him. Somewhere in the distance, a dog started to bark.

Wilder snorted. "Evidently, so has that dog."

"I've had my memory wiped, I've been attacked my demons, I stabbed a human-spider-hybrid thing through the heart with a magical sword, I was led on a wild goose chase by a troll doll..." I sucked in breath after breath, oxygen hissing through my teeth.

"Don't go frothing at the mouth, Purples."

"And I've had to put up with your awful personality for far longer than any sane human could tolerate!"

"Didn't you mention something about meds?" Wilder asked, tilting his head to the side.

"You're such a piece of—"

"We better get you inside, Purples," he interrupted. "Once you're in, you'll be rid of me."

I clenched my fist around my key. "Will you do that alteration thing on me again?"

"Up to you, though it's probably a waste of time. You'd be better off finding that pill bottle of yours."

I was far too exhausted to argue with the guy, so I stalked up the front steps and unlocked the door. Inside, it was dark and stank of mould. The house was so old, it seemed like it was rotting away most days. The owner of the flat downstairs was far too cheap to do anything about the dampness of the house, even though Jackson had been asking for years.

"It smells like a wet cat in here," Wilder said, wrinkling his nose. "Which flat is yours?"

"Upstairs." I climbed upward, completely agreeing with his assessment. When I reached the landing, I stopped dead in my tracks, a shiver racing over my body like something cold had rushed past me. Placing my foot on the first step of the next flight, I saw the front door to the flat was open.

"Usually people lock their front doors," Wilder said, stating the obvious.

"Duh."

"Wait here," he said with an authoritative grunt.

Ignoring him, I ran up the last dozen stairs and pushed into the hallway beyond.

"Jackson?" I called out to the dark apartment. "Jackson?"

A thump from within drew my gaze to his bedroom door and I rushed forward, passing my room before reaching his. The air temperature fell the farther I went, causing my breath to vaporise. It wasn't *that* cold outside and the radiator should be on.

Nudging open Jackson's bedroom door, I saw a writhing mass on his bed and yelped. I flipped on the light and a rush of brightness filled the space and my yelp turned into a cry.

"Holy shite!"

Jackson was lying on his bed, fully clothed, twisting and turning, his sheets a tangled mess beneath him. He gritted his teeth and turned his head, muttering under his breath. When his gaze met mine, his eyes were completely white.

An arm wrapped around my waist and yanked me backwards. I slammed into a hard chest and began to wriggle.

"I wouldn't go in there if I were you," Wilder murmured against my ear.

"Let go of me!" I exclaimed, desperate to get to Jackson. He was overdosing or having a fit or *something*. I didn't want to acknowledge the bit where another person had blank eyes just like that earlier in the evening.

"Your friend has been possessed."

I broke free of Wilder's grasp and turned to glare at him. "Possessed?"

He flipped his knife in his hands and pointed the tip towards my best friend. "That's what that is, just so you know."

"*But…*"

Wilder raised an eyebrow, unimpressed over the whole scene, which only made me want to slap him. *Hard.*

"His head isn't going to turn around is it?" I asked, glancing over my shoulder.

Wilder shrugged, picking paint off the doorjamb with his knife. "It might."

"It might?" I shrieked. "Get it out of him!"

"Wait, a moment ago you were telling me all the things that were wrong with me, and now you think it's a completely sane thing to go around asking strangers to perform exorcisms. Where was the part where you accepted all of this, because I think I might've missed it."

"Can you get it out of him or not?"

"Would it be such a bad thing to leave it where it is?"

"*Yes!*"

"I mean, look at him." Wilder gestured to the bed where my best friend was writhing and foaming at the mouth. "He has a Call of Duty poster on his wall. How old is he again?"

"He's a professional gamer," I said, clucking my tongue. "Wilder, *please.*"

"Well, that's all you had to say," he declared, pushing off the wall and pocketing his knife.

"Wait… What?" I stared after him incredulously as he stood at the foot of the bed, looking rather intimidating in his leather biker jacket.

"Manners get you a long way in life," he drawled. "They can charm you right into an exorcism if you're lucky." He clicked his fingers. "Now, hand me that limited edition Witcher sword."

"Huh?" I picked up the sword leaning against the wall. "You're not going to…"

"Pfft," he said rolling his eyes. "I couldn't even cut through butter with that thing."

"What do you need it for then?"

"Nothing. I just wanted to see the look on your face."

"You're such an arsehole."

"I've been called worse, sweetheart. You'll have to try better next time."

"*Hunter*," the demon said, its voice hollow. He spat at Wilder, who just stepped to the side. The saliva missed him and he cracked his knuckles. "You think you can win? This body is *mine*."

"Yours you say?" he replied with a laugh. "You can't even get up."

The demon cackled, licked its lips, and went for its crotch. I gasped and covered my mouth as it pulled out Jackson's—

"Don't look at him, Scarlett," Wilder said. "Demons are all about violent masturbation in front of the possessed's loved ones. It thinks it's shocking, but I guarantee your friend is already intimately acquainted with jacking off."

"I don't want to know. Just get that thing out of him!" I exclaimed.

"Put the penis away, Infernal," Wilder said, holding out his hands. "And leave this human before things get messy."

"*Never!*" it shouted, its eyes flashing silver as it bared its teeth.

"They always say never," Wilder muttered before he began to chant something in a strange language. *Was that Latin?*

I edged out into the hall as Jackson began to thrash, throwing his head from side to side. Wilder clenched his fists and the demon's back arched away from the mattress, its arms and hands twisting as its mouth gaped open. The bed shuddered, scraping across the floor a few inches to the left, then back to the right.

I glanced at Wilder, but he hadn't moved. His

hands were still raised and coiled into tight fists, and his gaze was locked on the demon.

Jackson let out a wail as he was pushed back onto the bed by an invisible force, then his mouth opened and a plume of black smoke rushed out.

The smoke hit the ceiling, then pooled in the corner, writhing and emitting sparks of electricity. It sent out long inky tendrils, looking for a crack to escape through.

"Kill it!" I cried.

Wilder pulled out his crazy sword and I flinched as it sprang into life, showering the room with white sparks. Luckily for us, nothing caught fire, but the demon began to pulsate, emitting a dull rumbling that sounded a lot like an angry growl.

He edged towards the cloud as it snaked across the wall, holding the sword at the ready. It was searching for the window, wrapping itself around the curtains.

Wilder thrust, the demon roared, and the window shattered. The demon shrieked, then flew out into the night, tumbling and turning until it dissipated.

"You let it get away," I said with a *humph*.

"At least it's gone," Wilder shot back, "and out of your geeky boyfriend."

"Jackson is not my boyfriend."

"He's not, huh?"

A thump banged against the floor as I tried to catch my scattered wits.

"*Shut the hell up!*" the neighbour boomed, his voice carrying through the floorboards. "*People are trying to sleep down here!*"

I glanced at Wilder.

"Sorry about the window," he said with a shrug. "Have you got insurance?"

Shaking my head, I climbed onto the bed and smoothed Jackson's hair from his brow. He was burning up and sweat prickled his skin. He was unconscious to the point of being in a coma, and no amount of shaking brought him around.

"That's not going to help," Wilder drawled.

"What's wrong with him?"

"There's no question about it now," he declared. "You'll have to come with me."

"I think we've had just about enough quality time together," I said, checking Jackson's pulse. *Thready.*

Wilder snorted. "You *and* your lanky friend."

I shook my head. I was so done with this bad acid trip. "We're not going anywhere with you."

"He was possessed," he stated. "The demon likely fed on his soul at least a little. That's why he won't wake up."

"It fed on his soul?" I shrieked, almost falling off the bed.

"Calm down, Purples. We can fix it. Don't get your knickers all twisted in a bunch."

I fisted my hands into my hair and resisted the urge to burst into tears. "Did it follow us here? Was it waiting for me?"

"After all the shit we've been through tonight?" Wilder glanced away. "Probably."

"Why? What did I ever do to it?" I sniffed, my throat burning. "Where do they even come from?"

"There's a world that exists alongside yours," Wilder said. "A secret world that threatens to plunge yours into eternal darkness."

"*How cliché.*"

"It may be a cliché, but it's also very real. Those demons you saw? Those are only the tip of the iceberg."

I stiffened at his analogy, unpleasantness tingling down my spine. Memories were like icebergs…

"I'm beginning to suspect that demon wasn't at that pub yesterday by chance," he went on, throwing a glance at Jackson, "especially now."

"Why? I'm a nobody… I'm…" *A messed up woman with a mental problem.*

"It could be any number of reasons," Wilder said. "I denied it, and this was its revenge, or its fixated on you, or—"

"Or?"

He shrugged and grasped Jackson's wrist. Pulling my comatose best friend across the bed, he leaned forward and dragged him over his shoulder like he weighed nothing. Maybe it was another magic trick.

"C'mon, Purples. We've got a long walk ahead of us."

"We're walking?" My feet were throbbing from a day pinging back and forth across the city *and* the midnight marathon around Moorgate. The thought of walking while trying to transport Jackson was too much.

"Fine. We can get a taxi, but you'll have to hail

one for us," he said with a pout. "No one will stop for a guy with a body slung over his shoulder."

Downstairs, Wilder hid in the bushes while I scouted oncoming traffic for a taxi. Dawn was on the rise as the sky was already lighting up. Glancing up at the flat, I grimaced as the curtains in Jackson's room fluttered through the broken glass. Not only was I going crazy, but I'd dragged my best friend into it too. *What a night.*

In the distance, I spied the light of an available black cab and I raised my hand. The indicator flashed orange as the car pulled off the side of the road and stopped beside me. Too tired to care, I climbed in the back and the driver leaned around and peered at me through the Perspex partition.

"Where to, love?" he drawled, his Geordie accent harsh against my ears.

"Um..."

The taxi rocked as Wilder appeared, the weight of both him and Jackson making the car dip.

"Oi!" the driver exclaimed. "You can't bring him in here!"

"It'll be fine," Wilder said, setting Jackson down on the seat between us.

"No, it won't! Get 'im out!"

"*Listen.*" The demon hunter leaned forward and tapped his finger against the partition. "Look here. That's it..." The taxi driver's expression slackened, and his gaze fixed on Wilder's fingertip. "You can't see us here and you definitely won't be able to hear what we say." The man nodded, his mouth gaping open.

"You're going to drive us directly to Battersea. Cringle Street. Got it?"

The man turned and began to drive, pulling out onto Kentish Town Road and almost sideswiping a bus.

"Bloody hell!" I exclaimed. "What did you do to him?"

"He'll be fine, Purples. We've got places to go and he'll get us there faster than our feet."

This Light thing was getting out of hand. I didn't know anything about it, but in books and movies people always said magic had consequences. Wilder seemed to use his abilities without any thought other than what it could get him. I found him more arrogant the longer I was in his presence.

Jackson was still out cold when I checked him, though when I pressed my fingers against his neck, his pulse was strong.

"You didn't mention God," I said.

"When?" Wilder asked, raising an eyebrow.

"Aren't exorcisms meant to be performed by priests? How can you be sure it worked?"

"There's no way in hell I'm a priest. I like sex too much."

My cheeks heated and I glanced at Jackson.

Hastily changing the subject, I asked, "What was with the troll doll?"

"It was a failsafe," he replied. "If my alteration didn't hold for a third time, it'd lead you back to me."

"You weren't too pleased to see me, though."

"I didn't want to deal with it," he stated. "And it did look like you."

"You don't know what to do with me, do you?" When he didn't reply, I added, "That's okay, neither do I."

"It won't be my decision," he said after a moment.

"What do you mean?"

Wilder glanced out of the window, watching an early morning London flash past as we crossed the Chelsea Bridge.

"Wilder?"

"I'm just a soldier, Scarlett," he murmured. "The Naturals will decide what to do with you, not me."

In that moment, I knew I was nothing more than a problem to Wilder. A stupid woman with too many issues to count, a history of poor decision-making skills, and a possible immunity to his weird magic. Whoever the rest of these Naturals were, they sounded like a real riot, but if they could help Jackson…

I rolled my eyes and grasped his clammy hand. He needed help and this was the only was he could get it. I guess there was no two ways about it. *Time to climb into the jaws of a lion.*

6

———

There were a lot of things I would have changed if I could go back forty-eight hours. Like ignoring the troll doll, calling the police when I saw Wilder stab that guy, and believing Jackson when he'd said no one was there. Another was following a demon hunter, who called himself a Natural, through the dark city streets while he carried my best friend over his shoulder like a sack of potatoes.

Glancing up at the towers of the Battersea power station, I shivered. My breath blew out in a plume of vapour in front of me.

"Where are we going exactly?" I asked. "We're not going to recreate the cover of Pink Floyd's *Animals* album, are we? Because I'm fresh out of inflatable pigs."

"We are going to the Sanctum," he replied. "The Naturals home turf."

I glanced around the rundown street that sat in the shadow of multiple tower blocks. "Here?"

"We can't exactly list our phone number, you know."

We turned down a dark lane, the rising sun casting murky shadows over everything. Wilder stopped outside an old factory and pushed open the wire gate.

"Wait, this is your headquarters?" I stared up at the abandoned building and didn't get it. Was it an underground facility or something? Who the hell were these people? "It's a pile of shit."

"You still don't get it, do you, Purples?" He grasped Jackson as he lifted his free hand and pressed it against a door that had a *no trespassing* sign nailed to the wood.

It creaked open and Wilder stepped inside, leaving me no choice but to follow. *So demons were a thing, as well as possessions and exorcisms… oh and magic. Were ghosts real too, because this place looked haunted as fu*—

My breath caught as I found myself inside a place that looked anything but decomposed and abandoned —it was posh as.

We stood in a foyer of bland slate-colored stone, the floor shining with slices of veiny black marble. Overhead, an elaborate domed skylight let in the dawn, filling the space with orange-tinted sunlight. A small metal plaque was screwed to an otherwise plain wall ahead of us. Footsteps drew my attention and I turned before I had a chance to read what it said.

A man melted out of the shadows and strode towards us, not looking too pleased with our appearance.

"Wilder, what's going on here?" he barked.

He was dressed in black from head to toe. A tight black T-shirt clung to a muscled torso, then came the black trousers and combat boots. I warily eyed the hilt tucked into a holster on his belt. It was another of those funky arondight blades Wilder carried. How many of these Natural people were there?

"Calm down, Brax," Wilder snapped. "I'm in the middle of a crisis here. I need Ramona."

He crinkled his nose in distaste. "What is that thing on your back?"

"That's my best friend!" I exclaimed, my annoyance levels running at an all-time high.

The man Wilder had called Brax glanced at me, his confusion clear. "What's she doing here?"

I bristled at Brax's tone as he gestured to another man waiting in the wings, who immediately rushed off deeper into the building, his boots thumping against the marble.

"I'd be careful with that one," Wilder said. "She bites."

"Hard," I added with a glare.

"You were meant to check in hours ago," Brax went on, ignoring me completely. "What have you been screwing up this time?"

I made a face. Wilder must be the delinquent bad boy who constantly gave the middle finger to authority. Looking him over, I could see how it fit. Smart mouth, a distinct lack of respect—he had all the hallmarks of an anarchist.

"I've been reluctantly saving people from

demons," he drawled. "Can I put this thing down yet?"

"Where is he?" a woman asked, striding into the foyer. She was just as happy to see us as that Brax guy was. "Where is the human?" She was almost as tall as Wilder, her auburn hair pulled back into a severe braid, and her attitude was as sour as a lemon on a hot day.

"Ramona," Wilder said to the woman as she came to a halt in front of us. "He was possessed by an Infernal. It's chomped at his soul, I'm afraid."

She pursed her lips as she looked at me, then immediately disregarded my presence. Why did they keep doing that?

"An Infernal?" She seemed worried about this and glanced at Jackson.

"There was nothing I could do at the scene," he went on. "He needs—"

"Understood." The woman clapped her hands and two men with a stretcher appeared.

I watched numbly as Wilder set him down and Jackson was carried away.

"Wait," I called out. "Where are you taking him?"

The woman lingered, narrowing her eyes. "To the infirmary," she stated. "He'll get the care he requires."

My skin crawled as I realised I was as unwelcome here as a fart in an enclosed space. My gaze bounced about the room, from one pair of untrusting eyes to the next.

"Wilder," I rasped, tugging at his sleeve.

"You don't have to worry about your geeky

boyfriend," he said. "Ramona will look after him and once he's better, he'll wake up at home none the wiser."

"No, that's—" The room tilted.

"He won't remember being possessed, Purples. His soul will be repaired good as new."

"No, it's not that."

"Not what?"

My vision blurred around the edges and a low hissing sound echoed in my ears. *Great, just my luck.*

"I don't feel so good," I muttered just before everything went dark.

7
<hr>

Awareness came back slowly.

My eyes cracked open, revealing a room awash with soft light. Cream walls and a leather chair sat in the corner. A soft bed and a feathery pillow. I felt like I'd sunk into the mattress and was fused there. I closed my eyes again, hoping the next time I opened them, I'd be in my own bed. How long had I been asleep? I remembered passing out, but nothing after that.

"She's had a rather eventful few days," a female voice said. "She'll wake when her body is rested enough."

"So it wasn't anything demonic?" Was that Wilder?

"No, merely human exhaustion. Besides, she wouldn't have been able to cross the threshold if she were harbouring a demon."

"Point…"

"From your report, she's been through a great deal. Our world is confronting, but to this extent?"

"I know." There was some rustling, but no one spoke for a while. "I'd like to be present when you test her."

"Wilder, you know I can't allow that."

"She's been through enough, and I'm a familiar face at least. If I—"

"I won't be manipulated," the woman snapped. "You know the parameters of your involvement here and they do not extend that far. The Codex doesn't allow it."

An uncomfortable silence stretched on for a while until Wilder said, "Understood."

There was more rustling and the sound of a chair scraping back.

"You better decide what mask you're going to wear today, Greer, because she's awake." Heavy footfalls crossed the room, then the door slammed shut, signaling that Wilder had stormed out. I had no idea what his role here was, but it seemed like he'd been demoted and wasn't happy about it. Why wasn't I surprised?

The gig was well and truly up, so I opened my eyes. At first I didn't see much at all. Whoever was in the room with me was at my back, so I had a second to acclimatize before I turned over.

I glanced around, but it wasn't like any posh hospital or hotel room I'd ever seen. Focusing on the woman sitting next to the bed, I realized I was staring, but it was hard to look away.

She was the image of a supermodel. I decided she was Cindy Crawford with her long legs, silky chestnut hair, a beauty mark on her cheek, and perfectly symmetrical facial features. In comparison, I felt like a cockroach lying on its back, waving its feet around because it couldn't get up.

"Welcome back, Scarlett," she said, flashing her perfect teeth. "How are you feeling?"

"Who…? Where…?"

"I'm Greer," the woman said with a smile. "I'm in charge of the Sanctum and protector of the Codex."

"The what?" I rubbed my eyes. Were all demon hunters part-time catwalk models?

"Don't worry, there'll be time to explain everything." She wasn't unkind, which just rubbed salt into my physical insecurities. I could see why Wilder had his hackles up, though—the sweet bordered on sickly.

"I-I had the strangest dream," I muttered.

"I assure you, this is all very real," Greer said. "I can sense you're still trying to come to terms with this upheaval, but you can't deny the things you've already seen. Infernals, possessions, exorcisms…"

I watched her with trepidation as she raised her hands and held them over me. Her brow creased as if she were trying to sense something in the surrounding air, then she placed her hands on her lap and flexed her fingers.

"Wilder was right," she said. "You have no Light, nor are you manifesting."

"What did he say?"

"He told us everything, though I suspect he's held a few things back. He's like that."

Hearing it didn't instill much faith in me, either. I didn't know a single thing about these people, or their politics, but I needed answers without locking myself unknowingly into some magical contract I couldn't get out of. What a conundrum.

"Where's Jackson?" I began, deciding to start with something obvious. "Is he…?"

"Your friend is recovering in the infirmary," Greer said. "His soul has been restored, though he needs bedrest. Possession is an exhausting experience."

"He'll be okay?"

She nodded. "Perfectly."

I sighed in relief, my breath whooshing out. That was good news, but I wouldn't be completely satisfied until he was out of this place and home where he belonged, and me… Well, I wasn't sure where I belonged now. Always pinging from place to place, that was my MO. Fitting in was a foreign concept, and now there were magical troll dolls in play—who knew which way was true north.

"Has anything like this happened to you before?" Greer asked.

I snorted and sat up, scooping the blankets around myself. I wasn't wearing much of anything, which meant someone had the fabulous job of changing my comatose body. *Blergh.*

"I gather that's a no."

"I've never seen any clouds of black smoke puff out people's mouths or had a demon chase me through the street before, so no," I replied with an air of sarcasm. "I think I'd remember if any of those things had happened."

"Usually people don't."

I rolled my eyes. The alteration thing, of course. It didn't work on me, so I definitely knew I hadn't run into a demon before. I wondered how common it was for there to be attacks.

"The sword… Wilder said I shouldn't be able to use it, but it worked."

Greer nodded. "That is correct. Arondight blades only activate for those who possess Light. It's very unusual."

I sighed. Lately a lot of things had revealed themselves to be unusual. It was hard to keep up with all the developments.

"Wilder believes the Infernal are interested in you for more than possession," she continued. "In light of this, we'd like to conduct some tests in order to determine the cause of your apparent skill, for lack of a better word."

I tensed. "You want to experiment on me?"

"No, nothing as sinister as that," she replied with a sweet smile. "The only explanation we can see is that you indeed have Light, but it's hidden. We'd like to try to bring it forth. In either case, we'd prefer to ensure your safety before allowing you to return to your normal life."

The Cindy Crawford-lookalike didn't say it, but I got the distinct feeling I had no choice in the matter. This was probably payment for them helping restore

Jackson's soul. Wilder never said anything about the fine print and I scowled.

"What do you mean by Light? Are you angels or something?"

"No," she replied with a chuckle. "Nothing as outrageous as that. What you refer to as magic, we call Light."

"And magic isn't outrageous?" I muttered, looking around the room.

Above the bed was a skylight set with stained glass in the shape of a woman in a flowing robe clutching a sword. It accounted for the strange hue to the room, but the closer I studied the image, the more I realised it wasn't Catholic. It didn't seem to have anything to do with the religions of the human world.

"Who is that?" I pointed to the skylight. "Is that your version of God?"

"We don't follow religion here," Greer said, watching me closely. "Only the battle between Light and Dark."

"Demons?" I asked. "Like the one Wilder and I fought?"

She nodded. "There is a constant push and pull for dominance. Every minute of every day, all that stands in the way from that balance tipping into Darkness, are the people you see here and those like them around the world."

"The Naturals?"

"Yes."

"And they all have this… Light?"

"We are all born of Light," she replied.

"Wait, so you can't learn it? You have to be born that way?"

"Or made, though a Natural hasn't been created in hundreds of years." Greer glanced at me, a frown creasing her perfect forehead. "Who were your parents?"

"I… They died when I was young. Wait…" I held up my hand. "What do they have to do with any of this? I don't even understand why I'm here. I don't have any of this Light you keep mentioning. Apart from being able to see Wilder the jackass when I was apparently not supposed to, and being able to hold a magical sword or whatever, I'm not anything special. I'm just an emotionally scarred twenty-five-year-old who missed her birthday because of *demons*. I fainted in front of a bunch of strangers, and I woke up in an unfamiliar bed. *And* here you are telling me awful bedtime stories. If this is a hidden camera show and I'm being punked, please put me out of my misery."

Greer laughed. *Ugh. Even her laugh sounded like angles singing.*

"You're very—"

"Surly?" I finished for her. "Don't worry, I've heard that before."

"Recently, I take it."

I nodded as I spotted the troll doll sitting on top of a pile of clothes in the leather armchair. My phone, wallet, and keys were beside it, and my boots were on the floor. Someone had polished them, which was borderline blasphemy. Kick-arse boots should always look beaten up and scuffed to hell and back. How else were people to know you meant business?

"Are you well?" Greer asked. "I'll show you more of the Sanctum, if you wish, and take you to see your friend."

"That'd be great." I sighed in relief and glanced around the room.

"I have some new clothes laid out for you," she said, gesturing to the pile of clothes on the armchair. "We salvaged what we could, but some of your clothing was ruined, I'm afraid."

"Oh. Thank you."

"I'll come back shortly to collect you," she said, rising to her feet. Realizing she was wearing an elegant black pantsuit with a shiny black silk blouse and sky-high heels, I raised my eyebrows. Corporate Natural? Business wear for demon hunters must be a thing.

Once I'd showered and scrubbed the grime off my body, I dressed, glad someone had the foresight to give me jeans that fit and a plain black T-shirt. Donning my leather jacket and shoving my feet into my boots, I glanced at the troll doll. That thing was following me everywhere.

Just as I reached for it, the door opened. I shot to my feet awkwardly and combed my fingers through my damp hair.

"Much better," Greer declared, gesturing for me to follow her outside. "I trust the clothes fit?"

"Yes. Perfectly, thank you."

Greer led me through the Sanctum, explaining

things as we passed. We were in the residential part of the building where all the demon hunters had their rooms. There was enough accommodation to house over a hundred people, but less than a third of them were occupied. There was a fully kitted out infirmary —where Jackson was being cared for—training facilities, briefing rooms, an array of computer systems to help in the hunt for demons, a library, armoury, kitchens, and even a garden on the roof. There was a vault and a holding facility specially designed to keep demons in—especially the black inky smoke type—in the basement.

The building had hints of medieval architecture mixed in with modern touches. Paintings and epitaphs were displayed in common areas, and the halls were hardwood with insanely long carpet runners over top. Every so often there were displays of weapons—swords, spears, shields, and halberds— unlike anything I'd ever seen. Some blades looked like they were forged out of crystal rather than steel, and the designs painted on the shields didn't look like any coat of arms I'd ever seen.

The Sanctum looked more like a museum than a demon hunter headquarters. I almost expected to see those little ropes cordoning off sections tourists weren't allowed to go into and dudes with walkie-talkies poised to tell people off for inching too close to the artefacts.

After reassuring me there weren't any demons currently being held down below, Greer took me to see the Naturals training area. The room looked like any other gym, though it was dark. The walls were painted black and the mats underfoot were a smoky grey. Spotlights lit up certain areas, while others were left to writhe in the shadows.

I watched as two men twisted and leapt, their blades colliding in a shower of sparks. It was surreal and completely mesmerising—they were like dancers putting on a performance on stage, like shadows armed with arc welders.

"Naturals train from the time they are children until they day they die," Greer explained. "We never stop learning, knowing that our enemy is always one step ahead."

"I can tell." The way the men anticipated each other's movements was otherworldly. It was like they were a second ahead of the curve before the curve had even thought about curving. "The swords… what are they exactly?"

"They are arondight blades as you know," she replied. "They are weapons forged with Light, whose sole purpose is to slay Darkness. They are one of the few things in this world that can banish a demonic soul forever."

I shivered, remembering how I'd stabbed the spider demon creature with Wilder's arondight blade. It'd burst into flames the moment its heart had been pierced. I guess it'd been damned to Hell or wherever they went when they died for real.

"What is Arondight exactly?" I asked. "Is it like some special metal?"

"Arondight was the magical sword wielded by

Lancelot in your Arthurian legends. Our arondight is made from a mixture of crystal, quicksilver, and carbon extracted from meteorites, then forged with an intricate web of Light at temperatures far greater than humans have been able to create themselves. The original blade has been long since lost, but its secrets lingered long enough for us to be able to forge our own."

"Lancelot?" I made a face and sighed. "I suppose it isn't so farfetched considering… you know, demons and shit."

Greer smiled. "It's not so much about the man who wielded it, than where it came from and what it could do."

"Slay demons?"

"Yes, though the blades we forge in its image are pale in comparison to the relic itself. If we had Arondight itself, then the balance would greatly tip in our favour, but that's another story. A very long story."

"Where is it?"

"Arondight was lost a long time ago."

"Oh…"

I watched the two demon hunters as they continued their fight, never once breaking formation or striking one another. Only their blades touched. Curiously, they were also showering the room with white sparks like Wilder's sword. When I'd picked up the blade, it'd glowed purple for me. I had no idea why that might be, but I had the feeling it might've been something Wilder left out of his report. I had more reason to trust him than Greer, so I decided to keep my violet hue to myself… for now.

"Ah, here's Romy," Greer said, drawing my attention away from the fight.

"Morning, Greer," a tall, wisp of a woman said as she came to join us. "Is this Scarlett?"

I gaped as she looked me over. Yet another Victoria's Secret model stood before me, all lithe, perfect, and, well, just *perfect*. Her black hair was pulled back into a severe ponytail, though it fell in long luxurious waves. Impossibly long lashes framed her icy grey eyes and her skin was flawless ivory. Unlike the other hunters I'd seen, Romy had black and grey tattoos which snaked up both her arms and along the left side of her neck. Geometric patterns made up of dots, blocks of black ink, and lines upon lines formed the intricate designs.

"Scarlett, I'd like you to meet Romy," Greer said, nodding towards the woman. "She's one of our recently graduated hunters. I've asked her to help you with whatever you need." Which I knew was code for babysit the untrustworthy human who may or may not be here to destroy us all.

"It's okay, Greer," I said with a smirk. "I know how these things work. You've got shit to do and someone needs to watch me in case I get sticky fingers."

Romy chuckled, earning herself a stern look from Greer.

"We are fighting a war, Scarlett," she replied. "We must not take any chances… even with ourselves."

She glanced across the room and I felt a blast of cold air tickle my neck like someone had just turned on the aircon and I happened to be standing under the vent.

Following her gaze, I tensed as I saw Wilder talk to another hunter. He looked different today, less disheveled and more solider-like.

"I trust you'll make sure Scarlett has something to eat?" Greer asked, turning back to Romy. "Then a trip to the infirmary is in order."

The hunter nodded, snapping to attention. "Yes, ma'am."

Greer offered me one last smile before she floated from the room, off to perform some mysterious official task I'm sure. There was something untouchable about her, like she held herself on a pedestal above the other Naturals. Well, she was the leader, but there was something I didn't like about it. This whole place, the way I was being given a personalised guided tour, assigned a minder, had a friend given preferential medical care… There was something off about it.

"I don't get it," I muttered. "If I can't have my memory altered, then why am I being told all this?"

"There must be something about you because you've already seen too much," Romy said with a smile. "It's not for me to ask."

I grimaced and looked for an exit, much to her amusement.

"Don't worry," she said. "Greer knows what she's doing. She must have a good reason for bringing you into the Sanctum like this."

"What are they going to do with me?"

"She'll consult the Codex," Romy replied. "Then possibly test you for Light."

"What's the Codex?" I asked, ignoring the part about being poked and prodded like a poor lab rat.

"It's an ancient text that tells us of the origins of Light," she explained, "and the Naturals code of conduct, give or take a few metaphors."

"So it's like your version of the Bible?"

"Kind of." Romy smiled and nodded towards the training mats. "What do you think?"

"It's very impressive." My gaze settled on Wilder, who hadn't noticed us standing there yet. His fingers curled into the hem of his T-shirt and he dragged the material up and over his head, revealing just how hard his chest was. He was lean, muscled, and one hundred percent—

"Is that drool?" Romy asked with a chuckle.

"No," I snapped a little too quickly. "It's just… What's his deal? He's got an attitude that screams troubled past." I was great at spotting the wounded ones because it took one to know one and all of that. We were brilliant at masking our pain with humour and arseholery.

"Wilder…" She sighed, her gaze following him across the room. "He's not like the rest of us."

"Meaning?" I asked, startled at the pang of jealousy that stabbed me in the heart.

"Perhaps that's a story he ought to tell you."

I snorted. "If I don't die on the autopsy table."

Romy laughed, the sound echoing through the

training room. Heads turned to stare and I flushed, not liking the attention.

"You're cool," she declared. "Are you hungry? Let's go to the kitchen."

I glanced back across the room. Wilder caught my eye and stared at me, though his expression gave away nothing.

"Uh, I think I'd rather go to the infirmary first," I said. "I want to see how Jackson is."

"Sure thing!" Smiling brightly, she guided me towards the exit. "So, is he your boyfriend or something?"

"Huh?"

"The human. He's pretty…" She searched her mind for a word but couldn't come up with anything.

"No," I said with a scowl, "he's not my boyfriend."

"Just as well, I doubt geek is your type," a masculine voice declared behind us.

I spun on my heel and shot a withering glare at Wilder, who'd forgotten to bring his shirt with him. "I thought I recognised the arsehole tone in your voice."

"I'm one of a kind." Glancing at Romy, he added, "I've got her from here."

"Nuh-ah," she said, waving her finger at him. "I've got my orders, Wilder. Back off."

"I'll fight you for her," he said with a grin, "one-on-one."

"That's cheating," Romy said with a pout. "You're a higher rank than me."

"Can you put on a shirt already?" I declared.

"Why?" His lips quirked. "Embarrassed by finding all this attractive?"

"*Don't make me vomit.*"

Romy sighed and grabbed a T-shirt from a passerby. "Here. But I'll be back in ten minutes and I expect to find Scarlett in the infirmary."

Wilder smiled triumphantly and pulled the T-shirt over his head. "You heard her, Purples. Let's go."

"Why do you care?" I asked as we stepped out of the training area and into the hallway. "You just wanted to dump me here and not deal with me, remember?"

"First rule in life, Scarlett, is don't trust anyone."

"Not even your own kind?"

"*Our* kind."

I snorted. "You think I'm a fancy pants Natural? Impossible."

"It's not out of the realm of possibilities," he stated.

I wasn't up for a debate over how weird I was, so I fell silent as he guided me through the warren of hallways and rooms. The Sanctum must be massive, but it was oddly devoid of activity.

When we reached the infirmary, I glanced through the windows and spotted Jackson. The whole room was open and lined with beds dormitory style, and medical equipment was scattered here and there. At the far end, a curtain had been drawn around one bed, and what I assumed were nurses flitted back and forth. None of them were paying much attention to my best friend at all. Was he just a routine case, or was it something more sinister? Prejudice? Maybe.

"Was it the same demon as Blond Tips?" I asked.

Wilder frowned. "Who?"

"The guy from the pub. Was it the same demon who possessed Jackson?"

"Both were Infernals, but it's impossible to tell if it was the same one. They all look the same."

I glanced through the door, beginning to get really worried about what happened next.

"So I figured out this isn't a hallucination," I said.

"Took you long enough."

I bit my tongue and shook my head. "It's clear I'm not welcome because I'm different," I went on, crossing my arms over my chest. "I can see the way people have been looking at me and it's only been five bloody minutes."

"I know," Wilder murmured. "I get it."

I glanced up at him and was surprised to see how troubled he looked. Romy had mentioned something about Wilder being different from everyone else, but something told me not to ask about it. Not yet, anyway.

"They want to test me," I said. "What does that mean?"

"Greer wants to see if you have any Light," he explained. "You weren't supposed to use my arondight blade, and you're immune to alteration. You're an anomaly, Purples, and they want to understand why."

"Or work out what side I'm on."

"I didn't want to say it like that, but yes. It's a real possibility."

"I'm not a demon," I stated, bristling with annoyance. "I'm not some secret weapon here to destroy you all from the inside."

Wilder tensed and lowered his gaze. "Not knowingly."

I snorted, seriously offended.

"That's what they want to figure out, Scarlett."

Then why show me everything? Was it all one giant ruse? If I was naïve and life hadn't taught me that all people were awful when it came to the crunch, I would've blindly accepted all of this. Acceptance and lack of questioning was the kiss of death in my book. One way or another, everyone had a motive. The only exception to that was Jackson. He was good, kind, honest… and nothing like these Naturals.

"I can't trust anyone," I whispered.

I fully expected Wilder to tell me I could trust him, and part of me wanted him to, but all he did was grasp my shoulders and turn me towards the door. "You better go see your boyfriend."

"He's not…" I sighed.

"You better tell him that then." Wilder shoved me and I practically stumbled into the infirmary.

Heads swivelled as the door slammed behind me and my cheeks heated.

"Scarlett!"

Spotting Jackson's waving hand, I scurried across the infirmary, shying away from the unwanted attention.

"Hey," I said, dragging a chair to the side of his bed. It made an awful scraping sound and everyone turned—*again*—and glared as I arranged myself.

"Hey," Jackson said with a weak smile. He looked paler than usual, and a little grey around the edges. He was propped up in bed and had those little round white stickers on his chest with coloured wires running out of them. The machine next to his bed displayed some numbers and a graph that looked like a heartbeat, but it was irregular.

"They said that squiggly line is my soul," he said as I squinted at the readings. "Messed up, isn't it?"

"This whole thing is crazy," I agreed. "How are you feeling?"

"Like shit warmed up."

"An eloquent way of putting it." I smiled, suddenly shy in front of the one person I trusted the most. Wilder had pushed me off balance again and it was infuriating.

"I've heard a lot of crazy stuff," he said, glancing across the room. "They said I was possessed by a demon. Scarlett, that's some weird shit, but I'm missing time like I blacked out. Just like you did…"

"It's cool," I reassured him. "I wasn't possessed. My story is, well… *different*. What do you remember?"

"I don't remember, that's the point." He shook his head and rubbed his eyes. "I was walking in the front door of our flat, then I woke up here. It was weird as hell. That rather unapproachable doctor told me I'd been possessed by a demon and after that, I seriously thought I was in an asylum. I still don't know what to believe, but I've got a mad sore throat. I didn't do anything weird, did I?"

"Um…" I shook off the image of his possessed body trying to grasp his *you know what*. "No, you didn't do anything."

"Scarlett… Am I…"

"Unfortunately, everything they told you is true. Demons, demon hunters, possession." I made a face, then proceeded to fill him in on everything that'd happened to me in the last two days. I left nothing out, even explaining the significance of the ugly troll doll and the missing time I'd experienced, even the encounter with the creepy spider-like demon on the tube.

"That explains why you were talking to yourself," Jackson said, resting his head back on the pillow. "And why you ran off at breakfast."

"I'm sorry."

"I know." He glanced around and waited until a nurse walked past. Once we were alone again, he murmured, "What are you going to do? You don't seriously trust these people, do you? I know they helped me, but they must want something in return because I don't think this place is part of the NHS. Do you think they take Bitcoin?"

"I don't know," I whispered. "Answers are just more questions in this place."

"Scarlett…"

"They're going to test me for powers or something," I blurted. "Wilder thinks I might have some of that Light they're so crazy over, which is why I was able to use his sword."

"Wilder? The guy who almost got you killed?" He scowled, pouting like a sulky teenager.

"Stop that," I said, swatting his arm. "He saved your life."

"And it cuts me up that I was saved by a guy like him." He pouted. "I don't like the way he looks at you."

"The way he…? Ugh. He looks at me like I'm a piece of shit on his boot."

"You're so clueless," he murmured, closing his eyes.

"Clueless or not, I'm out of here the second they get their payment. Not that I'm sure I've got much to go back to other than job hunting," I said with a groan. "I've missed one shift already at *8-bit* and ran out on another."

"Missing one shift? I think you'll be fine."

"That's if they ever let us out of here."

Jackson paled. "What do you mean?"

"I don't want to blindly trust them, but something weird is going on." I grasped his hand and squeezed. "I don't know what to do."

"You'll figure something out. You're the strongest person I know."

"Even with the meds?"

"Even with the meds."

I groaned and closed my eyes, realising I hadn't taken any of my prescribed pills for days now. Oddly, I hadn't had any episodes yet—no flashbacks, dreams, or mood swings—but I'd been comatose for most of it. If they were going to test me, maybe I should say something. Ugh, I was so confused.

"Who is that?"

I opened my eyes at the sound of his surprised question and I glanced up at Romy, who was walking towards us.

"I'm Romy!" she said brightly. "Nice to meet you."

"Well, her outsides are not like her insides," he said, his eyes almost popping out of his head.

"Don't be fooled by the exterior, human," she declared. "That's the first rule of demon hunting."

Jackson glanced at me and I shrugged. This place was full of juxtapositions.

"Are you hungry, Scarlett?"

I glanced at Jackson and he nodded towards the door. "Go," he said. "I'll be fine."

Romy cocked her head towards the other side of the room where the surly doctor I'd met on the way into the Sanctum was writing something on a fancy tablet computer. "Ramona's a bitch, but she's a great doctor. She'll watch out for your friend."

"See?" Jackson said with a smirk. "I'll be fine with the surly doctor."

I rose to my feet, but hesitated. I had that weird vibe again, like something invisible was breathing down the back of my neck.

"Go on," he prodded. "When you find out what's going on around here, you can come back and fill me in."

"All right," I said, stretching out the words. "Don't go anywhere okay?"

"Where would he go?" Romy said with a laugh. "He's tethered."

"Yeah, Scarlett, I'm tethered." He poked at the sensors stuck to his chest.

"No, silly," Romy declared, "you're *tethered*."

Jackson and I exchanged a worried look.

"Hurry back?" he asked with a squeak.

He didn't have to ask me twice. "As fast as I can."

8

———

R omy didn't let me stray on our way to the kitchen.

We passed more displays of weapons I desperately wanted to look at, but on my fifth attempt, she threaded her arm through mine and practically dragged me through the Sanctum. When we finally arrived, I wasn't surprised to find the room looked like a medieval banquet hall with all the trimmings, with a touch of modern convenience.

Through the open window, I could see the long galley-style kitchen with stainless steel appliances. There were three long tables that could easily seat at least twenty people a piece and a buffet-style spread of pre-prepared food in the dining room. People moved back and forth along the wall of food while others hurried in and out of the kitchen. It must be lunchtime.

Romy grabbed two plates off the warmer at the end of the buffet and began to fill them with salad, much to my horror. Five varieties of lettuce, garnished with purple onion, carrot, cucumber, those little cubes of crunchy bread, and a slimy layer of dressing. She bypassed the soup, a decent-looking stew, and the pile of bread and rolls, and found us a seat at one of the tables.

"There aren't many people here," I said. "Greer mentioned that only a few rooms were occupied?"

"Yeah, the Naturals aren't what they used to be," Romy said, setting the plates down. She slid into a chair and gestured for me to sit.

"Why?"

"The world is more accessible, I guess. People can go anywhere and do anything. Why would they want to be stuck in this place and risking their lives when they could be on a holiday in Ibiza?"

"That's irresponsible," I muttered. "Do they know there are demons and shit out there?"

"Someone else is taking care of it." Romy rolled her eyes and pouted. "Becoming a Natural is hard work, Scarlett. Not everyone is cut out for it."

I could understand that. We lived in a world of fast food, Netflix and chill, and five-second attention spans. Dedication wasn't something that was nurtured like it used to be. Even I had trouble finishing things I'd started.

Chairs scraped against the tiles beside us and plates were dumped on the table next to ours. Three more Naturals joined us—two men and a woman—and I glanced at them nervously. Romy seemed to be a social magnet and without her, I was sure there'd be a five-meter exclusion zone around my current location.

The woman smiled, flashing her ultra-straight teeth. She was another lean, athletic-type, with flame red hair and freckles for days. Her green eyes bordered on shiny emerald, and if it weren't for the scar that split her left eyebrow in two, she'd be flawless as well.

The men were much more rugged. The blue-eyed guy beside me had disheveled blonde hair and a standard black T-shirt that was torn at the collar. The other dude was sporting a full beard and man bun, but he looked way too tough to be a hipster. His muscles bulged and the fork he held in his hand looked like a dollhouse prop.

"Is this Wilder's new pet?" the blond guy next to me asked with narrowed eyes.

"If you're searching for my second head, I'm afraid you're going to be disappointed," I drawled. "I left it at home."

Romy and the other Naturals burst out laughing, and the man scowled.

"That's Valeria, Martin, and Aloysius," Romy said.

"Aloysius?" I asked, raising an eyebrow at the beefcake opposite. The name didn't fit at all, and I wondered why his parents had been so cruel.

"Don't get me started. Call me Alo, *please*." He winked and shoved a forkful of salad into his mouth, a shred of carrot getting stuck in his beard.

"We all trained together," Romy said to me. "Alo is a year older than us, though."

"What's the deal with that?" I asked, rubbing the condensation off my glass with a finger. "Training?"

"We're selected when we're children," Valeria replied, her Irish accent thick and juicy. "Then we train in the art of killing demons. Using our Light, weapons, theory, that kind of thing."

"We're elite warriors," Martin said with an air of arrogance. "Just because someone has Light doesn't automatically make them cut out to be a Natural."

Romy nudged me under the table and made a face, signalling Martin often liked to get up on his high horse and have a gallop.

"So, you were unlucky enough to have an encounter with Wilder," Alo said. "And you survived?" He whistled as he speared a cherry tomato with his fork.

"What's that supposed to mean?" I asked, watching as the juice from the tomato splattered across his plate.

"People say a lot of things about him," Valeria declared, "most of them bad."

"Yeah, they say his mother was raped by a demon."

"*Martin!*" Romy exclaimed.

"Well, they do." He shrugged, not masking his obvious dislike for Wilder.

"Wilder's a bit of a mystery," Valeria said to me. "No one knows for sure, but we know he's on constant probation."

From the sound of it, his tentative standing was due to much more than just his dislike of authority that he'd made constantly clear from the way he'd spoken to Greer that morning.

"Speak of the devil," Alo declared.

"That's an awful idiom," Valeria said. "I wish you wouldn't use it."

"Scarlett."

I glanced up at the sound of Wilder's voice, wondering what I'd done to deserve so much of his attention today.

He glared down at me, ignoring the other Naturals. "It's time."

"Already?"

He nodded.

I pushed my chair back and rose to my feet, my stomach churning like I was about to go to the executioner's block and that bland salad was my last meal, served to me by a mother who thought she knew best, but not really.

"Thanks for the… uh, *food*," I said to Romy, who smiled in return.

"Don't mention it."

Their eyes were glued to our backs as Wilder led me from the dining room and out into the hall. I didn't know how he put up with the snickering, the snide comments, the distrust. The longer I was here, the more I wanted to know what was up with him.

"Wilder?"

He grunted.

"Don't grunt at me," I grumbled as we passed a

display of what looked like an older style of arondight blades. They were only ornate sword hilts, but knowing how Wilder's worked, I assumed the pointy bit was deactivated.

We turned into an alcove and descended a flight of stairs. Overhead, an ornate chandelier hung, the crystal reflected shards of light from the open skylight. Unlike the one in my room, plain glass was open to the grey sky beyond.

"Did you want to ask me something, Purples?" Wilder asked with a smirk.

"I want to ask you a lot of things, but you're not exactly in an approachable mood."

"I'd spit it out if I were you. We don't have much time." *Well, that didn't sound ominous at all.*

"Is it… Is it going to hurt?"

He laughed and shook his head. "No. It's not an autopsy, Purples."

"May as well be," I drawled as we turned into a darkened hallway in the bowels of the Sanctum.

"It's more emotional than psychically painful," he said after a moment.

"You've had this test before?"

"Everyone who trains to be a Natural has to be tested."

We stopped outside an ominous-looking door, but he didn't reach for the handle. Instead, he turned towards me. "Tell them about your meds."

• • •

"Why? I don't see what that's got to do with anything." I'd debated it, but after talking with those other Naturals, I decided to keep as much to myself as possible. I didn't want to get rostered on the rumour mill if I could avoid it. Who knew how long I'd be stuck here. I suppose it all depends on what they find in their fancy tests.

"It could be blocking your abilities."

"If I have any at all," I muttered, "which I doubt."

"You have something," Wilder declared.

"Anyway, it doesn't matter. I haven't taken any in days. I'm *wide* open."

"And you don't feel any different?"

"Hmm, let me see." I gestured around me. "Two days ago, I was just a socially awkward mental case, and today, I'm standing in an invisible building full of demon hunters, but thanks for asking."

"You're welcome." He smirked, and the urge to slap him rose again.

"Wilder…" He turned and raised an eyebrow. "Those other Naturals…"

"I know what they say about me," he stated. "And I don't give two flying fu—"

"Wilder," Greer said, stepping out of the room, "that's enough."

I glanced at him, an unexpected wave of panic bubbling in my gut.

"You'll be fine, Purples," he said, inclining his head. "You don't need me, you made that clear the other night."

The other night? He must mean the spider demon. I stared after him as he spun on his heel and stalked away, his boots thumping against the carpet.

"Scarlett."

I turned back to Greer, who was holding the door open for me. "Why isn't he allowed to come?"

"Wilder's involvement at the Sanctum is governed under a strict set of guidelines. They do not extend here."

"Oh…" Looking back down the corridor, I saw that he'd already disappeared.

Stepping inside the room, I swallowed hard when I saw a scary-looking chair in the middle of what looked like one of those Victorian-era operating theatres I saw at a museum once. The restraints were bad enough on their own, but the bench seating? Whatever happened here was a spectator sport.

"I understand you've already met Brax and Ramona," Greer said, gesturing to the other people waiting. "This is Aldrich. Along with Brax and myself, we make up the governing council for the London Sanctum. Ramona is the head of our medical team."

"There's more than one Sanctum?"

She smiled, gesturing for me to sit on the scary-looking chair. "Many more. Demons know no bounds, and neither do we."

I eased onto the chair, eyeing the restraints, but no one made a move to put them on me. It alleviated my stress slightly to know there might not be any agonised thrashing in my near future.

"How are you feeling?" the man Greer had

introduced as Aldrich asked. He had kind eyes and a fatherly presence about him that made me ease back into the scary chair.

"Tired. Overwhelmed. Pick your adjective," I replied.

He smiled, his eyes crinkling with thready crow's feet. I wondered how old he was, though he certainly looked older than anyone else I'd seen around here.

"Discovering another world existing alongside the one you already know is much to take in," he agreed. "Not to mention the adventures you've had."

"I'm not sure adventure is the right word."

Brax snorted and leaned back in his chair. I decided I didn't like him, and it wasn't all about the way he'd greeted Wilder and I when we'd first arrived. No, Brax had a look on his face that said it all—old-school way of thinking, disapproval at having humans in their secret Natural hidey-hole, possible dislike of women who have any hint of a backbone. The list went on.

"What we want to do today," Greer began as she folded gracefully onto her chair, "is to determine the source of your apparent ability, and why the Infernal was so interested in you."

I nodded, already knowing the overlying reason I was sitting in the scary chair. Though I was wary of the underlying motives for the poking and prodding. I didn't know this world, which made the three people in front of me dangerous and unpredictable. I felt like I owed a little to Ramona since she had saved Jackson's soul and all.

"The scar on your face," Brax began, cutting right to the chase.

"I don't know how I got it," I replied before the question could go any further. "It's something I've always had."

"There's no way of discerning what made the mark," Ramona verified. "It's too old to scry."

"Scry?" I asked. "What's that?"

"It's a technique used to determine how a wound was made," the doctor explained. "In some cases, the information can be invaluable for treatment."

I wasn't keen to learn about what nasty demon-like creatures required specialised medicines, so I let it slide. They couldn't tell me anything about my scar anyway.

"You mentioned that you don't remember your parents," Greer said. "How old were you when they died?"

"What do they have to do with this?" I asked, squirming in the chair.

"In most cases, Light is inherited, but as you know—"

"I wasn't made," I declared. "I haven't been experimented on or whatever. I'm just *normal*." My whine sounded lame, even to me.

"Your abilities have come from somewhere," Aldrich said. "We're merely attempting to find the cause. We're not trying to harm or humiliate, but to help you, Scarlett." He knelt before me and smiled, his eyes warm. "Anything you could tell us could help determine why the Infernal targeted you."

The line between trust and answers was so fine that I was having trouble keeping on one side or the other.

"I… I have dreams," I began, my throat constricting, "of my parents."

"What are in these dreams?"

"I… I must be three or four years old. My mother asked me to hide…" I glanced at Greer, who nodded. "I was in a box, and it was dark… so dark."

"Then what happened?"

I shook my head, the image of my dead parents too confronting. My eyes began to fill with tears and all I wanted to do was crawl back into that box. It was dark, safe, and nothing could get in. The recollection always brought me to my knees, like their death was my defining moment. My breath caught and my throat twisted and burned, my eyes filled with tears.

"Scarlett…" Aldrich soothed, "can you tell us what happened next?"

"There were sounds," I said haltingly. "Thumps, cries… Then the lid opened. There was a man I'd never seen before. His eyes were white and his teeth… they seemed to go on forever. Sets of razor-sharp points over sets of more razor-sharp points. He lifted me out…" I glanced at them, hesitating. What happened next was a purple flash of light. What it did, I didn't know, but I knew it was linked to the colour Wilder's arondight blade had ignited with when I'd activated it. He hadn't seemed to mention it to anyone, and I was loathed to as well.

"And?" Aldrich prodded.

"Nothing," I replied. "Then nothing."

"Scarlett, I believe you just described what we call a Balan," Brax said.

"I don't know what that is."

"A Balan is a greater demon with the power to take on a human form without the aid of possession," Greer said looking thoughtful.

"But I…" I swallowed hard, then tried again. "But I've never seen a demon or anything until the other night. Wilder tried to wipe my memory three times and it didn't work. If I'd seen something like that before, it'd stand to reason I'd remember, right? Of course, my memory is sketchy back when I was a kid. Who knows if it's real or just the stylings of a four-year-old's overactive imagination? I always thought my dreams weren't real."

"She has a point," Brax said.

"What do you mean, you thought your dreams weren't real?" Aldrich asked.

"I…" Wilder's words came back to me. *Tell them about the meds.* "I take pills. For my hallucinations, my mood… I have for most of my life."

Brax *humphed* and Greer's eyebrows rose.

"It's possible the human medication has blocked any ability she might have," Ramona said. "When was your last dosage?"

"A few days ago," I replied warily.

"I suggest we test her," Ramona said to the others. "We can extend the delve for immunity and blocks, as well as a standard Light test."

Greer nodded. "Proceed."

My heart leapt into my throat as the chair began to recline. It didn't stop until I was lying flat on my back and all those scary thoughts I'd had about having my chest cracked open flooded back.

I watched Ramona's every move as she turned and picked up a strange silver device from a tray and slipped it onto her hand. It appeared to be a shiny round disk, with loops on the back for her fingers to slip through. The metal fit snugly into her palm as she held it over me.

I was offered zero explanation as she began to move it along my body. The device never once touched me, her hand hovering strangely in the air. After a moment, I fancied I felt something. A hum ringing in my ears and a slight vibration through my fingertips.

A jolt of electricity zapped through me and I gasped, unprepared for the abrupt jolt. My thoughts muddled and my awareness shifted.

Mummy! Daddy!

Shut up, you little brat.

The voices echoed through my mind, the world tinged with rings of purple.

"There's no sign of demonic tampering," Ramona confirmed, her voice echoing from far away. "And she indeed possesses Light, though it's been subdued. It's most likely due to the medication she's been taking, but I can't confirm that until her system is completely clear."

"What did you do to me?" I asked as my wits started to come back. It felt like I'd been out for only a second, but it must have been a while. Whatever that little silver disc was packed a punch.

"The disorientation is normal," Ramona said to me. "It will past in a few moments."

"Tell her," Aldrich commanded.

"I believe you were never ill, Scarlett," Ramona said, dropping some of her surliness. "What your doctors thought was a mental condition, was merely your Light manifesting. Without anyone to guide you, it was a logical conclusion."

"You mean…?" I didn't know whether to laugh, cry, or ask for another round of pills to stop the hallucinations from spreading to my lymph nodes.

"There's nothing wrong with you," she said as the chair came back up. "And there never was. Apart from a strange immunity to some forms of Light manipulation, I don't see any medical reason you should continue to take those pills. I would recommend a full physical to confirm with one hundred percent clarity, but that's up to you."

"Then it's as we expected," Aldrich stated. "The Infernal was tracking her because it caught the scent of her dormant Light. Nothing more."

He looked disappointed, but I was ecstatic. It meant I could get out of here and go home with Jackson. I wasn't implanted with a secret weapon, I wasn't possessed by a demon, and I was definitely not stark raving mad. This was real and I wasn't sick. All this time I'd just been a mad as hell teenager that'd been pissed off that her parents had been killed.

"Does this mean we can go home? Me and Jackson?"

Greer nodded. "As long as you don't reveal what you know about the Sanctum."

I snorted. "Who would believe me?"

"Your friend will be required to have his memory altered," Aldrich said. "He is not immune, and we have to abide by the Codex."

"Codex-schmodex," I declared. "As long as he's safe."

"He'll wake up tomorrow and be none the wiser," Brax confirmed.

"Thank you for your cooperation, Scarlett," Greer said. "You may go."

"Wait… That's it?" I asked, my eyes wide.

"That's it."

I stood, not sure how I should feel. Perhaps used might be an adequate word, but the lack of answers left me empty. Sitting on the sidelines, I waited as someone went to fetch Jackson. In a few minutes, we'd be out of here and on our way home. So why did I feel so slighted? It didn't make any sense.

When we finally passed across the threshold of the Sanctum and stepped into the human world, I glanced back but I never saw Wilder again.

9

———

When we arrived home, Jackson shuffled upstairs like a zombie.

Five minutes after he had his memory wiped, we'd been let out of the Sanctum, bundled into a black cab, driven home, and that was it. Our adventure was over.

Staring up at Jackson's bedroom window, I wasn't surprised to find it'd been fixed. I guess I should be thankful he had his soul restored along with the pane of glass Wilder had shattered. The only payment I had to give was enduring their tests and creepy round of questioning that revealed I was different, but not really. Useless Scarlett had been kicked out again.

Sighing, I went upstairs, checking every shadow for puffs of black smoke. When I peered into Jackson's room, he looked lost sitting on the end of the bed. I wondered if that's how I looked after Wilder had attempted to screw with my memories.

"Hey," I said, leaning against the doorframe. "You hungry?"

Jackson perked up and smiled. "Starving."

His reaction relieved a little of my anxiety. "I'm going down to the kebab shop. You want your usual?"

"Yeah. You want some money?" He patted his pockets and his expression dropped. "I can't remember where I put my wallet…"

"That's cool. My treat, okay?"

He relaxed and flashed me a smile. "Thanks, Scarlett."

Outside, the city looked different. The sky was darker, the shadows were longer, and it had nothing to do with the sun going down and me missing yet another shift at *8-bit*.

The kebab shop was a beacon of light in an otherwise tumultuous world. Stepping inside, I was immediately scowled at by the owner, a pudgy, six-foot-three Turkish man with a moustache of epic proportions.

"Yes?" He thumped his fist down on the counter and cocked a bushy eyebrow.

The guy had a reputation for being abrasive and demanding, but I supposed he had to be when they stayed open until two a.m. and served a long line of drunks looking to get something to soak up the excess alcohol. His real world, no bullshit approach was reassuring in an odd way.

"Can I have a large lamb donor, a large chicken kebab, and two large fries?"

"Yes. Eighteen-fifty. Pay there." He jabbed a

meaty finger at the cash register and turned to make up my order.

I paid, dropped the one pound-fifty change into the charity box chained to the counter, and sat on the bench. Watching people come and go, my thoughts naturally drifted to the creature that'd been lingering on the tube. He'd appeared to be just another guy on the commute home or to wherever, but the moment I ran… I shivered, remembering how he'd appeared out of nowhere in the tunnel and tried to grab me.

The cracking of bones, the whites of his eyes, the clicking sounds it made in the back of its throat. The Naturals just tossed me back into the world, knowing what awaited me. I felt like a worm wriggling on the end of a hook.

A prickling sensation quivered over my body and I was jerked out of my thought pattern. Turning towards the shop windows, I tensed as my gaze connected with a woman who was standing outside.

She was a normal-looking corporate clone on her way home from a boring day working at some office. A posh leather bag was slung over her shoulder and her woollen coat looked like it might be from a designer label. Her blonde hair was pulled back into a sleek ponytail, and her make-up was beige and bland. Normal, right? Not from the way she was staring at me, though.

Glancing around, no one else seemed to notice her. The kebab shop workers were busy taking orders and cooking. Customers were staring up at the menu, and passersby were engrossed in their own business.

I turned back to the window and the woman smiled, her eyes rolling.

"*You*. Order."

I glanced back at the counter as the burly kebab shop man thrust a plastic bag full of food at me. Taking it, I smiled weakly, my stomach twisting and turning. Glancing back at the window, I noticed that the woman had disappeared.

Swallowing a pile of vomit, I knew I couldn't stay in here all night, so I took a deep breath and left the shop. Outside, I looked up and down the street, but the woman was well and truly gone.

Scowling, I made my way home, the bag of kebabs and chips swinging back and forth. What use was having Light if it was blocked like a pile of sewerage stuck in a toilet? Did I just pretend that I couldn't see demons roaming the streets of London? That'd be a tough call if they all stood around staring at me like complete weirdos. How could I ignore that?

I looked back over my shoulder as I strode down Kentish Town Road, wondering if half the demon population of the world was bearing down on me. One fear had been replaced with another.

Don't be silly, Scarlett. They wouldn't have let you go home if they thought you'd be in danger. It sounded more absurd the more I thought it.

One thing was certain. I'd never look at the world the same way again.

Saturdays at *8-bit* was dance party night.

I stood amongst a packed crowd, my mind elsewhere as music thumped through the air, making my bones vibrate. A girl dressed in an elaborate cosplay snaked past me, her papier mâché angel wing almost smacked me in the face.

When I'd shown up ready for work, I expected to be blasted for missing my last two shifts, but it was business as usual. Howard, the owner, had just sailed right past me, a bee in his bonnet about the drunk who threw up behind the pinball machines, and didn't even pause to tell me how irresponsible I'd been. I smelled a little Natural mumbo jumbo, but I wasn't complaining. I needed the job.

Things seemed too unresolved and empty, and I couldn't shake the feeling. I didn't know anything about the mysterious Balan demon who'd appeared in my memory of my parents' death, nor did I understand what it meant to have Light. The only thing that'd happened since leaving the Sanctum was me developing one heck of a trust issue, but that was nothing new. Only the levels had changed from human arseholery to full-blown demonic.

It was tough not having anyone to talk to about it. I was itching to tell Jackson about the fact that my parents might've been Naturals, or at least have Light they passed to me, but he didn't remember anything. When he'd woken up that morning, he was back to his usual perky self, chattering about some big gaming tournament that was coming up. They'd wiped him clean like a whiteboard, while I was stuck with the permanent marker.

What got me was the fact that they didn't seem to care I might've been attacked by a demon as a child. They'd kicked me out rather fast. I wonder why that was?

"*Scarlett.*"

I jumped a mile when a hand tugged at my wrist. Spinning, I almost collided with Jackson.

"Don't do that!" I exclaimed, clutching the dirty glasses against my chest.

"You were staring off into space again," he stated.

"Huh?" I ducked as the papier mâché angel came back for round two.

He glanced around and tugged me to the side of the room. Princess Peach smiled down at us from the spray-painted mural on the wall and the glasses in my arms teetered wildly.

"I was just checking to see if you were…" He gave me a look that was all creased forehead and narrowed eyes.

"You have to be more specific," I declared. "I don't speak fluent pointed looks."

"Well, you've been acting a little strange lately," he declared, glancing around again. "You ran out of here the other night, and you ran out on me at breakfast." Was that sweat beading on his forehead? "Scarlett, have you stopped taking your meds?" he added, keeping his voice hushed, even though no one had any chance of overhearing us with the music at the volume it was.

I felt the blood drain from my face and it took everything I had to hold on to the glasses. Of course, he thought I was on the slow decline into insanity. He didn't remember anything about the Naturals or the things I'd told him on the way home about my test results. He still believed I was regular old Scarlett Ravenwood. Honestly, I was still debating that fact myself.

"I…" I fumbled and looked over my shoulder. I didn't want to lie to my best friend, but maybe this was one of those moments I had to—for his safety and mine.

"*I know.*" He looked like he was about to have me committed.

"What do you mean, *you know*?" A pang stabbed me in the gut and a little piece of me hoped he'd remembered our adventures. It was selfish because he was far better off not knowing about the time he was possessed by a demon. Especially when I involuntarily saw his willy in a prelude to *you know what*.

"Your pills didn't flush all the way down the loo."

I groaned and rolled my eyes. The first thing I'd done after we'd scoffed down those kebabs was lock myself in the bathroom and dumped my meds into the toilet and flushed. The water pressure was obviously on the fritz if a few of the suckers had stuck around in the cistern.

"I don't need them anymore," I stated.

"Who told you that? A doctor?"

"Yes, as a matter of fact." I pouted and turned on my heel, weaving through the crowd. The beer glasses got heavier in my arms like it was some kind of analogy for the string of lies I'd have to tell my best friend from now on.

"I don't know what kind of crackpot you saw," Jackson said, clearly not done with his well-intentioned intervention, "but it's clearly not helping."

"Jackson, I'm fine," I said as I put the stack of glasses down on the bar. My melancholy was less to do with the medication and more to do with the world being infiltrated by demons. "I know you're just trying to look out for me, but I'm cool."

He gave me a disbelieving look and ran his hand through his hair.

"This is something I've gotta try, okay?" It was my turn to give him a pointed look. "I've been struggling with this my whole life, and I don't want to rely on those pills forever. I don't want to become dependent, and if there's a way to cope without them, I have to try it."

He pursed his lips but nodded.

"Thank you."

"We'll talk tomorrow," he said as he was jostled by an overenthusiastic Overwatch character. "I've gotta practice in the morning for that tournament, but I'm free after that."

"The thing at the *O2* arena?"

"The one and the same. If I win, we're going to Aruba."

"Aruba?"

He shrugged. "Don't know where it is, but

everyone always says they're going there in the movies."

I laughed and shooed him away. Leaving the glasses for the staff out back to clean, I went out into the pub for another pass. I didn't mind the nights I was out on bussing duties, it saved my vocal cords from being screamed raw and my feet were actually less numb after my shift. It did put me into the direct firing line of all the drunk weirdos, but the positives outweighed the negatives.

Dodging a table, I spied a few glasses that'd been dumped on the windowsill. Sighing, I made a beeline for them, but knocked my shoulder against someone who'd danced their way into my stratosphere.

"Excuse me," I muttered, holding up my hands.

The man-boy stopped and stared, making me squeamish. He was wearing a costume of some anime character I didn't recognise. He'd put on a blue synthetic wig, school boy uniform, and held a giant foam sword. The bouncers loved those, *not*. They were constantly checking the clientele for concealed weapons. Mostly they were plastic and rubber, but occasionally people had lifelike replicas. That was another story of stupidity I didn't want to get into.

He bumped into me again and smiled when I glanced up. If he was about to hit on me, then this was so not the way to go about it. He wasn't exactly dressed for seduction.

"Hi," he said, his gaze meeting mine.

I tensed when I saw his completely white eyes. He might've been wearing a pair of coloured contact lenses for all I knew, and the lighting in here wasn't that great since we were running a club night. Saturday brought out all the cosplayers, gamer geeks, and left of centres for a night of getting off their faces. Contact lenses were part of the illusion, which didn't help now that I knew demons were roaming about.

"Can I help you?" I shouted over the music.

"Do you work here?" the guy asked, smirking strangely.

I wanted to put it down to him being socially awkward because I knew all about that, but since my trust quota had shorted out days ago, I just shrugged.

"Cool hair," he said, reaching out.

I jerked backwards. "Look, I'm busy here and I'm not interested, okay? You're not my type."

"What *are* you interested in?"

"Uh, *men?*" I made a face and started to turn away. That's when he curled his fingers around my wrist. "Let me go, or I'll have security forcibly remove you."

"I'd like to see them try."

Wrenching my arm away, I edged towards the bouncer who was scanning the crowd. Raising my hand, I waved.

"We know you can see us, Scarlett," the guy drawled, his voice rasping. "We're watching."

My heart dropped, and my breathing stalled. For a full five seconds, I was positive I'd died from shock until he tried to grab me again.

"That's enough of that." The bouncer appeared

from the midst of the flashing strobe lights and grasped the blue-wigged guy around the scruff of the neck. "You're out of here, you little shithead. No grabbing the staff."

The guy laughed as he was dragged through the startled crowd and blew me a kiss. Punters on the dance floor parted, letting the pair through, while I stared after them. I was shell-shocked. Did that just happen? First there was that creepy lady at the kebab shop and now…

"Scarlett!" Jackson pushed through the crowd and stood in front of me, attempting to protect me from the danger that'd already passed. It won him points, though, always did. "Are you okay? Who was that guy?"

"Just a dweeb that got handsy," I said, watching as the bouncer shooed the blue-haired demon down the street. "He was off his face."

"He didn't hurt you, did he?" He picked up my hand and began to examine my arm.

"It happens." I shrugged him off.

"Wow, what an arsehole. If I had seen him—"

"You would've gotten your lights punched out," I said with a snort.

"By that guy?" Jackson waved his arms wildly.

"I've never seen you punch anyone, like ever."

He rolled his eyes. "I could, you know."

"I don't doubt it."

Gathering the glasses from the windowsill, I stared outside, scanning the street. Busses flashed past on the High Street, people were walking back and forth, a cluster of police wandered through the shuttered market stalls, and a street vendor was selling baked pretzels from a little cart on the corner. It was a typical Saturday night in Camden Town.

I didn't catch a glimpse of a blue wig, which to be honest, wasn't much of a relief. I'd seen how that black smoke puffed about, so there was no telling where it'd puffed off to.

What was a girl to do? Picking up the dirty glasses, I turned back to the insides of *8-bit*. Get back to work, that's what.

After my first shift back at *8-bit*, after what I was dubbing 'the incident', I opened a note on my mobile phone and began to document any demon encounters and sightings.

I wasn't sure why since it wasn't like I could rock up to the local police station and hand it over as evidence, but maybe it had something to do with control. I couldn't protect myself, the Naturals had dumped me without any knowledge on how, so all I had was my own two eyes.

I saw a demon every day. Sometimes I caught two. There was one on the bus, holding the railing like any other commuter. He'd even gave his seat to an elderly man who'd climbed on at Regent's Canal. There was another in the dairy section of Sainsbury's comparing cherry and blueberry yogurts. I brushed by another in the market. When Jackson and I went to see the new

Marvel movie at the Odeon Cinema, there was one sitting two rows down and five seats across.

They didn't always see me, but when they did, they smirked like they knew a big secret that I didn't. They never approached, not after that guy tried to grab me at *8-bit*, and didn't attempt to harm me. It was almost like they were following my every move and wanted me to know it. Psychological warfare.

After the man who worked in the Off-license made a lewd gesture at me while his eyes rolled and his teeth snapped, I had to suppress the urge to Google exorcisms. I was at my wits' end.

I was standing outside of Camden Town tube station, the wintery night chilling me through my leather jacket, when I decided I had to go back. My first thought was of Wilder and the way he'd just disappeared after all that trouble he went through to get me away from Romy to have five minutes to talk. He'd argued with Greer about being present for my test. Then… he'd just dumped me.

I was angry, hurt, and pissed off. I was all the things I should've been when I was still inside the Sanctum.

"*I can't do this shit anymore,*" I muttered to myself.

Pulling the troll doll out of my jacket pocket, I held it in my palm. Its plastic face smiled its cheesy grin, its painted eyes stared blankly back at me. Curling a finger around the tuft of purple hair, I thought about Wilder. Was he on the prowl tonight? I shivered as his image came to mind.

C'mon, I silently urged the toy, *Lead me back to him*

again. Just like you did last time, you little heat-seeking missile. I held it for so long, the only heat it generated was from my hands.

I wasn't ready to give up though, so I scanned my Oyster card and descended into the tube, retracing the route I'd taken when I'd first searched him out. I walked down laneways, I circled museums and galleries, I went to an antique bookstore in Soho, I passed the stage door of a theatre in the West End, I crossed a church cemetery, and traipsed the Tower Bridge. I stomped by the Tower of London but I never once caught a glimpse of the elusive Wilder.

I did see more of my white-eyed friends, though.

They were dancers at the theatre, shadowy figures traversing laneways, an elderly woman on the tube, the priest at the church, a random person passing me on the bridge. They were everywhere, and the Naturals were nowhere to be seen.

The longer I wandered, the clearer it became that whatever spell Wilder had put on the troll doll was long gone.

What was the point? I sighed, my eyes brimming with unshed tears. I'd never be a part of anything, always a victim, never winning, just holding my head above water, waiting for the wave that'd finally drag me under.

Wandering down the street, I realised I was approaching a familiar location. The *Hung, Drawn, and Quartered* stood before me, a shining beacon of warmth in the icy darkness of my self-pity.

I'm going in there, I thought. *I'm going in there and if he's not inside, I'll just get something to drink and maybe something to eat. Then I'll go home. I'll go home and fill my prescription tomorrow.* It would be better to forget than to deal with not being able to control my own safety. If I was on my pills again, then the demons would leave me alone. Seemed logical.

Stepping into the pub, I scanned the tables, searching for the familiar leather jacket and messy hair that belonged to Wilder. Déjà vu shivered down my spine as my fingers coiled around the troll doll. He wasn't there, but I could feel him. Taking another step, I lingered, my gaze finding a form I recognised.

He was leaning against the bar, his shoulders slumped. Raising his beer glass, he threw his head back as he downed the last sliver of brown liquid, then slammed it back down. Nodding at the bartender, he turned, then froze when he saw me staring at him.

"Took you long enough," he drawled.

Nothing had changed about him. He was still wearing his leather biker jacket, worn jeans, tight black top, and gruff smirk.

"I see them everywhere," I replied, blurting out the first thing I could think of. "At the supermarket, on the bus, *where I work.*"

He narrowed his eyes and stepped closer. Grasping my arm, he wrenched me around and practically dragged me out of the pub and onto the street.

"You shouldn't have come here," he said, his voice low and threatening.

"Let me go!" I pulled out of his grasp and shoved him.

"You're playing a dangerous game, Purples."

"I have no way to protect myself. I can't fight them, they follow me everywhere, I want…" I swallowed hard, "I want to be one of you."

I didn't realise it until that moment that wanting to fight meant joining the Naturals, but as soon as the words left my mouth, I knew. I'd never felt that kind of conviction before. Always drifting, always just existing pay day to pay day, always lacking a purpose. I wanted to fight.

I wasn't on any medication, so I figured my Light would have a chance to manifest properly. If I had access to it, then maybe I could do something. The way the arondight blade had clicked into place in my hand had been exhilarating and the more I dwelled on it, the more I wanted to feel it again. In that moment, I'd been powerful and for someone who'd always struggled her way through life, it was everything.

"You want to be one of us?" Wilder mocked. "More than human?"

"I think we already established the fact that I already am."

"We train from birth to become Naturals." He turned his back on me and started to walk away. "It's too late for you. Go home, Purples."

It was a slap in the face. One minute I was told I was special, the next he said it didn't matter. The old Scarlett would've swallowed her tears, tried to hide her embarrassment, and melt away, but I wasn't her anymore. Not after the moment I'd seen a demon stalk me in the lane behind *8-bit*.

"It's too late for you to grow a heart, Wilder, but it's not too late for me to learn to fight," I shouted. "When I couldn't tell you people what you wanted to hear, you dumped me on the street like I was trash, and I'm here to tell you I won't stand for it."

Tearing the troll doll out of my pocket, I threw it at him with all the strength I could muster. It slammed against his back and fell to the ground, tumbling over and over until it came to a rest by his boot.

Wilder stopped dead in his tracks and turned. His expression was made up of pure anger, and his eyes flashed silver.

"Take me to see them," I said, determined not to let him intimidate me.

"You really are a piece of work," he muttered.

"*Takes one to know one.*"

He hissed through his teeth and raked his hands through his hair. "I need to find a new drinking spot."

"And I'll just find that one and the next and the next. If that doesn't work, I'll just go to the Sanctum myself."

"They won't let you in, Purples. The moment you cross the threshold, you'll just be in an old factory with a flock of pigeons that'll shit on your head. You can't just walk in and make demands."

"They know me," I said, recalling what the demon at *8-bit* had said. "They know my name, they know where I work, and they know I can see them. Either I fight back or—"

"Or?" Wilder prodded, daring me to voice my ultimatum.

"Or I go back on my meds." I shook my head and glanced away. "That way I'll block out my Light for good. Without it, I can't see them. Maybe in time I'll forget you even existed."

"You'd give up your Light?" He looked shocked, like I'd suggested amputating a limb.

"I never knew I even had it!" I exclaimed, throwing my hands into the air. "Even if I did, they told me it's blocked. By the meds or whatever, who the hell knows? But it doesn't change the fact that I'm being stalked by demons in the supermarket. *At the produce section of the supermarket*, Wilder." I sighed for what felt like the billionth time that day. "If I can't fight, then what have I got?"

He stared at me, his expression giving nothing away. I was an annoyance he didn't want to deal with —he'd said it once and I could feel the words rising in the back of his throat again.

Scarlett Ravenwood, you are a broken toy nobody wants.

I cracked, then I turned sharply before he could see it on my face. I strode away from him towards the tube station, every step tearing through the life purpose I'd had for a full two minutes. *New high score, Scarlett.* It was fun while it lasted.

"*Wait.*"

I stopped, my heart beating double time.

"I can't promise anything," Wilder said behind

me, "but I can take you to the Sanctum. The rest will be up to you."

I turned, hope causing me to float. Metaphorically, that was.

He grimaced. "Don't make me regret helping you, Purples."

I shook my head. "You won't."

10

———

Wilder phoned it in. He literally took a mobile phone out of his pocket, called some unknown person, and said, "I'm bringing her back in." Then he escorted me back to Battersea, making me walk the entire way.

"What do I say?" I asked as we walked down the lane towards the Sanctum.

"Don't ask me," he replied.

"Well, how does it normally go? You know, for all those kids who go off to train."

"They're asked if they want to be a Natural, they say yes or no, and that's it."

"That's it?" I made a face. "That can't seriously be *it*."

"If you're looking for the secret handshake, I'm sorry to disappoint you, but there isn't one."

I sighed, my stomach churning.

"If you're so hell-bent on becoming a Natural,

just tell them what you told me," he added. "Though I'd recommend turning around and going home. This life isn't a picnic, Purples. It's Hell on Earth."

"If I go home, I'll have to go back on my meds again."

Wilder stopped and ran his hand through his hair. Cursing, he turned and glared at me. "Don't pull that shit with me, got it? I don't do manipulative ultimatums."

"I wasn't—"

"*You were.*" His eyes shone silver for a moment, then he blinked and they were clear again. "You don't have to do anything, you know that? You're not forced to drug yourself into oblivion. There are a million other things you could do, Scarlett. A *million* other things. There are people out there who aren't so goddamn lucky."

He had a point, but my only defensive manoeuvre at that moment was smart-arsery. "Who? Like you?"

He let out a frustrated grunt and turned. He stomped off, forcing me to borderline jog to keep up.

"What's with your eyes?"

He didn't answer, he just kept on striding down the lane.

"Wilder?"

"*Shut up,*" he hissed. I guessed our conversation was over then.

When we entered the Sanctum, two Naturals were waiting for us. They looked like Tweedledee and Tweedledum, they were so similar—black trousers, tight black T-shirt, matching boots, jackets, the whole kit. Must be their Natural uniforms. Black commando gear wasn't exactly inconspicuous.

"They're waiting for you in the library," the man on the left declared.

They stepped forward, and I gathered they were my assigned escorts for the evening, but Wilder held up his hand.

"I'll take her."

"Our orders—"

"I know what your orders are and I'm relieving you of them," he barked, sounding all authoritative.

The Naturals didn't look too pleased, but they stood down and allowed us to pass.

Wilder led me through the Sanctum, his expression guarded. I still got that pissed off vibe from him, so I kept my mouth shut, not keen on repeating the reprimand he'd given me outside. At least not when I was about to pitch myself to three of the most intimidating and powerful people I'd ever met.

When we arrived at the library, I wasn't sure what I was expecting to see, but it wasn't what I was presented with, not by a long shot. Maybe I thought there'd be a few beat-up computers and a squeaky metal carousel with a couple of new release books covered in clear contact paper. Oh, and a magazine rack full of dog-eared copies of Cosmopolitan and Glamour from 2004 and some scratched DVDs available to check out, and a few threadbare metal shelves with more contacted books donated from the local charity shop.

Yeah, it was nothing like that at all.

Ironically, the place smelt like old books. I wasn't sure how to describe it, but it was like walking into a musty secondhand bookstore and stuffing your nose into the open pages of a yellowing Mills&Boon novel and inhaling—slightly crazy and mildly addictive.

Our boots tapped on the hardwood floors as we walked the length of the room, passing glass cases with artefacts sitting daintily on faded red velvet, and rows upon rows of shelving that went from the ground to ceiling, each shelf packed with books. Red, brown, and black leather-bound tomes of all shapes and sizes were lined up, some had writing on their spines while others didn't. A window sat in each alcove on the left, and beyond, I could see the Battersea power station doused an orange hue.

Glancing in one of the display cases, I saw an array of taxidermied moths. Some were tiny little brown creatures, and there was one huge specimen that had creepy looking eyes on its wings. Shivering, I walked on, following Wilder right to the end of the library.

The rows of shelving ended, and the room opened up into a circular space. Above, another domed skylight topped the building, and within, the floor dipped into a circular depression. Three steps down and we were in a seating area with crimson leather couches and armchairs and rich crimson carpet underfoot. Around the walls were Greek columns, and sixteenth-century style portrait paintings of people in big puffy collars and pants, holding swords and riding rearing stallions.

I didn't get a chance to study the library in more detail because Greer, Brax and Aldrich were waiting for us in the centre of the room. All the effort I'd gone to hold in my nerves and not puke into the nearest potted plant went straight out the window. My hands started to shake and I curled my fingers into tight fists —anything to look strong. I wanted to be a Natural and I gathered that meant a certain kind of tact when it came to shitting myself.

"Scarlett," Aldrich said, his voice echoing in the cavernous space, "we didn't expect to see you back."

Neither did I at first, especially since I was livid at the fact that they'd dumped me so abruptly, but miracles happen.

"I've come to ask..." I glanced at Wilder, who shrank back into the shadows. "I want to fight. I want to be a Natural."

They glanced between themselves so intently that I wondered if they could communicate telepathically.

"I've been through a lot in my life, not just the past two weeks," I went on. "Finding this place, being tested for Light... All the things I've been struggling against my whole life has finally made sense. I can see clearly, you know? But I can't do anything on my own. Since I left, I've been followed, harassed, and baited by demons. I can see them and there's nothing I can do as I am now, but there is a way. I can learn to be a Natural. I can help you fight them. I can protect myself and others."

"Being a Natural isn't all glory," Greer said. "It's a gruelling way of life. We constantly battle Dark forces and risk painful death in pursuit of protecting the living from evil."

"I understand," I replied. "I don't expect this to be easy."

"There are years of training involved," Brax said. "Not only in combat techniques, but mastering Light, demonology, and studying the Codex."

"Before you can even touch an arondight blade, you'll be required to pass rigorous training," Aldrich added. "It will be a long time before you'll be ready to face the Dark as a Natural."

"I get it," I argued. "I get that I have a lot to learn. I get that I missed out on manifesting the way everyone else does. I get that I'm at a disadvantage. But I'm willing to work at it and put in what's required." I glanced at Wilder, who lingered in the shadows, his arms crossed over his chest. "If my parents were still alive, I'm sure I would have chosen this when I was meant to."

"How do you know?" Brax asked, his skepticism clear.

"Because I know," I declared, thumping my fist right over my heart. "Ever since I was brought into the Sanctum and I stopped taking those pills, I can feel it. My calling was taken the day I was orphaned. Now I see this place and the demons out there… and *I know*."

Brax glanced at Greer, who stared at me unblinking. Whatever she was thinking was a mystery.

There might be three people who led the Sanctum, but Greer was the one in charge. She guarded the Codex—the most sacred relic of the Naturals, after all. Aldrich was older and possessed his own brand of wisdom, Brax was a wall of strength and harsh judgment, but Greer was all those things and more. If she chose to overrule the others, I was sure they'd submit.

"Greer," I said, fixing my gaze on hers, "why bring me in here and tell me all those things if you were just going to let me go? I don't understand your Codex, but I want to. Isn't that something?"

She didn't respond, which caused my anxiety to rise.

"Are you ready to leave everything behind?" Aldrich asked in her stead. "Your friends, your job, your family?"

"I have no family. I…" I trailed off, my thoughts going to Jackson.

After all the disappointments, the multiple schools and foster families, countless friends who'd come and gone when I was too hard to deal with, he was the closest thing I had to a real family. He'd stuck around, no questions asked, and put in the effort to *really* know me. Could I leave him behind?

"You're not suitable," Brax stated. "Hesitation is an immediate fail."

"What?" I glanced between the Naturals, shocked at Brax's blunt answer. *I wasn't suitable?*

"Hesitation is the mark of death," Brax replied.

"Those who wish to become Naturals must answer without pause."

"I'm not allowed to think about it for even one second? Just one second to make sure that leaving my life behind is what I really want to do? You can't allow me that?"

"That was a decision you should have contemplated before turning up here and wasting our time," he said with narrowed eyes.

I glanced at Greer, who nodded her agreement.

"We are bound by the Codex, Scarlett," Aldrich reminded me. "Being a Natural is a lifelong commitment. There's a reason why we select children and don't train adults."

"You mean you get them while they're young and impressionable," I said, fuming, "before they can grow a mind of their own."

"Yet more evidence to support your unsuitability," Brax said, looking bored.

My mouth flapped uselessly as reality sank heavily on my shoulders. They didn't want me. I was unsuitable. The word left a dirty taste on my tongue and my whole life stretched out before me—dark, empty, and plagued by demons I couldn't ignore.

"Then give me something I can protect myself with," I pleaded.

"We cannot," Greer said.

"But I see them everywhere. They know me, Greer. They follow me, they taunt and harass—"

"That is their way," she replied. "While they sense your Light, they won't touch you."

Somehow, I didn't believe her.

"Wilder," Aldrich raised his hand, summoning him into the light, "will you please escort Miss Ravenwood from the Sanctum."

I wanted to shout at them, but I knew it'd only make me look even more desperate. I'd been rejected and knowing it'd happened in front of Wilder made it even more humiliating. I'd taken out that demon with Wilder's arondight blade, and before coming back to the Sanctum I'd thought it was amazing I'd been able to do it at all, but now… My greatest victory was a footnote that hardly rated a mention to a Natural.

Wilder stepped forward and gestured for me to follow him from the library. Putting my head down, I stared at my feet as I left the room, humiliation colouring my cheeks an awful shade of crimson. It felt like I was doing the walk of shame right through the Sanctum and everyone was pointing and staring, laughing at how desperate I'd been.

"No hard feelings, Purples," Wilder said. "Not everyone is cut out to fight the demonic scourge. You just don't have the chops."

"Did they have to be so cold about it?" I asked, fighting back tears.

"Tact isn't their strong suit."

He led me through a part of the Sanctum I'd never seen before. Dark, abandoned, and cold. It wasn't until he opened a door that I realised I was being tossed out the back entrance where no one could see me. I didn't know if I should be offended or relieved.

"Go out here, turn right, then you'll see the Thames," he said. "Bye, Purples."

I stepped outside, the icy winter night cutting right through me. Before I could turn around, the door slammed closed, causing me to flinch. The sound echoed around the cold, dark street, one hell of a punctuation mark on my failed life.

If I couldn't be plain Scarlett Ravenwood or a Natural, then who was I meant to be? Turning right, I walked down the street, my extremities as numb as my heart. The Thames came into sight and I almost felt like throwing myself in. *Almost.*

I wandered through Battersea, then across the river, lost and alone. I felt an existential crisis coming on and there was nothing I could do about it. Other than come to terms with my mediocrity.

Stopping by the Tate Britain museum, I sat on the steps and shivered, shoving my hands into my pockets. My breath came out in white plumes, vaporising in the chilly air. My fingers curled around the troll doll and I sank into my depression like I was wriggling in a pit of quicksand.

Taking it out, I stared at its ironic little face and scowled. Its purple hair was all messed up and I combed my fingers through it, fashioning the tuft into a point. It wasn't of any use anymore—Wilder had taken the spell off it—and all that remained was the reminder of the first time I felt truly special… until it was taken away.

C'mon, Scarlett, I thought to myself, *it isn't like you to throw a pity party. Get up, you sad sack. Get up and move forward.*

With a heavy heart, I set the troll doll down on the step beside me. Standing, I smoothed down my jacket, straightened my jumper, then went home.

What else was a girl to do?

11

I sat on a chair in the middle of the packed *O2* arena in Greenwich, London, a scowl permanently etched on my face.

Playing absently with the lanyard around my neck, I watched as an advertisement for a game company *Blizzard Entertainment* flashed on the big screen. Men and dwarves in suits of armour, elves with impossibly long pointy ears, and gnomish creatures wearing goggles fought against one another, summoning all kinds of computer-generated magic. It only soured my mood further.

You just don't have the chops. What? I didn't make the cut simply because I *cared* about my friends? What a steaming pile of—

"Scarlett! There you are."

I glanced up—my arse numb from the plastic seat—and forced a smile for Jackson as he appeared through the crowd. I never knew how… *populated* these things were. It wasn't just a row of computers and PS4s lined up along a wall. No, it was a full-on stadium packed with the latest bells and whistles. Exhibits and stalls from all the big gaming companies, testing areas where you could go and play the latest pre-release titles in beta mode, areas where you could meet the developers, and there were even cosplay competitions. The big draw card was the tournaments, which played out on the main stage with MC commentary and post-game interviews. It was an eye-opener, for sure.

"I'm in the finals!" he declared.

"What?" I exclaimed. "That's amazing!"

"Yeah, I'm up against Zero Remorse, so the odds of me winning are slim. He's like the best in the world."

"Wait… the guy's name is Zero Remorse?" I snorted and stifled a laugh. "Are you serious?"

"That's his gamer tag," Jackson retorted, rolling his eyes.

"Couldn't he think of anything less… dorky?"

"Scarlett!"

"Okay, okay." I waved him off. "What's the prize this time?"

"First place is a million pounds and a sponsorship deal, and the runner up gets a hundred thousand pounds."

My mouth fell open, but not before I almost choked on my tongue. "*A million pounds?* Holy shite!"

"Either way, it's a guaranteed one hundred k!" He

rubbed his hands together. "So when do you want to go?"

"Go where?" I frowned.

"To Aruba."

"Oh…" I trailed off and shook the cobwebs out of my brain.

In the two weeks since my utter humiliation at the hands of the Naturals, I'd been walking around in a daze. Most of it was my struggle not to fall into a shame spiral, and as a result, I'd been the worst friend in history. Total self-absorption, forgetfulness, that sort of thing. Jackson had been busy preparing for today's tournament, so he hadn't noticed most of what was going on, and the things he did, he'd put down to my adjusting to life without medication to control my mood.

Wilder was right about that part—I'd been using the excuse of going back on my meds as a snide tactic to worm my way into the Sanctum. I hadn't consciously realised I'd been doing it, but a part of me must have. I didn't want to earn my 'chops' with manipulation.

Jackson looked so happy, and he should be. He was one match away from changing his life forever. I should be right there with him, not sulking on the sidelines.

"Where is Aruba?" I asked.

"The Caribbean," Jackson replied. "How cool is that? Envision white sandy beaches, blue water, coral reefs, palm trees, and those drinks served in coconut shells with little umbrellas and slices of fruit. Let's stay at a resort with a swim-up bar. I've always wanted to wade up to a bartender in my swim trunks."

"That doesn't sound weird in the slightest."

"It's all the rage in the tropics."

"When is the final?" I asked, doing my best to drag myself out of my stupor.

"In about half an hour."

"Are you nervous?"

"Scarlett, it's weird. I'm playing the best I've ever played in my entire life. It's like someone flipped a switch inside me and I've got superpowers or something." He held up his hands and wiggled his fingers. "My reflexes are so on point today." He kissed both of his trigger fingers. "Papa needs a sponsorship and money to fix the damp problem in his flat."

"Stuff the dump," I said with a laugh. "If you win, you'll be able to buy a mansion."

"No, mansions aren't my style. Though I'd buy a better place, for sure. You'd have to come live with me, of course."

I made a face. "With all the hot chicks you'll have dangling off your arm? I'll be fine."

"Scarlett…" His expression suddenly became serious. "You know, I wanted to—" His phone buzzed in his pocket and he clucked his tongue. Taking it out, he glanced at the message. "It's time."

Smiling, I threw my arms around his neck and squeezed him tight. "Good luck. You're going to kick his Zero whatever arse."

"Remorse."

"Like I said, *whatever*. He'll definitely be a zero once you're done with him!" I pulled back and stuck out my tongue. "And I'm good for Aruba anytime."

"I'll pencil you in."

"Is there someplace I can watch?" I craned my neck, looking out over the organised chaos.

"Down the front." Jackson pointed towards the main stage. "There's some seating and they show the match on the big screen, too."

"Cool." I followed his finger and got the gist of it. "Now go and crush him."

Jackson melted into the crowd and I picked my way through the heaving mass of gamer geeks towards the front of the arena. Finding a seat, I glanced up at the stage as the final round began.

I could see Jackson up there, controller in his hands and a headset on his head. The other guy, Zero Remorse, was next to him. Turning my attention upward, I watched as whatever was appearing on their screens was beamed up for the entire *O2* to see.

I tried to follow what was happening, but I knew next to nothing about video games. This was Jackson's domain. He'd tried to teach me how to play Call of Duty once, but I kept dying in the tutorial mission. Apparently, it was the easiest part of the game to beat, but I couldn't wrap my head around it. After my tenth gamer death, he confiscated the controller and banned me for life. It was a little dramatic, but after all, this was his calling.

Chaos erupted in the arena and I glanced around, not sure what was happening.

"Did you see that?" some guy said next to me, tugging on the arm of his buddy's shirt. "He slammed Zero Remorse so hard!"

"Wait." I turned to face him, looking for some kind of clarification my puny mind could understand. "Who won? Jackson?"

The guy blinked at me, like he was surprised I'd be talking to him. "Yeah," he said after a second of stunned silence, "by like a million miles."

I jumped out of my seat, my heart galloping faster than a racehorse on race day. I darted blindly through the arena, looking for the side of the stage. Jackson won! He won!

Spotting his curly hair as he climbed down off the stage, I pushed past a startled security guard and threw my arms around Jackson's neck.

"You won!" I shrieked, forcing him to jump up and down. "You won! You slammed him so hard!"

He pulled back, grinning from ear to ear. "You bet I slammed him!"

"I had no idea what was happening, but you won!" I screamed and jumped up and down again.

"Scarlett, it was incredible. I mean, everything was so sharp. I was one step ahead of him the entire match. It was like I could see what he was going to do before did it." An official tapped him on the shoulder and nodded towards the stage. "Uh, I guess I've got to go accept my obscenely large check."

"Go," I said, pushing him towards the stage, "I'll wait for you. Then we'll celebrate."

I hung in the wings as Jackson gave his speech and

accepted his prize. I had the jitters as he gave some interviews, hardly believing my best friend's dreams had just come true. It was a whirlwind, and I stood amongst it all, watching as he lapped it all up.

Good, I thought. *He deserves this. He's worked so hard to get here.*

By the time we left the *O2*, it was almost midnight and the lights twinkled against the night sky.

"I feel like a million quid!" he exclaimed, throwing his arms wide.

I laughed, his excitement was so infectious that his euphoria spread to me. "Aruba, here we come!"

"Let's get out of here," he said, tugging me towards the tube station. "If I don't go home now, I'll be tempted to party until the sun comes up and I'll be broke from buying everyone rounds of drinks."

"You just won a bazillion dollars and you want to ride the tube home?" I asked, making a face. "Are you sure you don't want to splurge on a taxi?"

"I might be loaded now, but I still know how much things are worth," he replied with a chuckle.

"Once a tight ass, always a tight ass?"

"Something like that."

We laughed all the way down to the platform, throwing ideas around about all the insane things Jackson could buy. A giant in-ground ball pit, a suit of armour, a shack on a desert island, an atoll in the Pacific Ocean, a yacht with the name 'Zero Remorse', a diamond-encrusted toothbrush, a legit castle, or a million pounds worth of Bitcoin.

For the first time in two weeks, I forgot about the

demon scourge shadowing my every step and the way the Naturals had turfed me out of their secret headquarters. My anger and resentment had dissolved, and here I was with my best friend—the best of the best, with the purest heart—just happy for his success. My life was as basic as they came, and I thought of all the people who'd be jealous of Jackson's win and curled my nose.

"What's that look for?" he asked, nudging me with his shoulder.

"I'm just thinking about all the people who'll come out of the woodwork now that you're loaded."

"Yeah, I thought about that, too." He stared across the tube carriage at our reflections in the opposite window. "I'm not just going to blow it. It's tempting, but I don't want to be the guy who was on top, then winds up having to get a desk job to pay the rent in twelve months' time."

"You're so responsible," I said with a smile.

"It's one of my more endearing qualities. Besides, a million quid doesn't go far these days. Inflation is a killer."

We had to switch lines, then get off at Kings Cross because of weekend track works on the Northern Line, so we worked our way through the maze of tunnels and escalators. It was such a warren, it'd take us at least five minutes to get out of the place. Then we had to brave the bus to Kentish Town.

I attempted to stare past the wave of people walking the opposite direction, not daring to make eye contact with anyone. We strode along with the flow of foot traffic, turning into the concourse, and following the 'way out' signs. Bodies were going in all directions, darting through openings, and squeezing into tunnels and escalators.

I was jostled and a shoulder brushed against mine. My reflexes kicked in and I turned towards the man who'd ran into me and my expression fell. His eyes shone entirely white and a lazy smile spread across his lips. *Demon.* As abruptly as I'd seen him, the man disappeared into the heaving mass of commuters.

I stumbled and bashed against Jackson. He caught me with a startled look on his face.

"You okay? You look like you've seen a ghost." He craned his neck, trying to see what'd shaken me up. "Old boyfriend?"

My heart was slapping hard against the inside of my chest cavity. "Huh?"

"That guy who was smiling at you," he replied. "Because if that's your reaction to a guy flirting with you, you're in real trouble."

"Oh, very funny, wise guy." I threaded my arm through his and began to walk, stretching out my stride. I wasn't running, but it wouldn't take much to spook me and force me into full panic mode.

"Slow down," Jackson complained.

"I just want to get out of here." I glanced over my shoulder, but the tunnel was eerily empty behind us. "I'm creeped out for some reason," I added lamely.

"Ghosts aren't real, Scarlett. I know you love watching those TV shows about hauntings and stuff, but there's no scientific evidence to support the heebie jeebies."

"Just because science can't explain it yet, doesn't mean it doesn't exist," I argued, feeling a dramatic pout form on my lips as we got on the escalator to the surface. "People used to think the Earth was flat until someone sailed around it."

"Some people still think it's flat."

"Do you want me to make you a tinfoil hat?"

"Millionaires don't wear tinfoil," he shot back with a cheeky smirk.

I rolled my eyes and glanced back at him on the escalator. My eye caught on a man standing a dozen steps behind us, and instantly, I felt my blood chill. This guy was different. He was about our age, clean-cut, a young professional type, but there was something off about him. His eyes were normal, but I wasn't sure I could trust that nothing was lurking inside him.

He sensed me staring and glanced up, smiling when he caught my eye. I tensed, and quickly glanced away, my heartbeat speeding up once more. I'd had my fair share of adrenalin hits already today, so I dragged Jackson off the end of the escalator, powering towards the barriers, with my Oyster card in hand.

"What's the rush?" Jackson asked. "Claustrophobic?"

"Something like that." The sooner we were back in the flat, the safer I'd feel.

I slapped my Oyster card against the reader and

the gate squealed open as Jackson did the same at the next barrier. Darting through, I kept my head down as we took the last set of stairs, emerging onto the courtyard outside the station. Thousands of people bustled back and forth, heading towards the intercity trains, or back into the tube, or to the long line of bus stops on Euston Road.

I began to fret, cursing Transport for London for scheduling track works on the Northern line. I would've much preferred to take the tube home than a bus.

We nestled amongst the commuters waiting by the side of the road, watching for the red double-decker with the bright yellow number 214. I fidgeted, glancing around. Maybe we'd lost it back in the tube station.

"You can't escape us, Scarlett," a voice hissed in my ear.

I spun around, panic flaring as I stared into a pair of eyes, the irises completely obliterated. The man smirked, his face unfamiliar to me. *The demon from the tunnel had jumped bodies!*

Turning, I gasped as I saw a lady three steps away from us turn and smile, her eyes completely white. I tugged Jackson back the other way and yelped as a middle-aged man stared back at us with milky eyes. Was there more than one?

This wasn't harassment… not anymore. This was something much more sinister. *We had to get out of the crowd.*

"Scarlett, what's going on?" Jackson asked, forcing me to stop.

"Listen to me," I hissed, keeping my voice low. "We have to get out of here. *Now*."

"Uh, you're kind of scaring me…" he trailed off, the concern in his expression more infuriating than anything.

He thought I was tripping out, hallucinating, having a mental break, losing the plot. Any of those were apt descriptions, but the problem was, it was all real. It was a tinfoil hat free zone and a demon was body jumping to keep up with me. *Allegedly.* Who knew why, but I wasn't about to let it hurt us.

"Someone's following us," I said. "Please just… *follow me*."

"Following us? Like they want to rob us?" He glanced around. "Then we have to go back into the station and find the police."

"No! We can't go back in there. We have to get away from the crowds…"

"That's the complete opposite of what we should do, Scarlett." He looked around again and shrugged. "I don't see anyone. Are you sure you're not…" *Awkward.*

"*Please, Jackson,*" I practically begged, "just this once, humour me."

Reluctantly, he nodded, tensing when I threaded my arm through his.

We crossed the street, weaving through the mass of pedestrians. Why were there so many people out after midnight on a weeknight? London was always bustling, and usually that was an exciting thing, but not tonight. Tonight, it was a pain in both my arse cheeks.

We passed the ornate gothic façade of St. Pancras station, turning off Euston Road, heading north towards Camden. The air felt like it'd dropped a few degrees as we walked, our breath vaporising in white plumes. Jackson brooded next to me, his win at the *O2* forgotten.

Abruptly, a shadowy figure stepped out of the darkness and cut us off. Jackson squeaked as we skidded to a halt.

"You can't run," the man said, his voice rasping like it was disembodied. "We'll always find you."

Turning, we legged it down a side street, weaving past a few startled pedestrians.

"Scarlett!" Jackson cried, his breathing ragged. "What the hell was that? Did you see his eyes?"

"Don't look back," I said as we turned down another street. This time it was devoid of life, so the only person we had to worry about was the current body the demon had possessed. If we could lose it, we had a shot at getting home in one piece.

"Do you think he was on that zombie drug?"

"What are you talking about?" I asked irritably, my gaze raking all the dark nooks and crannies as we powered down the street.

"It's a drug that people get high on like E, but some people had a bad reaction to it and it turned them into living zombies," he said, hardly slowing down for a breath. "They go mental—biting, scratching… they're completely rabid."

"It's not a drug," I shouted, storming towards the next crossroads. "We need to get home. If we get home, we'll be okay."

"Wait!" His footsteps pounded on the footpath as he caught up to me.

Before he could say anything else, a figure stepped out of the darkness ahead of us.

"Is that…" Jackson trailed off as we stared at the man's unnatural posture.

He was all twisted. His head lolled to the side, his shoulders were hunched forward, and his arms hung limply. It felt like the demon possessing him didn't know how to work a human body or maybe it didn't have ultimate control over its host. Either way, it was a demon and we were screwed.

I didn't have an arondight blade or a fancy dagger to stab it with. I had no clue how to perform an exorcism or use my Light. It wasn't like I could dial the emergency services and ask them to dispatch a squadron of Naturals. I didn't even know Wilder's number—not that he'd come anyway. There was no cavalry. We were it.

"If we're about to die, then you should tell me what's going in as few words as possible," Jackson declared, his entire body trembling. "I'm six-foot, but I'm weedy as hell. I've got no muscle mass and I've never hit anyone in my life. Not even the kid who bullied me in high school. Worst I did to him was superglue his locker shut. Of all the people to be trapped in a life or death situation with, you had to get stuck with the coward who's only a hero in video games."

"This isn't the time for an existential crisis, Jackson," I said, edging in front of him. "He's possessed with a demon that's been following us since I brushed past it on the tube."

"*A demon?*"

"An Infernal. Or at least, I'm pretty sure that's what it is."

The man tilted his head to the side, regarding us with a smug expression. He knew he had us. The only way out now was to fight, and we had nothing going for us. I knew I said my life was basic, but I wasn't ready to give it up just yet, and I was especially not going to let another Infernal jump into Jackson's body.

"Scarlett," Jackson said, his voice wavering, "what do we do?"

There was only one thing I could do, and it was a long shot at best. I had to try to tap into my Light. Ramona had said it was in there, theoretically blocked by my meds, but I'd been off them for weeks now. There was no other option left but to try.

"Stand behind me." With my heart pounding, I stepped towards the demon. I didn't feel any different, so how could I be sure my Light was still inside me?

"Scarlett!" Jackson exclaimed. "*Don't.*"

I raised my hand and his voice cut off. Focusing on the demon, it grinned, its tongue darting out and wetting its lips. Oh man, the poor guy it was hitching a ride in. How the hell did I fight it without hurting him?

"I'm sorry," I whispered, reaching inside myself. "It's us or you."

I searched desperately for my Light, my anxiety threatening to overwhelm my senses. The demon took a step towards me, its eyes shining eerily in the glow from the orange streetlights overhead. Raising my hands, I prayed for a miracle, but nothing happened.

The Infernal laughed, and then lunged, tearing towards me with unearthly speed. A scream tore from my throat as we collided, the force sending us rolling past Jackson across the footpath. I cried out as I smashed into a red mailbox, pain burning through my side.

"*Let her go!*" Jackson shouted, fisting his hands into the demon's jacket.

It wailed, throwing my best friend aside like he was nothing but a rag doll. Jackson hit the ground with an *oomph* and blinked, dazed by the force of the blow.

Forcing myself to my feet, I launched myself at the creature with a desperate cry. Grasping its face, I roared, a rush of power exploding into life inside me. A surge of electricity flowed through my arms and into my hands. The demon wailed, the space around my fingers glowed purple with little bursts of lightning crackling in the surrounding air. It let me go, tearing away from my grasp, and fell. It crawled across the footpath with its skin steaming, handprints glowing purple on each cheek.

"Where do you think you're going?" I exclaimed, a surge of confidence forcing me into action. I strode after it, intending to wrench its smoky Infernal arse out of the body it was currently inhabiting. I had no idea how I was going to do it, but I was determined to try.

The demon leapt to its feet and screeched at me before it bounded off into the darkness. Its limbs flailed as it skittered away, moving at an unnatural speed. My muscles coiled and I made to chase after it with a heady sense of power flowing through my body, but Jackson grasped my arm, stopping me from being a reckless hero.

"Holy shit, Scarlett!" he exclaimed. "You shot purple lightning bolts out of your hands!"

I'd scared it off, but for how long? I stared at my hands and the world tilted a little to the left.

"I don't think I was supposed to do that." I stumbled, slapping my palm against the mailbox to steady myself.

"Are you okay?" Jackson grasped me around the waist and pressed his palm against my forehead. "You're burning up."

"I…"

"We have to get you some help," he said, his eyes darting up and down the street.

"I don't know…"

Jackson frowned. His glasses were askew and the left lens was cracked. "The Sanctum," he said after a moment. "We need to get you to the Sanctum."

I froze, confusion blending with the nausea that

was bubbling inside me. How did he know about the Sanctum? The Naturals wiped his memories.

Blood whooshed in my ears and my vision began to cloud. "Jackson… I think I'm going to pass out."

His grip tightened around my waist, then…

Nothing.

12

____

I was falling into darkness.

My limbs were lead and invisible quicksand coiled around my ankles, sucking me down into a bottomless chasm. I cried out, clawing at the nothingness, searching desperately for something to hold on to.

Out of the gloom, a hand reached out and grasped me around the wrist. Instinctively, I locked my fingers around my unknown saviour's forearm. I was pulled upward, farther and farther until a face came into focus. Warm eyes and dark flowing hair materialised before me.

"Mummy?" I whispered.

"_We'll always find you, Scarlett._" Her mouth opened, revealing rows upon rows of sharp teeth.

My eyes flew open.

It took me a moment to realise I was in a soft bed, my body practically fused to the mattress.

Above, the skylight was back-lit, the image of the

woman in a flowing robe became more and more familiar each time I saw it. She was clutching a sword with an elaborate hilt, the point resting by her feet. *Arondight.*

Turning my head, I was surprised to see Wilder sitting beside the bed. He was leaning forward, his elbows resting on his knees while he tossed his fancy little knife over and over in his hand. It went tip over end, his fingers catching it around the hilt before flipping it again. He didn't miss… not even once.

"You said I didn't have any chops," I rasped, declaring my return to consciousness. "Well, I chopped that demon into oblivion, so *ha!*"

"You used your Light and almost lost yourself," Wilder shot back, catching the knife without even looking. "It was reckless, not heroic."

His gaze met mine. I stared at him, not understanding. He spoke like I'd broken some sacred taboo without knowing, but that's what they got when they tossed me back unprepared.

"Light shouldn't be used without proper training," he went on, scowling at me. "It doesn't make you immortal."

"Duh," I said, rolling my eyes. The movement made my head ache and I winced. No, 'hello, how are you' from Wilder, just straight into the chastising.

"It's attached to your life force. That's why you feel like you've got a brutal hangover." He leaned back in his chair with a sigh. "Ramona boosted your vitality and brought you back. You've been out for a few days, most of them spent in the infirmary."

"How did I get here?"

"I carried you."

"Gross, I meant the Sanctum."

"Your nerdy boyfriend brought you here. And a nurse wheeled you here on a gurney. I wouldn't carry anyone anywhere."

"You carried Jackson."

"Your boyfriend was different. The Codex demanded it."

"He's not my boyfriend," I drawled. "And all I wanted to do was *go home*."

Wilder's eyes narrowed and he declared, "You were attacked by an Infernal, you used your Light to mark it, you passed out because you drained too much of your life force, and here you are. The other option was an irreversible coma in a hospital. The end."

That didn't sound like fun, but verbally sparring with Wilder wasn't much better.

"Did Jackson tell you that? What happened with the Infernal?" I wondered what Wilder meant that I 'marked it.' Marked wasn't kill and I was a little disappointed, though I hoped the guy whose body it stole was okay.

"We've been watching you since you left," Wilder replied with a shrug. "We know a lot."

"You were perving on me?" I tried to sit up but was forced back down when a stabbing sensation shot through my brain.

"It was for your safety as well as ours. You have to understand, Purples, we don't condone disclosure."

"You thought I was going to tell on you?" My

head swam with more than a blinding headache. "You *humiliated* me, and now you're accusing me of double dealing?"

Wilder rolled his eyes. "You're so dramatic. Maybe that's why your application was rejected."

"Just keep sinking the boot in. It's all you people have done since you showed up in my life."

"Have a cry, Purples. Life is hard. And guess what, it never stops being hard. You of all people should know that."

"Yeah, and I'm sick of it," I exclaimed, practically spitting at him. Five seconds after waking up and I was already eyeball deep in an argument with my least favourite demon hunter. "I'm not good enough to be a Natural. I'm just a freak who can't have her memory wiped. My Light finally showed up when I needed it and it almost killed me. What am I good for? Oh, that's right. I'm good for *bait*."

"Don't be so precious," Wilder stated. "It doesn't suit you."

"Was anything you told me true?"

"Everything you've heard was true, apart from the bit where a demon impregnated my mother against her will."

My mouth fell open and my cheeks turned red. I hadn't been the one to say it, but knowing Wilder knew what the other Naturals said about him? I stung on his behalf.

"Don't look so shocked, Purples. I've heard it all before."

"I'd be less shocked knowing why you were

following me but didn't seem to want to help when that Infernal attacked me and Jackson," I declared, my hackles well and truly in the upright position. "What was I supposed to do?"

"Not use your Light, that's for sure." He rolled his eyes.

"I can't believe you," I seethed. "You just dropped me into a snake pit without anything to defend myself with."

"You say it like it's my fault. I'm just a solider, Purples."

"That's a cop out and you know it, Wilder."

Wilder scowled, his psychopathic underwear model vibe coming back to the surface. "Here's the thing, Scarlett." He paused and met my glare. "*You* aren't special. *I'm* not special. Those people out there aren't special. We're cogs in a wheel that's been rolling longer than you or I have been alive. I'm talking thousands of years, and it'll go on rolling for another thousand or more after we're dust. Maybe it'll roll on forever, who knows? What I do know, is that none of this is about you and your sob story and it's definitely not about mine, so grow the hell up and do something about it. Nobody likes to go to a pity party, Purples. That's a surefire way to lose all your friends and then some. This isn't a personal attack, it's war."

"Then train me as a Natural, give me an arondight blade, and I'll *break the wheel*," I snarled.

"No."

"Stop telling me what to do."

"Someone has to slap you back into reality."

"I understand reality more than you'll ever know."

"Oh, you can't say something like that and not elaborate, Purples," he drawled. "Words are hollow around here. Face value is not a commodity we trade in."

"I wouldn't want to bore you with my broken past."

He shrugged and leaned his head back. "I'm due for a nap anyway."

"What's stopping me from going solo?" I asked, narrowing my eyes. "I can go underground and learn myself. I don't need the Naturals."

"Your Light would consume you for one—eat you up from the inside out. Without proper training, you'd do more harm than good. Not all demons are the straight forward stab and kill variety. Do you want me to start listing all the ways you can die a horrific death?"

I closed my eyes and turned my face away. "Why do you have to be so nasty all the time? It's like you want people to hate you."

Wilder's silence was deafening.

Glancing back at him, I was surprised to find him staring at the skylight, that strange silver glint in his eyes again.

"Where's Jackson?" I asked, knowing it was in my best interests to change the subject. Wilder was an enigma I wasn't sure I ever wanted to solve. "I want to see him."

"He's unavailable right now."

My mouth fell open. "What do you mean by that? You've locked him up, haven't you?"

"He's in the vault," Wilder replied with a nod. "It's for his own safety."

"Why? What did he do, other than try to save my life?"

"He shouldn't have remembered this place. Two of you in one package isn't very likely… unless you're contagious."

Ignoring him, I rubbed my eyes. "Why are they following me? You said you were watching. So…?"

"I have to let Greer know you're awake," he said, rising to his feet.

"Wait. That's it?"

Wilder raised an eyebrow. "That's it."

"Why won't you let him go?"

He snorted and turned. "And you say he's not your boyfriend," he muttered as he walked away.

"Why? Are you jealous?" I shouted.

The door slammed, the sound reverberating through the room. Slapping my hands over my ears, I wondered why they were so sensitive, and why Wilder had such a chip on his shoulder. He was right about a lot of things. I'd never admit it to his face, but he had a point. Heading out on my own would be stupid to the max. Fuelling myself with stubbornness would get me killed in five seconds flat.

Pouting, I slid out of bed. My head swam and my knees trembled, forcing me to hold onto the edge of the nightstand to steady myself. I was wearing an oversized T-shirt, which meant I'd been undressed while comatose for the second time. It was slightly embarrassing, really. I wanted to be a strong, independent woman who didn't need any help, but here I was.

Shoving away my embarrassment—with an added side of fury—I took a deep breath to steady myself. Wherever they were holding Jackson, I needed to get there and get him out. I wondered if they had demons in Aruba.

Before I could find my clothes, the door opened and Greer wafted into the room, smelling like a field of wildflowers. She raised an eyebrow when she saw me teetering beside the bed and laughed. Looked like adding insult to injury was one of her favourite pastimes.

"Oh dear," she said, "you shouldn't be out of bed, Scarlett."

Her tone was unsettling. She was doing her sweet as pie thing again, and knowing how abrupt and cold she was towards me in the library, I was far from trusting. Remembering Wilder's words when I'd first woken in this room weeks ago, I smirked. *What mask are you wearing today, Greer?* Or something like that.

"I want to see Jackson," I said, narrowing my eyes.

"All in good time," she replied, placing her hand gently on my shoulder. Gesturing towards the bed, she waited.

It looked like I was stuck for the moment, and I grimaced as I flopped onto the mattress.

"I understand Wilder let his tongue loose again," Greer said, sitting gracefully.

"I'm not exactly a fan of his right now." I scowled. "Humiliated and followed, attacked…" I shook my head, wincing as my dehydrated brain rattled against the inside of my skull.

"War is all we've ever known," Greer replied. "I was born into it, as was everyone else in the Sanctum. It's not the best way to live, but someone has to fight the Darkness. We do what we must to keep Light in the world."

"Don't tell me," I said, on the verge of stamping my foot. "In war there are casualties and that's what Jackson and I are. Bait in your thousands of years battling 'Darkness'." I air quoted the last part. "It's not right, Greer."

"No, it's not. But it's what needed to be done."

I snorted, my brain throbbing.

"We had to understand why you were targeted. While you were in the Sanctum, there was no way of knowing."

"So instead, you let me wander the streets, completely exposed. Now my friend has been attacked not only once, but *twice*."

"The Infernal was tracking you," she said, ignoring me, "that much is clear. You have something it wants." Her eyebrow rose like she expected me to know what the demon wanted with me and I shrugged.

"I have no idea," I said.

"It stands to reason it may have something to do with your parents," Greer stated. "Your memory suggests they were killed by a Balan, and I suspect it's what gave you that scar. It's not uncommon for the mind to block out traumatic events."

I raised my fingers and traced the puckered line that ran down the side of my face. It'd always been a part of me, a mystery begging to be solved. But with no way to even find a clue to get me started, I'd come to accept it was just this thing I had—a thing children teased me about when I was at school, a thing adults stared at, a thing that marked me as defective. Sometimes, I even forgot I had it, and those were the good days.

"We believe all these things are connected," Greer went on. "Your parents, the Balan, the Infernal, your Light, and your immunity to alteration. The Darkness is interested in you and possibly has been since you were a child."

"That's not creepy at all," I muttered.

"We hoped to lure them out and catch them in the act, but we didn't expect you to do what you did."

I snorted and shook my head.

"I know we've lost your trust, Scarlett, but war is war. We do what the Codex demands of us. It's the way of the Naturals."

"So what do I do now?" I asked, changing the subject. I knew I'd get no sympathy from Greer, just more ideology.

I was at my wits' end with this whole thing. Where did I go from here? Up, down, side to side? I was lost in that ocean of icebergs again, but this time it felt as if a shark was circling somewhere in the shadows, waiting to devour me.

"First, you recover," Greer answered. "Then we'll find out why those demons are so interested in you. We'll begin with your lineage."

"You'll help me find out who my parents were?" I scarcely dared to hope. If I knew, then maybe I'd have something else to remember them by other than their deaths. Maybe I'd know who I was supposed to be.

"Yes." She nodded, lowering her head slightly.

"What about Jackson?"

"That," she said, looking troubled, "is a more complicated predicament. One that's going to take more time."

My heart twisted and I straightened up, my headache forgotten. "Greer, what's wrong? I owe my life to him. He's all the family I've got. You have to stop skipping around and just tell me. What aren't you saying?"

Greer glanced towards the door and I wondered if she was about to give me the 'I have to consult the Codex' excuse she seemed so fond of. After a moment of silent deliberation, she turned back, her expression blank, and I knew her answer wasn't going to be what I wanted to hear.

"Greer?" My voice wavered.

"Scarlett, there's no easy way to tell you this," she said, taking my hands in hers. "Your friend is… well, he's mutating."

"Mutating?" My stomach dropped. "Into what?"

"We don't know."

13

R omy threaded her arm through mine as we walked through the Sanctum.

After Greer left, I was left to my own devices for an hour before Romy appeared. I showered and dressed, but besides smelling like flowers, I didn't feel any better.

Glancing at Romy's bare arms, I squinted, focusing on the designs that were etched onto her skin.

"What are all the tattoos for?" I asked, desperate for some conversation—anything to take my mind off what I was about to see down in the vaults. Jackson mutating wasn't the best news, and knowing it was all because of me... well, it made it even worse.

"They're cool," the Natural replied.

"So they don't do anything?"

"No. They just look cool."

"Oh."

"Light comes from within," she stated. "We don't need physical items to manifest it."

"But what about the arondight blades?"

"Those are different. Our Light activates the blade, but it doesn't power them."

We rounded another corner, then went down several flights of stairs.

"Romy? Have they told you anything about Jackson?" I asked, my voice echoing down the corridor.

"Not a lot," she answered. "I guess it's on a need-to-know basis."

"And you don't need to know?"

"No."

"Doesn't that bother you? Being kept out of the loop?"

Romy shrugged. "Sometimes, but things happen around here for a reason. If everyone knew why Jackson was locked up in the vaults, the reaction mightn't be one that's so… desirable."

"Oh." She had a point, though I wasn't sure if highly trained soldiers would have the same pitchfork mentality as the general public.

"There's a lot of prejudice towards anything demonic," Romy said, glancing at me, "even amongst the Naturals."

I thought about Wilder, how Martin and the others had talked about him behind his back. Was there such a thing as a good demon? The more I got to know him, the more I realised Wilder had a lot of secrets—his tentative position amongst the Naturals, how his eyes shone with that silver hue, and the way others treated him. It was as if he'd helped the enemy and was being punished for it.

I shivered as we walked into a hallway lined completely with a slate grey-coloured metal. I assumed it was all fancy metal because *demons*. The air had an eerie chill to it like a supernatural force had sucked all the warmth out. I couldn't pinpoint what was so strange about it. Maybe it was the presence of something, more than the absence.

Hoping it wasn't Jackson I was sensing, I tensed as Romy opened one of the dozen or so doors that lined both sides of the corridor.

I didn't want to be the kind of friend who looked at her mutating BFF differently, so I boldly stepped into the room.

I saw him immediately. It wasn't hard not to, considering most of the space was his cell. Bars separated us, running from the floor to the ceiling, leaving a small portion of space for visitors to stand and observe. There was no sign of an opening to the cell itself, which didn't bode well for Jackson. How was he supposed to get out?

Turning my gaze onto Jackson, he was lying on a simple cot, the brown-coloured blankets kicked onto the door. He looked disheveled and exhausted, like he'd been awake for three days straight. There were bags under his eyes and his skin was sallow, but he looked exactly like the Jackson I remembered. If I closed my eyes and envisioned it, I could almost be fooled into thinking it was release week for one of his favourite game franchises and he'd been up all night mastering a new open world.

"Scarlett!" Jackson exclaimed, shooting to his feet.

I lumbered forward and glanced at the bars with an uneasy feeling in my stomach.

"Jackson," I said, "are you okay?"

"I should be asking you that question." He went to push his glasses up his nose, but he wasn't wearing them and he almost stuck his finger in his eye.

"I feel like I've got an epic hangover, but I'm more worried about you."

Jackson grimaced, then looked past me at Romy. His cheeks flushed, and he leaned closer.

"I remember everything," he whispered.

"Everything?"

"Yeah. Unfortunately." He shivered and blushed again. "Scarlett, I'm sorry. I really thought you were…"

"Going crazy?"

"Something like that," he replied sheepishly, not looking me in the eye.

"Look, it doesn't matter. What's happening with you? Greer said you were…" I trailed off, not wanting to say it out loud.

"Mutating?" Jackson scoffed. "I'm freaking out here, Scarlett. They say I won't turn into a monster or anything, that my outsides will still look the same, but my insides? Who knows?"

I thought about what'd happened over the last few weeks, searching for the signs I'd obviously missed while being self-absorbed. He did look different, though I wasn't sure if it was because of the fortified bars or because he actually was changing.

At the tournament at the *O2*, Jackson had said his reflexes were sharper than they'd ever been, that he'd known what Zero Remorse was going to do before he did it. After the Infernal attacked us, and I'd been on the verge of collapsing, he'd suddenly remembered the Sanctum. Now his glasses were gone, and his weedy frame was filling out with muscles.

"What's going on?" I whispered, curling my hands around the bars.

"Ramona thinks the demon who possessed me did something to my DNA," he replied. "I'm developing an immunity to their magic or whatever it is."

"What? What does that even mean?"

"It means we're not going to Aruba anytime soon."

My heart gained weight, feeling heavy at the sound of his admission. Everything was changing and nothing was certain anymore. My future and his were completely in the hands of the Naturals. I'd wanted to join them, but now I wasn't so sure. Wilder was right about one thing, though—I wasn't special and I wouldn't be treated any other way... and that included Jackson.

"It hasn't been pretty," he murmured. "I've lost count how many times I've been poked and prodded. They even tried to flush this thing out of my system with their magic. It was the worst pain I'd ever felt, Scarlett. It's what I imagine being struck by lightning feels like, except lightning stops after a second."

"Oh, Jackson…"

"It's cool. Whatever they did seems to have made it go slower."

"But they hurt you."

"Don't be mad at them," he said. "They're trying to help, I think. Ramona wants to stop the mutation."

"Stop it?" I asked, frowning. "What about a cure?"

"I don't know about that. Have you seen these muscles?" He lifted his arm and flexed. A little muscle popped up and he looked so proud of it. Knowing how it developed left a bad taste in my mouth. Was there an upside to being mutated by a demon? I wasn't so sure.

"You want to be like this?" I looked him over, not sure if he was joking or not.

"Not exactly. I can afford laser eye surgery now."

"And a personal trainer."

Jackson smiled, but I noticed the expression didn't reach his eyes. Thankfully, his irises were still their usual shade of green.

"Are you…" I let the sentence fade away, my own fear stopping me from asking the hard questions.

"Scared?" Jackson asked.

I nodded.

"I don't know," he answered honestly. "I mean, I still feel like me. Just… better somehow. Whatever's changing inside me, I'm pretty sure it helped me win the tournament. I don't know how to feel about that." He lowered his head. "It kinda feels like cheating."

"You didn't know," I argued.

"No, but I also don't know what I'm going to be at the end of this."

My bottom lip began to tremble as tears formed in my eyes.

"Don't," Jackson whispered. "Think about Aruba, okay?"

I nodded, knowing I wouldn't be able to think of anything else but the trouble I'd gotten him into. He had to realise that this was my fault, right? If I wasn't weird and the Infernal hadn't targeted me, he never would've been possessed.

"What about you?" he asked, deflecting the conversation away from his predicament. "What are you going to do now?"

I shrugged. "No idea."

"You shot lightning bolts out of your hands and almost died because of it," he declared. "I think you better find out more about that, huh?"

"Always the level-headed one, aren't you?"

"I know what things are worth, remember?" He winked, then curled his hands around mine, which were still grasping the metal bars.

The air shimmered between us and he jerked away.

"What was that?" I let my hands fall away, squinting as the air returned to normal.

"There's a barrier," Jackson explained. "It's designed to keep demonic creatures in."

"What a mess, huh?" I felt a barrage of tears coming again and I swallowed hard. I wasn't a crier, but what else were people supposed to do in this kind of situation? Waiting around wasn't something I subscribed to.

Romy coughed to get my attention, the sound echoing around the vault.

"I think she wants something," Jackson whispered, flashing a half-smile.

"I'll come back as soon as I can."

"I know," he replied. "Go do you, then tell me how it goes, okay?"

I nodded and backed away from the bars, feeling awful for leaving him there.

"Ramona wants to see you," Romy said, closing the door behind us.

"Dr. Surly is in the house, huh?" I asked, glancing down the metallic hallway.

"Ramona's not so bad once you get to know her." She chuckled, her blue eyes sparkling as she nudged me away from Jackson's cell. "She's been working around the clock to figure out what's going on with your friend."

"Oh." I felt bad for my sassy outburst as we walked down the hall, our boots clip-clopping on the metal walkway.

To my surprise, a portable laboratory had been set up in the next room. Benches laden with microscopes, beakers and vials, little refrigerators, computer screens, and other bits and pieces were set up in a grid-like pattern. A whiteboard with complex mathematical formulas hung at the opposite end, and a man I didn't recognise furiously scrubbed out an equation before writing it again.

I had no idea what half of this stuff was for, but I got the feeling Greer wasn't lying when she said they were doing everything they could to help Jackson. A little trust began to filter in at the thought.

Ramona glanced up from the microscope she was peering through and rubbed her eyes. When she saw Romy and me, she rose and came to meet us. She looked exhausted, and the three empty coffee cups on the table were an indicator that there must have been a great deal of all-nighters.

"Scarlett, how are you feeling?" she asked, pressing her palm against my forehead.

"Tired. My head aches and my ears seem a little sensitive."

"That's normal," she replied with a slight nod as she let her hand fall away. "Overuse of Light draws from all the senses—sight, hearing, taste, touch, smell. You may feel a little overwhelmed for the next few hours, but you'll make a full recovery."

It was reassuring, but my thoughts were on Jackson.

"I'm not really worried about that, honestly," I stated as Ramona turned back to her makeshift laboratory. "How's Jackson?"

"We've managed to slow the transformation for now," she replied matter-of-factly. "But our attempts to stop the mutation have been thwarted so far."

"What does that mean?"

"It means he's taking on the characteristics of a demon. Sorry to put it so bluntly, Scarlett, but that's the reality of his situation."

I swallowed hard and glanced uneasily at Romy, who's expression was unreadable.

"Is he going to die from this?"

"Unlikely," Ramona replied. "I've determined his DNA was compromised when he was first possessed, though the contact was minimal at the time. Which is why it wasn't detected until now."

"The alarms went off when he walked into the Sanctum carrying you," Romy explained. "We have anti-demon measures set up all along the perimeter of the complex, and something inside him tripped them."

Remembering the first time we'd crossed the Sanctum's threshold, I frowned. Nothing had happened then.

"He wasn't yet sufficiently altered for the wards to identify the changes," Ramona explained, preempting my thoughts. "When we repaired his soul, it dampened the effects. I suspect that why it's taken so long for his symptoms to manifest."

I turned my attention to the medical equipment, not knowing where else to look.

"Don't worry. We're working on it as a priority."

"Thank you."

The door opened behind us and a man entered, wearing a full Natural uniform—black T-shirt, tactical pants, and combat boots. He whispered something into Romy's ear before departing, leaving me staring after him curiously. Something was going on.

"Scarlett," Romy said, "you've been summoned."

I scowled and made a face. "They couldn't wait a

day before handing down their verdict? They really like making people squirm, don't they?"

The Natural sniggered and nudged me from the room, leaving Ramona to her work.

"I can see why Wilder likes you," she said when we were alone again.

"Wilder hates me," I declared, my limbs going all wibbly wobbly. I was still over sensitive after my Light mishap. Yeah, that was it. I'd only woken up a few hours ago, so it stood to reason.

Romy laughed as we climbed the stairs to the upper floors. "He's shown an interest in you. He never shows an interest in anything other than killing demons, so I wouldn't be surprised if he's assigned as your mentor."

"My what?"

"Mentor," she replied. "He'll train you. Probably. You're a special case. A late bloomer, so they say."

"You think Greer and the others will ask me to become a Natural?" I blinked as if the repetitive motion would teleport me out of the Sanctum and back in time to the moment right before I met Wilder outside of *8-bit*. I could use a do-over.

"Everyone's saying so," Romy declared.

"There's gossip about me?" My cheeks heated and I started to fret. I didn't do well being the centre of attention. I liked to melt into the background where it was safe, and no one judged me for being slightly off-centre. That's why I liked working at *8-bit*, the pub where I was so fired from.

"Of course there is," she said as we finally turned

into a hallway I recognised. "A strange woman shows up in dramatic fashion with the Sanctum's black sheep? That's given us fodder for years to come and that's not even a quarter of what's happened in the last few weeks. Ah, here we are."

She opened the double doors before us and gestured for me to go on ahead while my stomach fluttered with a slew of new butterflies. Talk about constantly being judged.

Taking a deep breath, I stepped forward into an unknown future.

The library looked completely different during the day.

The windows were awash with light, drowning the rows upon rows of leather-bound books in a warmer hue. It didn't feel stuffy in here at all with the reflection of the stained glass playing across the floor. Even the macabre items in the display cases weren't so scary now that the sun had risen. I wished I could say the same for the three people waiting in the reading area in the back.

The room had been cleared for the occasion, and the spaces between the shelves were devoid of other Naturals. It didn't stop me from feeling as if a thousand pairs of eyes were scrutinising my every step, though. If I knew where the closest toilet was, I would've bolted right towards it.

By the time we reached the end of the room, my

heart was beating so fast, I'd stopped my search for the loo and was looking for a defibrillator.

I was surprised to see Wilder draped over a leather armchair, a look of complete annoyance etched on his face. He hadn't bothered to dress for the occasion, his knees showing through tears in his jeans and his hair had likely been scraped back with his fingers with a bit of spit to hold it. He looked like he'd just rolled out of bed and threw on whatever was lying on the floor. His lack of respect for the Naturals' chain of command was on full display.

Brax was glaring at Wilder with an air of disapproval as I approached, and the others—Greer and Aldrich—were watching me closely. I wondered where my nerves measured on the Richter scale—probably a twelve point seven.

"Thank you, Romy," Greer said, lifting her hand gracefully. "You are dismissed."

Romy nodded slightly, then strode away, her footfalls silent on the carpet.

"We trust you're feeling much improved?" Aldrich asked.

"Yes, thank you." I shuffled from foot to foot. "I'm sorry. I didn't understand what I was doing, and… Well, I had to do something."

"There's no need to apologise, Scarlett," Brax said. "It was unfortunate you had to use your Light so openly, and in such a manner, but what's done is done."

I was fairly sure he was telling me off, but it was so

passive-aggressive that he almost had me convinced that I was off the hook.

"One thing is very clear about this situation…" Aldrich began. "You can't go back to your old life, Scarlett. It's far too dangerous."

"You're saying I can't go home?"

"It would be unadvisable."

"So my only option is to stay in the Sanctum? I can't leave at all? Well, this blows." I blew a strand of hair out of my eyes.

"You came to us wanting to become a Natural," Greer stated. "Has that wish changed?"

My breath caught, and I forced myself to keep eye contact and not glance away. *Be strong, Scarlett, don't show them any weakness.* I'd dismissed Romy's earlier assessment as pure speculation based on gossip, but it seemed like it was true.

"I don't understand," I began with a note of skepticism in my voice. "I was under the impression my hesitation nullified my chances."

"You must forgive my harsh response," Brax said. "But it was necessary."

"To your bait scheme," I shot back without missing a beat.

He nodded, pursing his lips. It seemed Brax didn't like being talked back to. Duly noted so I could challenge him again.

"And what about Jackson?" I demanded. "What will happen to him if I refuse?"

"This conversation is about *you*, Scarlett," Aldrich

stated. "Your concern for your friend is admirable, but what do *you* desire?"

"I…" I glanced at Greer, but she was as stoic as ever.

"You spoke with great conviction when you last approached us," Aldrich went on. "Do you still wish to fight the creatures who've tried to harm you? The creatures who've harmed your friend?"

I turned towards Wilder, but he wasn't looking at me. He was picking at his fingernails, looking bored out of his mind. Honestly, it was a little insulting.

"What other choice to I have?" I asked, narrowing my eyes.

"You can choose to do whatever you please, Scarlett," Greer replied. "If what you truly want is to go back to your old life, we cannot stop you. We don't recommend it, but you're free to go at any time. The Sanctum is not a prison."

It felt like passive-aggressive manipulation but staying here and becoming a Natural *was* what I wanted. *Man, these people were good.*

"Fine," I said. "So be it. I'll train."

Greer smiled, looking a little too pleased for my liking. Turning to Wilder, she snapped her fingers.

"I'm not a dog, Greer," he drawled. "I don't come when you whistle."

"Wilder," she said, ignoring his insult, "you are assigned as Scarlett's mentor."

"Excuse me?" That got his attention. He straightened up in the armchair, his fingernails long forgotten.

"Why else did you think you were here?" Brax asked.

"As a reference on her résumé," he stated, biting back as hard as he could, "not petitioning for a job I don't want."

His words stung, but why would I expect anything else? I wanted to like Wilder, but he just kept pushing everyone and everything in the opposite direction as hard as he could.

"This is not open for discussion," Greer declared. "The Codex demands all Naturals have the highest level of understanding. You are the most qualified to assist Scarlett in her journey."

"So, that's it? The Codex has spoken?"

She nodded and turned her attention back to me, leaving Wilder to stew in his own juices. "Welcome to the Sanctum, Scarlett. Your path won't be easy, but in time, I hope it will be rewarding."

Aldrich and Brax stood, each shaking my hand like it was a mystical signature on a contract.

I was in. I was going to get what I wanted all those weeks ago. I was going to learn how to fight and take my life back. This was the purpose I was searching so hard for. Maybe this time I'd find out who I was meant to be.

"Are we dismissed?" Wilder rose to his feet and glared at me. So much for celebrating, then.

"Go," Brax said, waving his hand. "*Please.*"

Wilder strode away, his boots thumping against the carpet. He was a whirlwind of annoyance that I was forced to jog to keep up with as we left the library.

Greer was right—my path was going to be hard if I had to deal with Wilder's temper tantrums day in, day out. *Why did he hate me so much?*

Once we were in the hall, I sighed and a smile crept across my lips. The same burst of adrenalin that'd seared through my veins the night I'd confronted Wilder outside of the *Hung, Drawn, and Quartered* overcame me. What did they call it? Passionate victory. *Good choice of words, Scarlett.*

"Don't smile like that," Wilder snapped.

"Why not? I won. I'm finally going to learn who I am."

"Here's the thing, Purples," he said with a sneer. "This isn't a victory for you. I'm being punished and so are you. Get that through your scarred little head."

"*Low blow.*" I pouted and rolled my eyes. "What did I do to get into trouble? I can understand you being in the doghouse with your stellar attitude, but me? I get they were arseholes, but now they're giving me what I want, *and* they're helping Jackson."

"You talk back, you used your Light openly, you're different, and your friend is being mutated by demon DNA that has rendered him impervious to alteration. Do you want me to keep going?"

I scowled and shook my head.

"They're being nice to you because you've got something they want. The sooner you understand that, the better off we'll both be. We're tiny cogs in a much larger machine, remember?"

"I've got something they want?" I scoffed. "Like what?"

"They know something's different about you, but they don't know what." He twisted his finger around a lock of my hair, painfully pulling against my scalp. "There's more going on here than either of us know."

"That hurts, Wilder." I narrowed my eyes, uncomfortable at his proximity. He was totally within kissing distance.

He sneered and let me go, putting space between us.

"You think I shouldn't trust those three?" I glanced over my shoulder, but we were alone. "What are they called anyway? The council, elders, tories?"

"Arseholes."

"What did they do to you?" I asked straight up. "Or should I be asking, what did you do to them?"

"Maybe one day I'll tell you," he said darkly. "But for now, don't trust anyone, Purples. Not even me. If there's only one lesson I can get through your thick skull, then make it that one."

"I don't understand this world, Wilder," I argued. "I don't…"

He turned and stepped into my personal space again, lowering his lips towards my ear. He was so close, I could smell his cologne again—spice, male sweat, and something else… something metallic.

"A demon who can alter human DNA has been stalking you," he murmured, his breath tickling my ear. "Then add in all those other things, the Balan who was present when your parents died, your purple

Light, and your immunity to alteration, and you've got one hell of a conspiracy beginning to take shape… and you're at the centre of it."

"But… you said I wasn't special. And how do you know about my parents?"

He ignored me, much to my ire. "There's one of those things they don't know about yet."

I drew in a shaky breath, the gravity of the situation finally making sense. Was I right to keep the hue of my Light a secret? It was looking that way, but Wilder also said not to trust anyone, including him.

"Something more is going on, and they're going to try to use me to get to you," he whispered.

"This is going from bad to worse," I murmured, trying not to panic.

I had no idea what to do. Did I escape, play along, or confront them? It wasn't an easy decision, not with Jackson still locked up in the vaults at the mercy of his strange mutation.

"You've been given permission to train," Wilder said, straightening up, his voice returning to its normal volume. "So that's what you'll do."

I had no other choice but to agree. I'd gone from being special, to being kicked out and used as bait, then welcomed back into the fold by Greer, the protector of the Codex, herself. There was more to this than I understood… and I intended to force Wilder to help me. I'd learn everything I could, train every second I was able, I'd forgo sleep if it meant I could master my Light. Then, when I'd gathered my strength, I'd find out the truth about everything.

There was no way in hell I was going to let anyone make me their tool.

"Fine," I hissed, "I'll train. I'll play along, but if you think, even for one second, that I'll—"

"Don't be so dramatic, Purples," he interrupted with a smirk. "It's not all about you."

He strode off, whistling to himself, leaving me in the middle of the hallway, staring after him in shocked silence. *What the hell just happened?*

"Wait!" I cried. "Where am I supposed to go? What time do we start? Do I need a textbook? *Wilder!*" He disappeared around the corner, leaving me standing all alone. "Wilder?"

14

———

The Sanctum was eerie at five in the morning.

The building was rather empty most times, but even more so at an hour no one in their right mind should be awake at. Well, unless you'd been out all night and were finally dragging yourself home. I'd had more than my fair share of those experiences.

Last night, Wilder had sent me a text message—I had no idea how he had my number—demanding my presence on the third-floor at this precise, and ungodly, hour. I'd thought I'd seen everything the Sanctum had to offer, but it appeared I'd missed one vital part—the gallery.

I peered into the first room, tucked away in a lonely corner of the third-floor, and I couldn't help but feel like I was some place I shouldn't be. Art galleries were cool and all, but this one seemed private and not for outside eyes. I was now a Natural in training, but I still felt as if I existed just outside the sphere of belonging.

The room was dimly lit, the charcoal grey-colour of the walls darkening it even further. Paintings hung at precise intervals, each of the ornate golden frames lit with tiny LED spotlights. There were a mixture of portraits, landscapes, and battle scenes, each differing in era and style. Men were depicted with ruffled collars, suits of armour, and riding rearing stallions. Surprisingly, the women were much the same. An odd dress showed up in a portrait or two, but there were sword-wielding maidens amongst the male soldiers on the battlefields too. *Hm, they were a progressive lot.*

My footsteps echoed softly as I walked through the first room, wondering about the people around me. They were obviously Naturals, but who were they?

I moved into the second space and found more paintings, which were larger, taking up most of the space on the walls they hung on. Wilder stood in front of a landscape of a castle, the canvas at least a foot taller than he was.

He was wearing his standard black T-shirt, the material clinging across his chest, leaving nothing to the imagination. Were his biceps bigger? They seemed bigger.

His gaze lowered as I approached, and I squirmed, feeling self-conscious. Wrapping my arms around my middle, I glanced at the painting, wishing I'd had a baggier T-shirt. The Natural 'uniform' was very *clingy*.

"You're late," he snapped, his voice loud in the silence.

"Why are we here?" I asked, staring at the painting.

"If you truly want to be one of us, then you have to understand where you come from," Wilder replied. "Let's call this History 101." He pointed at the image. "What do you see?"

The painting depicted a grand castle on a rocky plateau which overlooked rolling green fields and forests. Stone walls and towers stretched up into the blue sky, and red and gold flags twisted in the imaginary wind. Banners hung either side of the gatehouse—three gold crowns on a field of crimson—the open portcullis leading into the inner bailey where a series of mounted knights were assembled. It was a detailed snapshot of a grand medieval fortress.

"A castle?" I wondered what the catch was.

"Wrong. It's not just a castle, it's Camelot."

I raised my eyebrows. "I've come to terms with the whole demon and Light thing, but Camelot?" I wanted to scoff because everyone knew Arthurian legends were just that. Legends.

"The stories are mostly fabrications twisted by the ages, but the people who lived there were as real as you and me."

"They were Naturals?"

Wilder nodded and moved me to the next painting. It was a portrait of a woman with long flowing hair, her blonde tresses twisted into braids and dotted with tiny white flowers. She stood within the waters of a blue pond, her cream robes draped around her body and disappeared into the water. The background was a forest of emerald green, untameable and filled with the promise of fairies and wild beasts. In her hands, she held an ornate sword, its tip disappearing into the waters at her feet.

"She's the woman I see everywhere," I said. "She's in the skylight in my room. Who is she?"

"That's the Lady of the Lake."

"Really? It's getting very Arthurian in here," I declared.

"Our history has been fictionalised for human consumption many times over the years," Wilder drawled. "There's a hint of truth in it, but they left out the demons and focused on the knights and romances."

The word 'romances' sounded weird coming from Wilder, and I found myself flushing at the thought of him 'romancing' someone.

"Who was she?" I nodded towards the painting.

"No one knows for sure," he replied with a shrug. "We do know she gifted both Excalibur and Arondight to the Naturals."

"Wait, there's two swords? I thought there was only Arondight?"

"Our history says Excalibur was destroyed. Not long after, Arondight was lost, but that's another story."

I blew a loose strand of hair out of my eyes. "You don't know very much."

"Much of our history was lost in the cataclysm of 1185."

"Cataclysm?"

"The Naturals of Camelot were able to defeat the first wave of demons that invaded Earth, and those battles were the basis of the Arthurian legends, but the enemy wasn't gone for good. When the demons inevitably rose again, they caught the Naturals unawares. The scourge overran Camelot, and all those within were wiped off the map. Excalibur was shattered, the Naturals were splintered, and the demonic horde has been on Earth ever since."

Greer had told me about the delicate balance between the two forces when I'd first arrived at the Sanctum. Over a thousand years had passed, and the Naturals had never been able to fully recover their power. I gathered they needed Excalibur and Arondight, and since the former was supposedly shattered, I understood why they wanted to find Arondight so badly.

"The Holy Grail?" I asked, thinking about the stories I knew.

"They were searching for Arondight, not the Grail."

"Oh… What about before?" I wondered. "Where did the Naturals come from?"

Wilder shrugged. "This is all we know. Our origins are lost."

I frowned as a wave of sadness washed over me. To not know where your people came from must be awful. I knew all about that and knowing that the history of the Naturals before me was just as hazy didn't fill me with the reassurance I was craving.

Instead of wallowing, I changed the subject.

"Where does the Codex come in? I asked Greer about it the first time I was here, but she didn't say much."

"The Codex was created in the ashes of Camelot," Wilder explained. "It's the only record we have of our faith, history, and origins. It contains all our secrets, our triumphs… and our failures." He gestured to a third painting that depicted men and women overlooking an ornate tome on a table. Rays of light shone from its pages, marking it as a holy relic. "It is protected here, under the care of Greer. She was appointed to decipher and govern its power so we might live to fight another day."

"What's with you and Greer?" I asked.

"There's nothing with me and Greer."

I rolled my eyes and glanced away, studying the sword in the Lady of the Lake painting. He challenged her at every turn, was abrasive as hell, and if I wasn't mistaken, she secretly liked it. The notion of a forbidden affair popped into my mind, and I was taken aback by the pang of jealousy that stabbed me in the heart.

"We like to push each other's buttons, Purples," he shot back. "Challenging authority gets me off."

Yeah, got him off inside her.

I swallowed hard, brushing away my stupid hormones and turned to face him. "So what now, boss? Do I have to write an essay about the history of the Naturals?"

Wilder smirked and walked away, gesturing for me to follow. "In these rooms are paintings of notable Naturals and the battles fought over the last thousand years. This is our past, and it shouldn't be forgotten, but we have the future to worry about. Things are changing, the balance is tipping, and we need to be ready."

I clenched my fists and nodded, though a twist of dread tightened my stomach. I'd seen some confronting things in my journey to the Sanctum, but something told me those were nothing compared to what else was lurking out there.

Wilder led me downstairs to the gym, my footsteps dogged by images of demons and burning castles. Were things really that dire? I didn't understand how demons could exist while no one knew about them.

As I weaved past a weight machine, I was suddenly aware that I was being watched. Forced to cross the room and bear the brunt of curious stares from a few early risers, I focused on Wilder's back. I didn't like being the anomaly, and I especially bristled at the thought of being the subject of the Sanctum's gossip. I wished Romy had kept that tidbit to herself.

Before I panicked and broke into a full-on sprint, Wilder closed us in a private room, cutting off my escape route. At least we were alone. There were so many questions I wanted to ask him—like why my Light was a funky colour, whose side was the right side, and was I in some kind of danger from within the Sanctum. The mention of conspiracies and secrets hidden in my past were burning a hole in my 'need-to-know' pocket.

Blowing out a sigh of relief, I studied the room.

Racks of weapons lined one wall, and I approached them, all the pointy bits intimidating as hell.

"These are the basic tools of a Natural," Wilder said, gesturing to the array. "While we have few specialised weapons that mortally wound demons, it's beneficial to learn how to fight with everything and anything."

I stood in front of a display of ornate hilts. Some were pure metal while others were wrapped with leather, but all of them had a cross guard and pommel like a traditional sword would.

"These are arondight blades?"

He nodded. "There are several styles. While any Natural can activate one, hilts are forged to fit the grip of their owners. They are a very personal weapon."

"So, I'll get my own?" I asked, running my fingers across the hilts.

"In time." He nodded to the next rack. "These daggers are made out of cold iron. When pierced in the correct fashion, demons are forced out of the possessed."

"Cold iron? What's that? You refrigerate it first?"

"No, it means it's iron mined from a meteorite that fell to Earth."

"Why is it cold then?"

Wilder pinched the bridge of his nose. "It's not literally cold, Scarlett."

I snorted and picked up a dagger, feeling the weight of it in my palm. Wilder must've used one of these on Blond Tips that fateful night outside *8-bit*.

"When do I get to learn how to use them?"

"Not today." Wilder snatched the dagger out of my hand. "So far, you've proven yourself to be nothing but a Mary Sue, and quite frankly, I call bullshit."

"That's insulting," I said. "I'm pretty sure I can't do everything, thank you very much. If anything, I'm Scully and you're Mulder."

"I beg to differ," Wilder declared, "I'm Scully and *you're* Mulder."

"No, I'm Scully because she's more level-headed. Mulder is the crazy one."

"From where I'm standing, you're looking like the crazy one in the equation."

"*Wilder!*"

"Let's see how Mary Sue you are, *Mulder*," he said, tossing me a wooden sword.

My fingers grazed it, and it slipped and fell onto the floor with a clatter. "See? There's no Mary Sue in this room. I suck at hand-eye coordination."

"Pick it up," he commanded.

Grasping the sword, I held it up. I had no idea what he wanted me to do with it, so I just stood there like a lump.

Wilder kicked off his boots and moved out onto the mat. "Try to hit me."

"Try to hit you?" I repeated lamely.

"You wanted to fight back. Well, Purples, show me what you've got."

I made a face and pulled off my boots, tossing my socks over my shoulder. Padding out onto the mat, I held the wooden practice sword up. How did I do this? Just swipe it at him? The thought of slapping him down was too good to be true, and I knew the catch was going to hurt, but I gave it my best shot anyway.

I swung with all my strength, and Wilder twisted, bringing his sword back to meet mine. They clacked together so hard that I lost my grip, the sword fell and I followed it.

I landed with an *oomph*, and he cocked an eyebrow.

"That was lame."

I groaned and scrambled to my feet. "I don't know anything about fighting with a sword. Well, except for the slice and stab part."

"This exercise isn't about that," he said. "It's about instinct. Now, try again."

I lunged, and Wilder's sword slammed into mine with a *clack*. I pushed against him, but the wooden hilt slipped from my grasp and I stumbled forward. A second later, I was whacked on the arse with the flat of his practice blade.

"*Ow*," I complained, rubbing my left cheek.

Wilder kicked my sword back towards me. "Again."

Picking it up, I readied myself for another arse whooping. This time, I waited and considered my options before striking, but when I finally took a swing, I was rapped on the side.

"Dead," he declared.

Grimacing, I felt anger start to rise and tried again. Then again and again. Every time Wilder knocked me down, I got back up, determined to not let him win. I landed on my side, jarred my shoulder, twisted my knee, fell flat on my back, bruised my arse, and hit my funny bone all before Wilder finally confiscated the wooden sword from me.

"It was a fluke," he declared, setting the swords back into the bracket on the wall.

"What was a fluke?" I demanded, panting and wiping the sweat off my forehead.

"Killing that demon on our evening run through Moorgate."

"Hang on a second, I—"

"I'm here to train you to become a Natural, Scarlett," he interrupted, his brow creasing. *Man, he was pissed at me.* "I won't listen to your excuses. I've been training my whole life, you've been here a single morning. If you don't want to die on your first mission, then shut up and listen."

I swallowed hard and shrunk away from him.

"Watch, listen, learn," he said, "and have a little patience. A sword is nothing without the wisdom to wield it."

Oh my God, he was Yoda. Yeah, if Yoda was a six-foot-two arsehole wrapped in punk rock hipster paper with an anarchy bow stuck on top, then I guess that's what Wilder was. I was beginning to see why Greer paired me with him, despite his ominous whisperings in my ear the previous day.

"Why are you looking at me like that?" he demanded with a scowl.

Realising I was staring, and had been for a full minute, I blinked. "What now, boss?"

He sighed and raked his hand through his hair. "Cardio."

"Cardio?" I imagined running on a treadmill and lifting weights, and my enthusiasm level dropped.

"*Cardio*." He narrowed his eyes, signalling it wasn't open for discussion, and snatched up his water bottle.

There were so many questions I wanted to ask him, but if we went out into the gym, we wouldn't be alone.

"But," I began.

"But what?"

There'd never been a chance to bring it up until now.

"Wilder…"

He turned and walked back towards me. From the look on his face, I gathered he expected I was about to make another excuse.

"Why is my Light purple?" I blurted.

He stilled and then picked up a strand of my hair. I tensed, the gesture too intimate for a guy like him. Especially when he made his annoyance at my presence abundantly clear every chance he got.

"Why is your hair purple?" he asked, and I shrugged. "*Exactly*."

"I never told anyone. I got the feeling that it wasn't… normal. Not that any of this is, but I don't think I can cope with being super-supernatural."

"Good, you should keep it to yourself. Around here, people who are different…" He sniffed and glanced away, his expression hardening. "You won't need to reveal your Light for some time. There're stages of training you need to complete before you can even think of learning those basics. We have time to figure it out."

"Am I in some sort of trouble?"

He shook his head. "No, but this is a complicated world, Purples. There's a fine line between Light and Dark, and no one ever took into consideration those that live in the shadows."

I narrowed my eyes and nodded. I got it more than he realised. Shadows didn't fit in a black and white world. They needed both light and darkness to exist and their mere presence threatened both worlds. There was something different about me, but until I understood where I fit in the hierarchy of the Naturals, I'd have to play it safe.

"Do you live in those shadows?" I asked, thinking about all the gossip I'd heard about him.

Wilder grunted and narrowed his eyes. "The less you know about me, the better."

"How old are you?"

"Thirty-one."

"Really? I thought you were pre-pubescent."

"You're not getting out of cardio, Purples. Adrenalin only gets you so far." He pointed towards the door. "*Out.*"

I pouted and strode past him into the gym where I became intimately acquainted with the treadmill. As my feet pounded and my lungs burned, I was painfully aware of the spectacle my presence had created. I was the elephant in the room, physically and metaphorically.

Ignoring the prying eyes, I focused on the wall in front of me. I couldn't lose my nerve on day one.

And Wilder… Could I trust him? I felt like we'd shared something after our reluctant adventures together, and I wasn't talking about the colony of butterflies I was incubating in his name. He'd warned me about exposing my Light, then implied that he'd help me.

Glancing over my shoulder, my stomach fluttered as I watched him lift a set of weights. His muscles tensed, and I swallowed hard.

Whose side was he on?

The next week went by in much the same fashion. Wilder beat my arse—in a non-sexual way—and I worked out until I either threw up in the corner or collapsed.

Mornings were for stretching, cardio, and strength training, afternoons were a mixture of hand-to-hand combat and theory like Demonology: How to Spot and Identify. We were nowhere near starting the unit on maim and kill yet.

I did know the smoke demons who possessed humans were called Infernals. The spider-like creature we'd fought in Moorgate was a lesser demon who impersonated a human but didn't use possession. Their bodies were solid and awkward, though they had little intelligence. Wilder called them foot soldiers, or 'cannon fodder'. There were also many kinds of greater demons. They were more powerful, smarter, had their own version of Light, and appeared to be just like us, though some had certain extremities that were very *demon*. Balan were one kind, but not the highest in the ranks of Darkness.

By the end of the seventh day, things had finally started to get easier as I settled into the punishing routine Wilder had set for me. My least favourite part was dinner. And lunch. Oh, and breakfast.

The kitchen had been given strict instructions on what food I was allowed to eat, so that evening, like a special snowflake, I collected my pre-prepared meal and turned to find some place to sit. Wilder had said something about muscle and protein and another thing about fat, all of which went over my head. All I knew, was that I was forbidden from eating anything that'd been dipped into a deep fryer or rolled in powdered sugar. *Pizza night was out then.*

Romy, Martin, Alo, and Valeria were sitting at the middle table, laughing and chattering amongst themselves. When Romy saw me balancing my tray and staring out across the kitchens, she waved me over.

"You okay?" she asked, raising her eyebrows as I perched gingerly in an empty chair.

"My bruises have bruises." I winced as I tried to find a portion of my butt cheeks that didn't hurt when I sat.

"He's a tough mentor," she replied, smothering a

laugh. "Sometimes I don't think Wilder knows what pain is."

"Then there's the bit where I suspect he lost his taste buds." I stabbed my fork into a spear of steamed asparagus and held it aloft with a grimace.

"Sucks," Valeria said.

"Huh?" My forehead creased.

"Having to train with Wilder," Alo replied.

"I'd rather choke on demon vomit than train with him," Martin added, sinking his boot in for good measure. "Be careful, Scarlett."

"Careful of what? His stellar personality?"

The Naturals laughed as if I'd told the funniest joke of all time.

"Be careful he doesn't lead you astray," Valeria explained. "Stick to the Codex and you'll be fine."

"Okay, is this the part where I panic?"

"Wilder has his own idea of what the Codex looks like," Romy said. "Don't stress too much about it."

"I'm being tested, aren't I?" I groaned and began to furiously slice the chicken breast on my plate. "I knew it."

"It's going to be harder for you, that's for sure." Alo shrugged and went back to his meal, shovelling food into his mouth.

I drifted off as the others started to talk about the comings and goings of the Sanctum. Scoffing down my dinner, I was hardly aware of their tales of demon fights, exorcisms, and routine patrols out in the city. Usually, I'd be all over it, but tonight my thoughts were on Jackson.

I'd been doing the bad friend thing again. Night after night, I'd only been able to drag myself to my room before I collapsed, so I hadn't been to see him since I'd recovered from my Light hangover. Wilder kept telling me he was fine and if anything changed, Ramona would let me know, but I'd made him a promise. I'd go to see him when I could, but a week? It was far too long to leave him down there alone. *Alone and mutating.*

Saying bye to the table to Naturals, I dropped off my empty tray and made my way downstairs, my thighs protesting with every step.

Two flights of stairs later, I shuffled into the vault and crumpled against the bars of Jackson's cell.

"You didn't come back," he said, not turning around.

"I'm sorry," I replied, my limbs like jelly. "They put me into training and Wilder's been brutal. I'm one big bruise."

"Wilder?" Jackson turned, and my heart sank when I saw the anger in his eyes—eyes that flashed *silver.*

I nodded and curled my hands around the bars. The metal was cool against my skin, but Jackson's glare burned straight through me.

"It's been a week since I've seen you," he said, "or at least I think it has. I haven't seen daylight in so long, I'm not even sure if there is a sun anymore. There could have been a nuclear holocaust for all I know."

"*Jackson...*" I shook the bars, but they didn't

budge. *Damn this cell.* "I'm sorry, okay? The schedule they've got me on is more than I can handle. Five in the morning until eight at night."

"You're going to be one of them?" He looked aghast and it kind of hurt.

"Yeah," I muttered.

"Scarlett…"

I waited, my eyes prickling with tears.

"Ah, Scarlett." A familiar singsong voice filled the metallic room, reverberating back and forth. "I haven't seen you in a while. How is your training going?"

I spun on my heel and came face to face with Greer. Perfect Greer, who'd come down from her exalted position sitting on the Codex to see my best friend.

"Fine," I said a little too sharply.

"I see Wilder has been hard on you," she noted. "That's good."

I stared at her in surprise, then glanced at Jackson. She seemed rather bitchy tonight. I was starting to sense I'd intruded on a pre-organised interlude. Was Greer interested in Jackson? Like, romantically? Absurd. It was just the demon thing. That's all. She was checking on him because her position demanded it.

"Jackson is doing just fine," she said with a sickly sweet smile. "Ramona has been able to almost completely halt the transformation."

"Really?" I glanced at Jackson hopefully, but his attention was on Greer. "That's great."

"She believes there will be no adverse effects," she added. "Perhaps some enhancements, but nothing negative."

"I don't need my glasses anymore," Jackson confirmed. "And I don't seem to need much sleep, though you look like you need it, Scarlett."

"He's right." Greer clucked her tongue. "You should get your rest. Wilder won't allow you to have a day to recuperate. Training never stops for a Natural."

"But…"

"It's okay, Scarlett," Jackson said. "You look exhausted. *I get it.*"

"Please don't be mad at me," I murmured.

"I'm not," he replied, edging towards the bars. "I'm angry now, but I'll get over it. This is a huge, scary thing for me. You've got your own transformation to worry about."

"I don't want to lose you."

"You won't." His voice held a promise. Glancing at Greer, he added, "Go. Get some rest. I'll be okay."

Reluctantly, I backed away from the bars, my heart heavy. This didn't feel right, which only made me stew over the warnings Wilder had whispered in my ear. Something was going on here. Something bigger than me, Jackson, and even Wilder.

As I walked away, I knew I was losing him, and life without Jackson wasn't a life I wanted to live.

15

———

I landed on my back, the impact forcing the air out of my lungs.

Gasping, I stared at the ceiling, my heart beating so hard it almost burst through my chest cavity.

"I can't believe I'm saying this," Wilder declared, standing over me, "but after showing so much promise, you're actually getting worse."

I wheezed, my brow creasing tenfold. After my visit to the vaults last night, I'd stewed over Jackson so much that I'd worked myself into a frenzy. We never argued. *Never.* I'd stared up at the skylight, studying the stained glass Lady of the Lake and wished I could have gone back in time and visited him more often. Or immediately left to hunt down the piece of trash who mutated him the moment I woke up.

So, due to all the stewing, I hadn't gotten any sleep that meant anything, but had gained puffy eyes and a foul mood. I'd brought them along to training, especially for Wilder. Now we had matching his and hers arseholery.

Rolling onto my side, I pushed myself up, my lungs searing. Wilder's way of training was so brutal, and I had to wonder who pissed him off as a child. I guessed he had his reasons for being the way he was, but he didn't have to take it out on me by flipping my poor bruised ego over his shoulder.

"Get up," he said. "Pain is—"

"Weakness leaving the body?" I interrupted.

"Sure. Let's go with that."

Scowling, I forced myself to my feet. Wilder wasn't helping soothe my foul mood, but what did I expect? A lollipop? Actually, now I thought about it…

"Get it off your chest, Scarlett," he said. "I don't particularly want to hear it, but at least then we can get on with more important things."

I wiped my brow. "Jackson's mad at me."

"Lover's tiff?" Wilder shot back with a smirk.

"How many times do I have to tell you? Jackson and I aren't a thing. We're friends."

"You're so blind, Purples. That nerdy little hybrid is in love with you."

"Yeah? Well Greer's been going to see him every day since he got here," I fired back. "She's very invested in him, *just so you know*."

His stupid smirk faded, and I knew I'd hit the right button.

"What's this really about, Purples?" he asked, his tone turning sour.

I sucked a sharp breath through my teeth. There

were so many things jacked up about our current situation, and it was difficult to keep up with all the plot points.

"Jackson's mutating into a demon hybrid," I declared. "And what about the Infernal who did this to him?"

"What about it?"

I threw my hands into the air and scoffed, "What about it? Bloody hell, Wilder. You kill it, that's what you do!"

He raised his eyebrows. "And that there is why you won't be allowed to leave the Sanctum any time soon."

"So, I'm a prisoner?"

"You're on probation. There's a difference. Besides, if you go out hunting with that kind of attitude, you'll get yourself possessed and locked in the vault, too. Vendettas don't usually end well."

I faced the rack of arondight blades and scowled. Maybe not, but at least those fools were doing something. That Infernal was harassing me. Maybe if I went outside the Sanctum…

"What good am I in here?" I asked. "Getting my arse beat, losing my best friend, and suffering through your constant barrage of insults. It's one humiliation after another with you people."

"There's your second problem," Wilder fired back, his voice rising. "You don't see yourself as a Natural. You see it as you versus the world. Has anything I've said to you stuck in that brain of yours?"

"Obviously not." I reached out, shielding the

movement from Wilder, and snatched the closest arondight blade. Slipping it down the front of my trousers, I let my anger percolate. "While I'm in here, the Infernal who ruined my friend's life is still out there. How many other people has it mutated? Ten, twenty?"

"Going after the Infernal is not your problem, Scarlett."

It always gave me the shivers whenever he used my name instead of Purples. Maybe because I knew he was being serious. Serious Wilder was bad news.

"So, your boyfriend is mad at you because you're busy training so you can hunt the demon who mutated him? Sounds like a really great guy."

I pinched the bridge of my nose. "He's not my—"

"If he's so short-sighted that he can't see the sacrifice you're making to protect humanity, then he's not worth it," Wilder stated. "Get over it and move on. He's dead weight."

"Dead weight?" I scoffed. "Clearly you've never cared about anyone but yourself!"

"And there's another reason why you're not leaving the Sanctum."

I grunted and glanced at the door. This was a control thing, right? My life was spinning into chaos and the only solid thing I had was hunting the Infernal who started all of this. I could get answers *and* revenge. Impatient or practical, who knew.

"I need to get out of here," I muttered, my body itching.

Everything ached. From head to toe, I tingled with

the need for action. It was a need that couldn't be sated by training alone. I couldn't see the results of training like I could the blood on a sword. Besides, I could go back to the flat and get some things. I could bring Jackson something from home. *Man, talk about trying to justify my crazy.*

I strode towards the door, snatching up my boots on the way. Wilder was oddly silent as I slammed the door closed behind me and stormed through the gym. Ignoring the other Naturals going about their training, I went back to my room, not even stopping to put my boots on until I'd closed myself inside.

Tearing through the chest of drawers, I pulled out the light woollen jumper I wore the day of Jackson's tournament at the *O2*. It seemed like years had passed since that night and I scowled. Pushing away the unwanted memories, I dragged the jumper over my head, laced up my boots and threw on my leather jacket.

Fishing the arondight blade out of my trousers, I slid the hilt into the inside pocket of my jacket, then stuffed my keys to the flat in the other. Glancing at my mobile phone, I hesitated. After a moment of deliberation, I left it behind.

The hallway was empty as I left, as were all the others as I made my way towards the exit. The air was stifling, the pressure heavy on my chest. I didn't know if that was metaphorical or not, but I had to get outside. Once I crossed the threshold, I'd know if this mission was crazy or completely and utterly brilliant.

The foyer was dark as I strode across the marble. I

pushed the outer door open with a violent jab, almost expecting an alarm to go off, but the only thing that happened was a blast of cold air buffeting through the gap and tugging at me with icy fingers.

I stepped over the threshold and onto the street. Glancing over my shoulder, all I saw was the illusion that protected the Naturals' home base from the human world.

No one tried to stop me. No one at all. It was a little too easy if you asked me, but I walked away all the same.

After weeks of being inside, the outside world had become a strange place.

Everything looked different, it smelled weird, and I didn't quite fit. As I walked towards the river, I knew it was me that'd changed, not the city. London was one of those places that was always the same, no matter how much time had passed. It was this ancient, heaving mass of Englishness that would survive anything—fires, wars, famines, demon invasions. It was the inhabitants who evolved.

Slinking down Kentish Town Road, I stuck to the shadows, avoiding pools of light. Whenever I came across another pedestrian, I crossed the street. The result had been an erratic zigzag across London, but I didn't know any other way to remain undetectable. Wilder hadn't even begun to teach me how to use my

Light, and I wasn't keen on repeating my first attempt.

As I approached home, I passed the kebab shop. It was lit up, late-night customers coming and going, all of them probably drunk. Honestly, I kind of missed *8-bit*. I hardly fit in amongst all the gamers but working there was the closest I'd ever been to liking what I did for a living.

Glancing up at the flat, I hesitated and stumbled a step before coming to a complete halt. The lights were on.

Ducking into the lane across the street, I flattened against the brick wall of the neighbouring building and focused on the windows.

It didn't make sense. Jackson was still in the vaults at the Sanctum and I was here. No one else had a key.

A hot poker of rage stabbed me though the chest as I watched for movement above. Someone was in our flat. *Our flat.* How dare a stranger go through our stuff. At this point, I seriously doubted it was a human burglar, so knowing a demon was pawing through my underwear drawer made me want to projectile vomit.

The arondight blade was heavy in my pocket. If I went upstairs, I'd have to be prepared to slice through anything that attacked me. Wilder was wrong about the way I'd killed that lesser demon—that was so not a fluke. I could do it if I had to and right now, it looked like I had to.

Don't think, Scarlett. Just do.

I tensed, my head tilting slightly to the side. Movement. Someone was behind me.

It was a gradual awareness, like a cold drop of water had oozed down my spine, chilling me as it went. Eyes were boring into my back, and warm, slimy breath tickled the shell of my ear. Reaching into the inner pocket of my jacket, my fingers closed around the arondight blade.

I turned slowly, tensing as the shadow behind me solidified. White eyes stared back at me, the male demon grinning from ear to ear.

"*Boo.*"

I cried out, tore the hilt free, and swung, willing the blade into life. On cue, the sword erupted in a shower of purple sparks, its metal links slotting together as it arced through the air.

The demon ducked, and the sword collided with the wall, sparks flying everywhere. Before I had time to react, his arm flew upward at an unnatural speed. Its palm slammed into my forearm, the force loosening my grip on the sword.

The hilt flew over my head, the blade disappearing as suddenly as it came to life. Metal clattered onto the cobblestones and skidded away, and panic took me.

A hand clamped around my neck and I was thrown against the wall. I collided with the brick, then my body swung the other way and I hit the opposite building with a thud. Dazed, I fell to the ground, my head cracking against the cobblestones.

The demon laughed and folded itself over me, its weight pinning me in place.

I cried out as its fingernails dug into my skin and

pried my eyelid open. He lowered his face towards mine, his tongue dangling out of his mouth. Was he going to lick my eyeball? *Man, now I'd seen everything.*

"Arondight," it hissed. "Where is it? *Where is it?*"

"I don't know!"

"You do know. *You do!*"

I gritted my teeth, desperately searching for an escape. The demon forced my head to the side, its tongue dipping dangerously low to my eyeball. It was the Infernal who'd attacked me and Jackson. It had to be.

"Infernal," I said. "You're the Infernal who's been following me."

"*Arondight,*" it hissed.

I squirmed, trying to work my way out of the demon's grasp, but he was too strong.

"Wriggle all you like, Natural, but you will tell me. Then I'll pry your skull open and fu—"

A scream tore from my throat as the Infernal flew to the side, rolling across the lane. It slammed into the wall, landing face-first on the ground.

"Get back," a voice commanded.

I glanced up at the silhouette, my heart beating wildly. *Martin.*

I scrambled away, my back hitting the opposite wall, and swiped at my face. The side of my hand came back smeared with red, the action making my face sting where the demon had tried to pry my eye open.

The Infernal was pushing to its feet as Romy appeared out of the shadows. Martin wrestled the creature to the ground, pinning it underneath his body. Then Romy lunged, burying her dagger deep into its chest. The Infernal wailed, its arms thrashing, and a plume of black smoke poured from the man's mouth and into the air.

Romy wrenched her blade free, dropped it, and snatched something from her pocket. Whatever it was, she held it high and the Infernal's smoky essence began to pull towards it. The mass writhed and sparked, hissing as it was sucked into the Natural's hand. Then, with a strange sucking sound, the demon was trapped.

Romy snapped the lid closed on what I could now see was some sort of vial.

"What was that?" I asked, sitting up. My gaze was locked on her hand, where I could see black smoke billowing inside its prison.

"Bloody hell," Martin cursed, glaring at me. He turned and began to search through the man's pockets. He pulled out a wallet and flipped through the contents, holding up a photograph.

"You're lucky we came along when we did," Romy said to me.

"Did you really just 'come along'?" I narrowed my eyes and hauled myself to my feet. Flaming embarrassment was now my middle name.

"Unfortunately, Wilder called us when you left the Sanctum," Martin declared, his pride obviously hurt. Obviously, being ordered around by the Sanctum's resident misfit wasn't his cup of tea.

"It took us a while to find you," Romy said with a shrug.

I glanced at the vial in her hand and wondered if this was another one of those moments where I'd been manipulated, but it was unlikely. My stupidity had given them an opportunity to trap an Infernal.

"At least we got it before it could escape," Martin declared. "There's an upside."

"But there's someone in the flat," I said, pointing across the street.

"An illusion," Romy explained.

"Demons can create illusions?" Glancing up at the windows, which were now dark. Frowning, I didn't get it.

"There's a lot you don't know yet," she replied. "There's a reason we do the things we do."

"Yeah, it's all fun and games until someone *loses an eye*," Martin drawled.

The man on the ground began to groan, and to my surprise, his chest was fine. Other than the hole in his shirt, there was no other evidence he'd just been stabbed by Romy's cold iron dagger. No gaping wounds or pools of blood to be seen. I didn't know how that worked yet, but somehow, I knew now wasn't the time for a lesson in exorcisms.

Martin knelt over the man and began to murmur, using his Light to alter and soothe.

"Don't worry," Romy said, "he'll be fine. Martin will send him home with new memories."

"But... if that's the Infernal who mutated Jackson..."

"He can tell," she reassured me. "We wouldn't send anyone away who was soul sick."

"Soul sick?" I scratched my head. "That's what you call it?"

Romy nodded and tucked the glass vial that held the Infernal into her pocket. "Let's get you back to the Sanctum."

Groaning, I leaned against the wall as the unknown man stumbled down the lane to the street beyond.

"You can't avoid it," Martin said, narrowing his eyes at me. "You're in big trouble. Better face the music now, than later."

Romy offered me a half-smile and began to walk away. I had no other choice but to follow them with my tail between my legs.

Wilder was right… Vendettas never ended well for anybody.

16

The lights of London twinkled across the river, the orange and white shimmering through the rising mists.

I sat on the roof of the Sanctum, my feet dangling over the edge. Below, the empty street was dark, the industrialised laneway shimmered where it met the side of the building—that must be where the invisibility illusion kicked in.

"Are you sulking?"

The sound of Wilder's voice grated against my raw heart and I winced. Humiliated wasn't the right word to describe how I was feeling. I wasn't sure there was a stronger word than that. Maybe I'd have to add an adjective to amplify the burning embarrassment at my failed romp through the city.

"Yes," I hissed, angling my face towards the shadows. There was no use lying. I was wallowing big time.

I tensed as he sat beside me, a little closer than

I'd like, his boots dangling over the edge. We sat in silence for a while, listening to the dull roar of the rumbling back and forth traffic. Sound echoed across the water, bringing the outside world to us, but our little pocket of London was isolated, even though we were in the centre of it all. Alone in a crowd—that was the curse of the Naturals, after all.

"You didn't think I'd be smart enough to see your sleight of hand?" Wilder asked.

"You saw me swipe that arondight blade?"

He snorted. "Of course I did."

I groaned and shrunk into myself. I knew I'd stuffed up and hearing it from Wilder made me feel even worse. It was news to me, but I hated that I'd disappointed him.

"Get over it," he drawled.

He leaned back and fished in his pocket. A moment later, he pulled out something and set it on the ledge between us. A shock of purple acrylic hair made my eyebrows rise.

"Where did you get that?" I asked, picking up the troll doll. The last time I'd seen it was when I'd left it behind at the Tate.

"I followed you," he said.

"That was like a month ago…"

"You didn't cry."

"No. I wanted to, but not out of self-pity or anything." I sighed, stroking the troll's hair into a point. "I've been kicked down a lot. Crying seemed pointless."

"It is pointless." There he went, handing out pointy passive insults again.

I closed my eyes and took a deep breath. Having a heart-to-heart with Wilder wasn't the most comforting thing in the world, especially when I knew I was probably going to get an epic knuckle wrapping from Greer and her cronies in the morning. "It's just... I feel so powerless being stuck in here."

"I know you want to find out why demons are targeting you, and get revenge for what happened to Jackson, but you won't solve anything by picking fights with every random bottom dweller you come across. You'll just get yourself possessed or worse."

"There's something worse than being possessed by a puff of black smoke?"

Wilder nodded. "Yeah, there is. It's called death."

His words conjured an image of my parents and I shivered. Sightless eyes were one thing, but when they belonged to your mum and dad? Stuff like that haunted people. It haunted me for sure. Now here I was, in the middle of something bigger and wilder than I'd ever imagined. Camelot, mythical swords, epic demon battles, knights, and magical women who lived in lakes... Yeah, it was wild all right.

"It wanted to know where Arondight was," I said, somehow knowing I could trust Wilder. There was just something about him.

He tensed and glared at me. "Arondight? Are you sure?"

"Wilder, a demon was trying to lick my eyeball at the time. I remember every detail." I jabbed a finger at my face, where the Infernal's fingernails had dug into my skin.

"You'd be forgiven for hallucinating," he quipped.

"It was traumatising. I'm an over-thinker. Traumatic experiences give me fodder for months. It asked me where Arondight was. *The* Arondight."

Wilder looked troubled, but he didn't voice his thoughts. At least not the ones I wanted to hear. "You shouldn't have gone out there, but at least we know why those demons were stalking you," he said.

I scoffed, "Dumb asses."

"There must be some reason they think you know where it is, *Purples*."

"Nuh-ah! Until you did your ninja shit with your sparky sword, I never knew what any of this was."

Wilder rubbed his hand over his face. "Did you? Did you, *really*?"

"What's that supposed to mean?"

"The memories you have of your parents' death… That Balan wanted something."

"You still think my parents knew where Arondight was?" My eyes widened.

"It's possible."

I looked out over the city and muttered, "Then why don't I remember?"

"You were a child who went through a traumatic experience, Scarlett. You likely blocked out most of it and simply forgot the things you didn't understand."

"If I knew…" I sighed and rubbed my eyes. It wasn't like I was keeping that part a secret. I genuinely didn't know squat about the Natural's magic sword.

Besides, Wilder had a lot of secrets, most of which I'd probably never know, but right now it was obvious he was keeping something important from me. He was all vague and deliberately giving me just enough to be satisfied. Seemed like he'd never met an overachieving over-thinker like me.

"What aren't you telling me?" I demanded.

He grunted and shoved his hands into the pockets of his leather jacket.

"*Wilder*. This is my life we're talking about. If you know something… well, I can take it."

"You're very intuitive, you know that?"

"Don't make me shove you off the roof."

He turned, picking up a strand of my hair. He was always doing that. What was so special about my weird highlights that he felt the need to keep touching me?

"Arondight had another name, actually it had many, but one was the Indigo Flame." He met my gaze and dropped my hair.

"Indigo?" I frowned, then my mouth formed an 'O' shape. "Indigo as in purple…"

"I think you came into contact with Arondight, and it altered your Light."

"Are you insane?"

"Only slightly," he replied with a smirk. "Even then, it's debatable."

I rolled my eyes and turned towards the city, my shoulders slumping forward. "That's just speculation.

Even if I did come into contact with Arondight, I don't see why that makes me any different from other Naturals. Apart from colouring my Light and giving my hair some killer highlights that don't need touch ups, I don't seem any different from the other Naturals."

"That remains to be seen."

I screwed up my nose. The longer I was in this place, the crazier it became. Everyone seemed to have their own motives—the Codex, Arondight, power, Light, influence, secret liaisons… Where did it start, and more importantly, where did it end? Evil geniuses always had an end game. What was Wilder's?

"If I knew where it was, what would you do?" I asked, watching him closely.

He didn't reply, which annoyed the hell out of me. He was weighing up his options before he gave me the answer I wanted to hear.

"Would you give it to Greer?" I prodded, going for an easy button.

He shrugged.

"Then what would you do?"

"I'd use it to end the demon incursion," he snapped. "I'd end this war once and for all."

I let out a *humph* and crossed my arms over my chest. "Good."

"Is there something you're not telling me?"

"Oh, so now you're turning my questions back on me?"

"Well?"

"If Greer had Arondight, what do you think she'd do with it?"

"You're avoiding the question, Purples."

"If she had it, do you think she'd use it to end the war?" I ignored him because there wasn't anything I wasn't telling him. Not really. If I told him I thought he was handsome and that I was developing a stupid crush on him, then he'd use it to taunt me for eternity.

"Why are you asking me?" He gave me his trademark blank 'I know nothing' expression.

I snorted and glanced away. "Maybe because I'm trying to understand what kind of person she is."

"Scarlett… do you know where Arondight is?"

I laughed and threw my hands into the air in exasperation. "No, I don't. Bloody hell." I felt the same anger that'd driven me to escape the Sanctum raise its ugly head again. "Why are you always so… so surly with me? Am I really that horrible?"

Wilder lowered his head and sighed. "No, you're not," he replied after a moment. "I'm hard on you for a reason, Scarlett. This life isn't easy for people like us."

I made a face that said 'WTF'. "Naturals? Or…"

"Both." He flexed his fingers and curled them into tight fists.

"Wilder…"

"Spit it out, Purples."

"Will you explain it to me now? Why your eyes shine silver like those demons?"

He sighed, letting his head fall back. Then he turned to face me, his eyes soft. It was kind of unsettling, how gentle he looked. Wilder had always been this strong, abrasive arsehole until now. And I simply didn't know how to handle it.

"I possess certain *qualities* that are inherent to demons, so people assume I was possessed as a child," he said. "But I was born this way, and no, my parents weren't demons. They were Naturals. I don't know why I'm like this. No one does. All I know is that I can do things other Naturals can't, all while being completely… Natural." He lowered his head. "People tend to fear things they don't understand. The closer to home they are, the worse it gets."

"What can you do?" I whispered.

"I can see in the dark without the aid of Light," he replied. "I can anticipate movement before it happens, and my stamina…"

My thighs clenched at the word stamina and I swallowed hard. "That's why you're so good at knocking me on my ass," I declared.

"No, it's because you're raw as hell, Mary Sue."

I snorted. "Do you want to know? I mean, why you're different."

He shrugged. "I stopped thinking about it a long time ago."

"Jackson was altered by his possession," I argued. "Perhaps—"

"It isn't the same," he interrupted. "My DNA isn't altered."

"What I was going to say *before I was so rudely interrupted* was that maybe something Ramona has found out might be able to explain why you can do the things you do. It mightn't be the same, but it might be *similar*. Don't be so precious."

Wilder snorted and raked his hand through his hair. "Bloody hell."

I sighed heavily. *What a day.*

"No one's ever talked to me like that," he stated.

"Like what?"

"Like I'm not contagious."

"Not even Greer?" The words were out of my mouth before I could stop them.

Wilder narrowed his eyes and studied me for a moment, the intensity of his gaze made me tremble. The last thing I wanted to think about was romance —especially not with Wilder—but my gaze dropped to his mouth anyway. *Traitor*, I internally hissed at my lady parts.

"Not even with her," he finally said.

"Were you—"

"Briefly."

I turned away before he could see the colour of my cheeks turn.

"A long time ago," he added, "before she was the protector of the Codex."

"You don't need to explain it to me," I said sharply. "Just a yes would've been fine."

He grunted, and then rose to his feet, stepping away from the edge of the roof.

"C'mon," he said, "it's late. I'll see you back to your room."

"I don't need an escort."

"Humor me, Purples."

I stood and dusted off my arse. "I'm in trouble, aren't I?"

Wilder nodded. "You'll be reprimanded."

"Great."

He led me off the roof and back into the Sanctum, closing out the chill of winter behind us. I stewed over the night's events all the way downstairs, mystified more about the way Wilder had opened up to me, more than the consequences of having my eyeball licked by a demon. Yeah, I was that weird.

We turned into the hallway where my room was located. It was past midnight, and it was dark and empty. Sometimes the Sanctum gave me the creeps when it was like this—all dark corners where ghosts lingered.

Wilder's arm brushed against mine and I tensed, quickening my steps.

"Scarlett."

I turned, gasping when I realised he was right behind me. When had he gotten so close?

I attempted to speak, but the words were stuck in my throat as he inched towards me.

"What?" I finally managed to whisper.

Wilder's gaze lowered to my lips, then his hands were on my face, his fingers twisting into my hair, pulling me close. Dazed, I melted against him, and let him kiss me. I was hardly aware of the world around us as I slid my palms over his waist.

His lips were soft against mine, his stubble rasping my skin as he deepened the kiss. His touch ignited my senses and I felt my Light simmer, the sensation flaring as his tongue twined with mine. As soon as we fully touched, he pulled away like he'd been shocked, his grasp loosening. *What just happened?*

A loud cough sent us ricocheting farther apart. Spinning towards the sound, I gasped as I saw Jackson leaning against the doorway of my room, his arms crossed over his chest, and a look of pure thunder on his face.

"Jackson," I exclaimed.

"Well," Wilder declared, rather snootily, "I can see you have another pre-arranged liaison. Let me give you two your privacy. I'm not into threesomes unless there's two women, just so you know."

"Wilder…" I sighed.

He glared at me and then stalked off down the hall.

"Great," Jackson drawled, "just great."

"What's going on?" I asked, facing him.

"I'm going home," he said glaring after Wilder. "I just came by to see you before I left, but I see you've already replaced me."

"What?" My mouth dropped open and my heart twisted. "No, Jackson. Never!"

"You're so blind," he said, shaking his head. "I tried to tell you for months how I felt, but every time…" He snorted and rolled his eyes. "Now I see I never meant that much to you."

Realisation slapped me in the face and I stood there like a moron, stunned by the fact that he, and everyone else, was right. I *was* blind. Jackson and I had been friends for years, and he was the only family

I had, without actually being biologically related. He meant the world to me, but romantically? I'd never seen him that way. You couldn't make someone love you and it never ended well, even with good intentions.

"*Jackson.*"

"Goodbye, Scarlett," he said backing away. "Have fun with," he glanced around and waved his hand with a flourish, "with your new life. Oh, and don't forget to use *protection.*"

"Jackson, please," I called after him. "Don't go."

But Jackson wasn't listening. I'd just broken his heart, after all.

He left me standing in the hallway, adrift and alone in a strange world, a victim of my own stupidity.

17

My stomach churned as I stood outside the gym.

I was going to be sick. Like, full-on, projectile across the room, out my nose sick. I hadn't been this nervous about seeing someone 'the day after' since the crush I had on David Ivans in high school went viral… for all the wrong reasons. Walking down the corridor past his locker to get to my regular English class was a nightmare for months afterwards. Ironically, I'd been teased over my inability to fit in and their choicest morsel of ammunition was a fabricated story about my supposed devil worship. *Man, if they only knew.*

Standing outside the gym, I felt like I was walking past David Ivan's locker all over again.

I could still feel Wilder's kiss burn against my lips, but unfortunately, I could also see the image of his back and Jackson's cold glare was seared into my retinas. I'd close my eyes, and like a horror movie, there it was painted on the back of my eyelids in full technicolor.

Jackson was into me. *Romantically*. I thought about kissing him and the image didn't mesh. I just didn't see him that way. What was I supposed to do? Force myself to love him? No, it wouldn't be real. Love like that was a privilege, not a right. You couldn't demand romantic love from someone.

I scowled, not sure if I was angry at Jackson for not telling me sooner, or myself. If I knew… I snorted. If I knew, I'd still have to let him down.

The closed door stared back at me mockingly. Knowing I'd only be punished with extra squats if I was late, I pushed into the gym and strode across the expanse, ignoring the accusing glares the other Naturals were firing at me. Squats were the worst.

I tensed as I edged into the private room where we trained. Wilder was shirtless in the centre of the mat, a staff in his hands. He was twisting and turning, his muscles flexing as he skillfully wove the staff around and around. I squirmed, slightly aroused, but mostly embarrassed.

When his pattern finally allowed him to turn, he straightened up and slammed the end of the staff on the mat.

"Wilder—" I began lamely.

"You've been summoned," he snapped. "Greer will see you in the conservatory."

"Conservatory?"

"Fourth-floor," he stated, turning his back on me.

"Wilder, can we—"

"I wouldn't keep her waiting, Purples," he interrupted. "Not after the stunt you pulled last night."

I closed my eyes and sighed. All I could think about was him kissing me and now it was ruined. In the cold, hard light of day, I was nothing more than a mistake to him. I hadn't felt this heartbroken over a guy since David Ivan had laughed in my face and called me Satan's bitch.

I knew this was about me going after Jackson and not him. In that moment, in true Natural form, Wilder expected me to choose and I hesitated... again. In his eyes, it was over.

Turning, I stalked from the room, determined not to let his reaction get to me. Right now, I was about to be roasted by the powers that be. Weighing the two— love and duty—I knew one predicament was more dire than the other.

I just didn't know which one.

***

The conservatory turned out to be a large sunroom that opened up onto the roof of the Sanctum. It was made out of stone, but the ceiling was a bubble of impossibly clear glass. Beyond, I could see the grey London sky, brimming with ominous storm clouds. What a metaphor.

Climbing the wrought iron stairs that spiralled around the inner circle of the structure, I sensed a pulse of power emanating above. I doubted it was

Greer, unless she was going to cast a spell on me the moment I walked in, and that'd be rather unfortunate.

When I reached the landing, I stopped in my tracks, not expecting to find a mostly empty room.

Before me there was a glass case, much like the ones museums' used to house their most precious artefacts. Bulletproof, two inches thick, seamless, and clear it was made to house something priceless. A pedestal stood within and resting on top was a book that… *shimmered*.

Movement drew my attention, and my gaze met Greer's. My heart leapt into my throat and my cheeks began to turn, what I assumed was a lovely shade of crimson. I'd been to the principal's office more times than I cared to remember, and endured detention and suspension without a care in the world, but this was in another league. For what felt like the first time in my life, I didn't want to be expelled because of my impatience or short temper.

"Scarlett," Greer said, gesturing for me to come closer.

I swallowed the lump in my throat and shuffled across the maroon carpet, my boots springing on the plush pile. The Naturals sure knew their flooring.

"Is that the Codex?" Unable to meet her gaze, I stared at the book, trying to focus on the strange shimmer.

"Yes."

"It's very… shiny."

"There are many copies of the Codex, but this," Greer placed her palm on the glass, "this is the original. They say there are secrets within secrets amongst its pages, more than can ever be found. Scribes can copy its words, but not its Light."

I knew this was going somewhere profound and not in my favour. The suspense was killing me. I wasn't sure if having Greer rage at me would've been any better, but I just wanted the axe to fall.

"Greer… last night, I—"

"If you truly want to be a Natural, then you have to abide by the Codex," she stated, cutting me off. "We're not the military, we won't conscript you into service, but the rules apply to everyone."

She was testing my resolve. I could chuck in everything and walk away, or I could stand up and take responsibility for my actions. Leaving the Sanctum was a stupid idea, and I put Roxy and Martin in unnecessary danger. Lifting my hand, I poked at the scratches on my face. *Where is Arondight?*

"What happened to the Infernal Romy trapped?"

"The Infernal is secure," she replied. "It will be studied and questioned."

If it was questioned, then it was only a matter of time before my purple Light was common knowledge. Then there was the little thing known as Arondight, a.k.a the Indigo Flame. What would happen to me? I didn't know squat about either of those things, but it wouldn't stop Greer and Co. from dragging me in for more tests. Wilder said he believed I'd come into contact with the blade as a child, and if the head honchos suspected that too, then I was afraid of what they'd do to pry the information out of me. The words 'withered husk' came to mind.

The more I thought about it, the less sure I was that I could trust Greer with those things, even though my understanding was absolute zero.

"You endangered the lives of your fellow Naturals," Greer said. "Any one of you could have been possessed. With the risk of mutation, it was reckless. To steal an arondight blade and leave the Sanctum…" She shook her head.

There was nothing to like about this situation, but I was better off here than out there without the proper training. It was glaringly obvious how green I was after facing off with the Infernal. I was an inch away from an eyeball licking after a single swipe of that arondight blade.

"What's going to happen to me?" I whispered.

Damn Wilder for putting doubt into me. Maybe he was the one playing me, not Greer. I felt a pang in my heart and wished Jackson was here, but I knew he wouldn't come back. I was on my own again and it sucked.

"Do you truly want to be a Natural, Scarlett?" Greer asked, watching me as I internally freaked out.

"Yes," I replied without hesitation, "I do."

"Then, let this be your punishment. You are bound to the Sanctum and confined to your training. No concessions will be available to you other than those Wilder deems necessary to your education."

"So I can't leave?"

"No. You cannot leave until your probation is

over. Those are the conditions of remaining a Natural."

"And how long is that?" I scowled and glanced up at the sky beyond.

"Until I say it's over," Greer declared, her tone clipped.

A wave of nausea prickled over my skin, and I turned to face the Codex. "What will happen to Jackson?"

"Jackson will be fine," she replied. "Ramona halted the mutation and there's nothing in her findings that suggest his mind is compromised."

"His mind?"

"We believe the mutation was designed to turn him," Greer explained. "Though, that is only speculation. We weren't prepared to allow the sacrifice of an innocent to confirm."

"That's kind of you." I made a face, her forthright explanation not entirely comforting. She'd shown a great deal of interest in my best friend, though right now it was hard to distinguish if it was her duty to the Codex, or something more personal.

"He is immune to alteration and other forms of Light manipulation," she explained. "His senses are sharper, his body stronger, and his impaired eyesight has been repaired."

The way she listed Jackson's improvements made him sound like a super-soldier. I could see how that was a problem for the Naturals. If demons were out there altering human DNA through simple possession, then the balance could tip in their favor *big time*.

"What does this mean?" I asked. "If possession can turn humans… If it can alter their minds…"

Greer smiled, her impossible beauty masking her underlying emotions. "Don't fret, Scarlett," she said. "Brax, Aldrich, and I are investigating the matter. There's nothing to worry about."

I didn't believe her for one second, but I was just the new kid, and I was now on probation to boot.

"Before you leave, I have a gift for you."

"I thought I was in trouble," I drawled. "Now I get presents?"

Greer crossed the room to a table I hadn't noticed before and picked up a black book. She smoothed her palm over the cover as if she was blessing the contents. When she stood in front of the Codex once more, she handed the tome to me.

"If you're to understand our ways completely, then you should have your own Codex."

Taking the book from her, I opened it and frowned. It wasn't the same as the original in the case, but Wilder had told me it contained the complete history of the Naturals after the fall of Camelot. There was no ebb of Light fused within its pages, it just had that new book smell.

I glanced over the passage I'd opened the book to. *Arthur sent the twelve Naturals forth in search of Arondight. Lancelot rode south, for he'd held the blade before. Galahad rode north, his blood singing him a different story.* Another omen.

I caressed my thumb over the leather cover and snapped the book shut.

"Thank you," I said, "for not kicking me out of the Sanctum."

"Not on a first offence," Greer replied. "Though, I sincerely hope there isn't a next time, Scarlett."

I nodded, holding the book close. I studied the Codex—the real Codex—and felt an urge to go flip through its pages. Wilder told me since Greer was the protector, she was the only one who could read from it, let alone touch the thing. Still, the more I focused, the more I was drawn towards it.

The Codex… it… Was it calling me?

"One day," Greer said, studying me closely. "Perhaps you will look upon it when you understand."

I looked at the stairs, the Light in the room starting to weigh heavily on my shoulders. "Am I dismissed?"

She nodded.

Clutching my copy of the Codex, I clattered down the stairs, a strange sensation beating in my heart.

18

———————

I didn't go back to the gym straight away.

Clutching the copy of the Codex Greer had given me, I wandered through the hallways. I hadn't been kicked out, but I didn't feel any better about what had happened. No, I felt worse.

Stopping in front of a marble sculpture of the Lady of the Lake, I sighed. Jackson was mad at me, Wilder's opinion wasn't much better, Romy and Martin probably thought I was a nightmare, and that wasn't even counting all the other things wrong with me. The only common denominator in all of this mess was Scarlett Ravenwood.

Opening my copy of the Codex, I flipped through the pages. Greer was always consulting the original, maybe it could help me make sense of everything. Understanding what the Naturals went through at the cataclysm might be a good place to begin.

Scanning the blocks of text, I was surprised at what it revealed. I kind of expected the Codex to be like the Bible, full of verses and metaphoric language, but it was like reading a non-fiction book, complete with pictures.

Hand-drawn images of Naturals in various scenes were laced amongst the text. Some pages appeared to be Medieval in design, then evolved through the ages—Renaissance, Impressionist, Art Deco. Checking the last few pages, they all ended sometime around the 1940s. Nothing since.

The Codex contained eyewitness accounts, discoveries, personal struggles, and everything in between. How did Greer consult this? It was like one giant logbook and without the Light the original emitted, I wasn't sure what to do with it. History wasn't my best subject at school, even though I knew humanity could learn a lot from their past mistakes. Teachers always wanted me to memorise dates, but numbers and I didn't mix.

Turning back to the first page, I read, *We were born out of the ashes of Camelot...* It seemed like a lot to live up to.

I snapped the book closed with a frustrated sigh and glanced up at the blank marble eyes of the Lady of the Lake. She stared back at me, her stone arm lifting a stone Arondight towards the ceiling. I wondered if she ever felt this rotten.

The dull sound of people talking echoed down the hallway and I turned. A group of Naturals rounded the corner, their black uniforms strange against the refined manor house backdrop of the Sanctum. Recognising Romy amongst them, I swallowed hard.

They were laughing about something, and for a moment I thought it might've been gossip about last night, but I shook my head. Best not to jump to conclusions.

Romy's expression turned sour when she saw me, and I shuffled from foot to foot. The other Naturals glanced at me and kept walking, but she hung back, her usual friendly demeanour nowhere to be found.

"Romy, I…" I trailed off, knowing anything I said was going to be lame to the extreme.

"You disrespected everything the Naturals stand for," she said, staring at me with hard eyes. "We don't endanger others, and we especially don't allow our personal feelings to cloud our mission."

"I didn't expect… I didn't…" I trailed off feeling like I was a five-year-old with a trembling bottom lip, not a twenty-six-year-old woman who should be trying to make up for her massive cock up.

"Look at it this way, Scarlett. There are so few of us left, that even the loss of one life grossly tips the balance towards the Darkness. If there's not enough of us left to fight, then the demons win and our struggle has been for nothing."

I lowered my head, my cheeks flaming.

"Read that," she said, gesturing to the Codex. "You might learn something about camaraderie."

"Romy! Are you coming or what?"

She glanced down the hall as a Natural I hadn't met before waved at her. Glancing at me one more time, she turned and strode away, leaving me standing beside the marble statue, feeling like I was two feet tall. It was David Ivan and the devil worship gossip all over again.

I watched Romy walk away and didn't turn until she'd disappeared around the corner. Then, I was alone again, the silence of the empty Sanctum deafening.

Sniffing, I walked the opposite direction, avoiding wherever it was Romy was headed towards. Had I blown my one and only opportunity to fit in? I'd never really belonged anywhere, and now I knew I was different, I'd hoped this place was it. Maybe it was a case of too little, too late. I was too old to become a Natural and I even then I was too weird. When would I catch a break?

My boots tapped on metal and I looked up. I'd been so wrapped up in my wallowing that I hadn't realised I'd found my way back to the vaults. Peering into the room Ramona had turned into a laboratory, I frowned. It was empty—no equipment or tables were inside, and there were no signs to say there ever had been. Sniffing, I could detect a slight metallic scent, almost as if someone had been smelting iron.

The smell conjured up the image of the cold iron daggers and I wondered where those were made. Surely not inside the Sanctum.

Leaving the empty room, I went back out into the hall. I knew I should've gone back to the gym by now, but I didn't have it in me to face Wilder. The look on his face... Well, it'd been chilling how indifferent he'd been, especially after that kiss. *The kiss that'd stirred my Light.* I couldn't even ask him if that was a thing now.

I peered in the various doors as I wandered down the metallic hallway. Behind each was a cell, much like the one Jackson had been quarantined in, with floor-to-ceiling bars and a greyish expanse of uncomfortable emptiness. There were zero prisoners in residence, which made me wonder where the Infernal was being kept.

Another door was set at the very end of the hall, and I stared at it, wondering why I'd never noticed it before. I thought about it for a moment, trying to recall if it was there the few times I'd been down to see Jackson. It was different from the others—taller, the window set above my head, and there was no door handle. Frowning, I held my hand up to the metal, pretending I knew what I was doing.

I didn't feel anything.

It was just a door I hadn't noticed before, unless someone was hiding its existence with Light. An illusion like the one that hid the Sanctum, maybe?

I wasn't sure how much more trouble I could get into, so I stood up onto my tippy-toes so I could peer through the window. Catching a glimpse of Greer, I gasped, almost slipping on my backside. I fell back onto my heels and immediately propped myself back up again.

A giant glass vial sat in the centre of the room, each end capped with silver, and the Infernal swirled within. It heaved, sparking angrily as it brushed against the edges of its prison. So this was where it went.

Other instruments and equipment surrounded the

vial, monitors flashing with graphs and numbers, recording data on the demon. She'd told me they'd research it to see if it was the same Infernal who'd mutated Jackson. It stood to reason they'd keep it hidden down in the vaults away from the rest of the Sanctum.

I was about to back away and leave while the going was good, but the Infernal spoke. "*Arondight*," it cried in a digital-like voice. There had to be some kind of computer hooked up to it to allow the puff of smoke to speak.

"So you've said," Greer declared, sounding exasperated. "Who is your master?"

"Did you like him?" the Infernal asked.

"Who?"

"The boy. *The boy*. I made him better."

I stifled a gasp. *Jackson*. It was talking about Jackson! So, I was right after all—the same Infernal *was* stalking me the whole time.

I glanced over my shoulder, but thankfully, I was still alone. The metal corridor afforded nowhere to hide, so if I was stumbled upon, I was so banned for life if wasn't even funny. Glancing back through the window, I knew I had to know what was happening. Not to satisfy my own curiosity, but to make sure Jackson got justice for what had happened to him. He might never speak to me again, but it didn't mean I should give up.

Greer tapped her fingernail against the glass, and the Infernal rushed towards her. Nothing happened, of course. It just bounced off the smooth surface and ricocheted back and forth like an angry bee caught in a jar.

"Human Convergence," Greer said, "that's what you're part of, aren't you?"

Human Convergence? What the hell was that?

"You should know… *Greer*."

"That's a loop I haven't been part of for a long time," she replied. "What's the end game, Infernal?"

"A better world," it declared. "*Better*."

"Darkness is not better," Greer snapped. "You will tell me all you know, *filth*, or I will make sure it hurts."

"Filth," the demon chortled. "Filthy in your bed, in your body. Filthy seed in your c—"

Greer slammed her palm down onto a button, shutting off the Infernal's foul tirade. Her head lowered, her hair hiding her expression.

Lowering myself onto my heels, I hightailed it back down the hall and out into the Sanctum, leaving the vaults behind. My head swam with new information, and I had no idea what to do with it.

Was Greer…? Was she a part of all this? Not on the side of the Naturals, but the demons? If that was true, then the Naturals were in big trouble and so was the Codex.

I wracked my brain trying to think of what I should do, but only one name came to mind.

Wilder.

Wilder would know what to do.

It was past lunchtime when I finally made it back to the gym.

Wilder had locked himself in the private room we usually trained in and was pumping iron. I edged through the door, my gaze fixed on his flexing biceps as the dumbbell went up and down.

"Wilder?"

He glanced up and glared at me. "You took your time," he snapped.

My fingers tightened around my mass-produced copy of the Codex and I closed the door behind me.

"Something strange is going on," I muttered.

"Something strange is always going on," Wilder shot back.

I rolled my eyes. "I mean with Greer and the demons."

Wilder snorted and promptly turned his back on me. He was still in a rotten mood which wasn't going to help what I was about to say go down any better. Maybe I should skim over the part where I spied on Greer mere hours after I'd been put on probation.

"I think that Infernal was sent out to possess people to alter their DNA on purpose," I said. "It attacked Jackson because it knew who I was and where I'd end up."

Wilder glanced over his shoulder and frowned. "You think it was trying to send a message?"

"They think I know where Arondight is. Attacking someone close to me is more than a show of power. Ramona stopped the mutation, but no one knows what would've happened if they hadn't. What if the demons were trying to *turn him*? When I suggested it to Greer…" I trailed off, biting my tongue.

"Greer what?"

"She brushed me off."

"So?" Wilder scowled and shook his head. "Greer has always had her own agenda, but she wouldn't allow—"

"And you call me blind!" I exclaimed. "She's hiding something, Wilder, and I don't think it's nice."

He grunted, his brow creasing, and he put down the dumbbell.

"That's it? That's all you've got to say? *Humph*." I crossed my arms over my chest and did my best Wilder impersonation.

"You know what?" he exclaimed. "I don't jump to conclusions. There's a difference between suspecting and outright accusations, Scarlett."

"Oh no, you wouldn't dare suspect the woman you want to bang," I drawled. "She couldn't be dealing with demons behind all our backs. She's far too pretty to be bad outside of bed. That's the only place she likes to inflict pain. Smack my arse, Greer. That's it, baby. Harder. *Harder!*"

"Shut up," Wilder snapped. "You sound like a child."

"Ever since last night, you've been pouting like one!"

He began to grind his teeth together.

"Listen to me," I gritted through my teeth, "something's going on with Greer. I overheard her talking to the Infernal Romy caught last night."

"You overheard her?" Wilder's eyes widened. "You're unbelievable, Scarlett. I gather you're on probation?"

"Yeah, but—"

"But nothing!" he exclaimed. "If you want to see out the day, you better start listening."

It was my turn to grind my teeth together. *I better start listening?* The irony was outrageous.

"Greer is the protector of the Codex for a reason. It's impossible for her to be anything else," he went on. My hands tightened around my copy of the Codex in an attempt to control my rising anger. "There's no way she could be working with the demons. It's impossible. The Codex would burn it out of her the moment she touched its pages."

"What's that supposed to mean?"

"It means Greer has to be pure of heart to even *touch* the Codex," he shot back.

"I don't believe you," I whispered.

"You'll have to speak up. I might have heightened senses, but I can't hear you through your temper tantrum, Purples."

"I said…" I gritted my teeth as my Light flared, *"I don't believe you."*

Purple light shot through my hand, burning a hole into the gym mat between us. Wilder stared at the smoking hole, his mouth hanging open. If I'd been aiming, I would've seared his chest until Light burst out the other side.

"I think you better leave," he said darkly. *"Now."*

"Wilder, I…" My heart twisted and I glanced at the hole in shock. "I didn't mean—"

"*Now, Scarlett,*" he barked.

Spinning on my heel, I fled the room. Rushing blindly through the Sanctum, I wasn't sure where I was going until cold air buffeted my burning cheeks.

The roof was empty, apart from one extremely anguished Natural in training.

Above, it was abnormally clear. Winter was finally mellowing into spring, but that only meant rain was coming. I wasn't sure which one I preferred—the constant chill or the constant drizzle England was famous for.

Sitting on the edge of the roof, I watched the sun go down, the orange orb disappearing behind the cloud bank on the horizon. It seemed like hours passed as I shivered, stewing in the juices of my own shame. I'd ruined everything. Could this day get any worse?

If Greer really was out to cause trouble, how could I prove it? The way Wilder had shot me down made me doubt the conversation I'd overheard. Maybe it was my ignorance forcing me to jump to conclusions. This world was still new.

What was Human Convergence? It sounded rather… ominous.

A screeching sound pierced the air and I slapped my hands over my ears, screwing up my face. What the hell was that? The alarms?

Scrambling away from the edge of the building, I stood, forgetting my Codex on the ground. Looking up, my mouth fell open as an enormous pillar of red light shot towards the sky, clouds billowing around it like they were circling a drain, before the beam disappeared into the upper atmosphere.

I didn't have to be a genius to know what was happening. The Infernal was downstairs, Greer may or may not be crooked, and the demons were obsessed with finding Arondight through me. Now, it appeared they had a way in, and it was sitting in a fancy jar in the vaults. It was a perfect storm, really.

The Sanctum had been breached… *big time.*

The alarms wailed again and the pillar of light flared. A split-second was all it took for the dome above the library to shatter, shards of glass flying into the air. I cried out, throwing my arms in front of my face as millions of tiny razor-sharp spears rushed towards me.

I guessed this was it. Crunch time.

19

I screamed as thousands of shards of glass rushed towards me. Throwing up my arms, I closed my eyes and said a prayer.

Don't hurt too much, I thought. *I've had enough for one day. Just make it quick. God? Codex? Lady of the Lake?*

The air pulsed in front of me and something brushed past my tense body, but the pain didn't come. Opening my eyes, I gasped as the last of a purple-ish shimmer faded, and a thousand spears of glass tinkled onto the roof.

Breathing heavily, I patted myself down, but I couldn't find any nicks or cuts anywhere. For once in my life, my Light had done what it was supposed to do. It'd actually worked—which was a feat in itself—but it didn't help what was probably going on downstairs in the Sanctum.

The pillar of red light still burned, piercing the library like a giant spear of flame. I knew there was some freaky shit out there, but this? This was the ultimate in supernatural bad news.

The alarms wailed once more before they were abruptly cut off. Swallowing hard, I pushed into the Sanctum and made my way downstairs, trying to remember what Wilder had taught me about emergency procedures.

I emerged into the main foyer, the marble glinting strangely. The pillar's light was emanating through the air, filtering through the skylight above. I wouldn't find any help here.

Turning, I let out a curse as I saw movement at the opposite side of the foyer. A humanoid creature lurched from the shadows, its arms and legs bent in awkward positions—a lesser demon. It used to be a woman, or it'd been attempting to pass for one. Its floral dress flapped all over the place and I copped an eyeful of its beige underpants a split-second before it saw me.

It skittered across the marble floor with a wail, its feet slipping and sliding. They really were clumsy creatures, but after tangling with one that night in Moorgate, I knew better than to underestimate its thirst for blood.

Rushing towards the display of halberds on the wall, I wrapped my fingers around a shaft and pulled. Wilder told me they were handy weapons on the battlefield in the Middle Ages, with their spear and axe combination, but not so much in modern times. It wasn't exactly a weapon you could tuck into your back pocket. The two-handled pole was a little too long, and the axe a little too menacing. I called it the stabby chop-chop pole. Needless to say, Wilder wasn't impressed with my creativity.

The halberd came loose, and the top end was so heavy I almost dropped it. Behind me, the lesser demon shrieked and its human-like voice freaked me out. Spinning, I brandished the halberd, eyeing my prey. *Now is so not the time to choke, Scarlett.*

The demon leapt and I swung, the axe flying. The sharp end smacked into flesh and the shock vibrated up my arms. A scream pierced the air as I let go of the halberd. It clattered to the floor as I dodged to the side, the demon landing in a bloody heap on the black marble.

It twitched, a clicking sound emitting from its throat, its white eyes open, and tongue lolling out the side of its mouth.

Wiping the back of my hand across my forehead, I backed away, melting into the shadows. That was only one demon. There'd be more. Lots more. Glancing at the halberds on the wall, I left them behind. They were way too bulky for close quarters fighting. I needed an arondight blade, *stat.*

I made my way through the halls, back to the gym where I'd last seen Wilder. He'd know what to do and there were actual weapons in there. There were countless displays of swords, shields, and ancient arondight hilts in the halls, but they were all useless. I couldn't be certain they'd work and right now, I needed certain.

Ahead, I could see the crimson light of the pillar

filtering through the stairwell skylight. I leaned over the edge and peered down to the lower level. It was hard to see in the dark, and with everything tinged red, it made visibility even worse. I just had to make a break for it.

I sidled down the stairs and into the hall, the emptiness of the Sanctum eerier than ever. The gym was just ahead, but it may as well have been five hundred miles away. This felt exactly like a scene from a horror movie where at any second, something would jump out at me, slashing a knife. I swallowed hard and glanced over my shoulder.

Maybe it was my heightened senses, but I hesitated when the sound of footsteps echoed through the murky darkness.

Something was patrolling the halls, but it didn't feel like a Natural. I tensed, knowing I was screwed if it was an Infernal or a more powerful demon. I had nothing to fight with that could take down one of those things.

I dashed down the hall towards the gym, knowing I'd find some arondight blades in the training room Wilder and I used. Wrenching on the door handle, I cursed. *Locked.* It was open before, but now it was sealed tight.

I could hear the footsteps approach, the sound booming louder and louder. Grasping the door handle, I begged my Light to come forth. I glanced down the hall, my heart beating wildly. It was going to turn the corner at any second. *Open. Please, open!*

The mechanism clicked, and I ducked through the

crack. Closing the door behind me, I pressed my palms against it, willing the same feeling to pulse back into the opening. I felt a wave of warmth heat my skin and I sealed the gaps and fused the hinges. Nothing was coming through that door any time soon.

Turning, I realised I'd walked in on a full-on barricade. The other exit was piled with gym equipment, blocking the way out, and a group of black-clad, arondight-wielding Naturals were milling about with their backs to me.

I recognised Romy, Valeria, Alo, and Martin amongst the group, as well as a few Naturals I knew by name only and others from my countless hours training in this very room. I studied all their faces, but the one I wanted to see the most wasn't here.

"Where's Wilder?" I asked, grabbing Romy's sleeve.

"Scarlett," she exclaimed, clutching her heart, "where did you come from?"

"I was on the roof when the dome exploded," I replied. "What's that pillar of light?"

"A greater demon has infiltrated the Sanctum," she explained. "Something or someone let it in, and now there are lesser demons all over the place."

"The Infernal. Has to be." I glanced at the door, and right on cue, it shuddered as something heavy slammed against it.

Romy nodded. "Alo was on duty when he saw the Infernal break free. It played us, Scarlett. It played us all."

"Greer?"

"It possessed her," Alo said, appearing out of the shadows. "Took control of her and forced her to drop the wards."

"We need to get her back!" I exclaimed.

"I know," Romy agreed. "If they have Greer, they can get to the Codex."

My body erupted in a cold sweat. I wondered if that's what the demons wanted, or if it was a smokescreen for something else. They were desperate to find Arondight, after all, and here I was, all purple and shit.

"Where do you want me?" I asked, ready to step up and fight.

"We're pinned down here," Valeria said. "We need to forge a path to the conservatory and form a ring of protection around the Codex. That's our first priority."

I glanced around the room, counting a dozen Naturals, but Wilder wasn't amongst them. If I knew him like I thought I did, he would have already gone after Greer. All he'd have to do was stab her with a cold iron dagger and the Infernal would be excised… but it wouldn't stop her from mutating. If the demon had sunk its claws in deep enough, it might already be too late.

I shook my head. If the demons wanted the Codex, then they wouldn't risk harming her. Wilder said she had to be pure of heart to even touch it. If her DNA was altered, they wouldn't be able to take it.

"Here," Alo slid an arondight hilt into my hand, "while it's not made for you, it'll work."

I stared at the hilt and bit my bottom lip. If I used it in front of the others, they'd know. Purple Light wasn't exactly normal, but I wasn't sure I'd get a choice.

The door shuddered again, and Martin and Alo rushed forward to brace it.

The remaining Naturals formed a line, brandishing their arondight blades. Romy shoved me behind them and braced herself. The door rattled violently, then screams pierced the air. The sounds of a fight echoed through the makeshift barricade, then as abruptly as it began, everything fell silent.

"*Naturals, stand down!*" a voice bellowed from the hallway beyond.

Alo and Martin glanced at one another, and then began to dismantle the barricade, dragging away the gym equipment. When the door finally opened, Brax and Aldrich burst into the room, both brandishing fully extended arondight blades coated with blood.

Aldrich spotted me and strode over, his fatherly demeanour gone. A ruthless warrior had taken over and he was kind of frightening. Behind him, the others were staring at the pile of lesser demons left sliced and diced in the hallway beyond.

"Wilder?" he asked.

I shook my head. "I haven't seen him since the dome exploded. I assume he's gone after Greer and the greater demon."

"How many?" Romy asked.

"Unknown," Brax replied. "We need to do a full sweep, but the Codex must be secured first." He barked orders, getting the Naturals into groups. Most were sent to the conservatory, and two pairs were labeled *search and destroy*, their mission to eliminate the lesser demons loose in the Sanctum.

"What about me?" I asked, glancing between the two men.

"You need to stay here," Aldrich replied. "I know you want to fight, but you're not trained for this."

It was a nice way of saying I was a liability, and I narrowed my eyes. "There's something else out there," I said grasping his forearm before he could stalk off. "Something… different. It was out in the hall that way." I pointed towards the exit I'd sealed with my Light. "It sounded tall and heavy, not like a lesser demon at all."

Aldrich nodded, his expression grim. "Thank you, Scarlett." Gesturing to Brax, he said, "Go secure the Codex. They've brought a Colossus with them."

Brax's eyes widened, which didn't instill much confidence in me. Seemed like I'd made it in here just in time.

"What's a Colossus?" I asked.

"There's a bloody Colossus now?" Romy exclaimed.

"I'll take care of it," Aldrich declared. "Now, go!" Turning to me, he grasped my shoulders. "Barricade yourself in the training room. I'll come for you once I've taken care of it."

"But—"

"Scarlett," he said, lowering his voice as the other Naturals broke away into their assigned details, "you and I both know this is more than an attempt to take the Codex."

"You… you know?"

He nodded once and then urged me towards the back room. "Arondight must not fall into their hands. Do you understand?"

I nodded. "Aldrich… I don't know where it is."

His eyes lowered. "I know, but it doesn't matter. They think you do."

Backing into the room, I didn't know what else to say. Aldrich closed the door and it slammed home with a thud, making me flinch.

It'll be okay, I promise. My mother's voice echoed in the back of my mind as I began to tremble. *Stay very quiet, and I'll be back soon.*

Aldrich was worried. I could see it in his eyes, but the way he'd cut through those lesser demons was phenomenal. He was a warrior in the literal sense of the word. He'd be fine. *But my parents weren't,* a little voice whispered in my ear.

I held up my hand, attempting to still the tremors. Where did my Light come from? It was just… there. When that Balan demon had lifted me from that box, I'd screamed… and purple light had blinded me. *I'd fought back.* Even as a child, I had the courage. I couldn't lose the plot now.

Glancing at the door, I gritted my teeth. I wasn't going to be locked in a box while everyone died, not this time.

I thrust my palm against the door and it blew

open, swinging around so fast, it slammed into the wall and cracked the plaster. *Holy guacamole!*

Grasping the arondight hilt Alo had given me, my heart raced as I strode across the gym and picked my way over the pile of lesser demons outside the door. There wasn't any time left to ponder the glory of the universe and how I'd been able to conjure my Light without passing out. I simply put it down to adrenalin. I'd hooked into my emotions, just like the night my parents died.

I made my way through the Sanctum, one eye open for the Colossus—whatever that thing was supposed to be—and any rogue lesser demons.

The library, I thought. *They're in the library.* The breach would be the best place the demons could fortify. The other Naturals would secure the Codex and sweep the Sanctum, but Wilder was out there on his own. I had to help him.

I ducked behind a marble statue of the Lady of the Lake as a group of lesser demons lumbered past, knowing better than to try to take them on solo. They didn't catch my scent, and the moment they were gone, I continued down the hall.

I saw the library doors were falling off their hinges when I approached. The air reeked like someone had washed a stinky dog, then lit a fire on a humid day and forgot to open a window. For a moment, I wondered if this was how Hell smelt, like a smoky wet dog. My nose wrinkled as I darted into the library and ducked behind a row of shelves.

There were no guards, so I managed to work my

way over the debris unseen. Overhead, the entire roof of the library was shattered. Rubble and glass were strewn all over the place, books were flung off shelves, and display cases were smashed to pieces. Above, the pillar had waned, but I now saw it was some kind of portal. It appeared to be a hollow tube, almost like a wormhole through space and time. *So that's how they got so many demons inside.*

Hiding behind one of the Greek columns surrounding the reading room, I peered at the scene before me.

Greer stood in the centre of the room, circled by six lesser demons. A dozen Naturals lay on the carpet in front of them, set out in a neat row, all of them unconscious. I tensed when I realised Romy and Brax were amongst them.

The Codex! They'd never arrived, which meant the book was unguarded… but there were two other teams out there sweeping the Sanctum, and Aldrich was facing off with the Colossus, so there was still hope. He'd make it back. I knew he would, but there was still no sign of Wilder.

A man dressed in a dark suit paced back and forth. His black shirt was unbuttoned, his brown hair was slicked back and brushed against his collar. If I'd seen him on the street, I'd assume he was just another run of the mill businessman who'd forgotten his tie— maybe a nightclub owner or concert promoter—but watching him wear a hole in the carpet in the Sanctum? He had to be the greater demon in charge of these shenanigans.

"They'll make fine additions to the project," the man said, his voice grating like sandpaper against an open wound.

I flinched, resisting the urge to slap my hands over my ears. Despite Wilder being pissed at me, I had listened to every word he said. Greater demons had the ability to manipulate their own kind of Light. He'd called it Darkness, but that was kind of obvious. I liked to call it Demon B.O. It must be using its voice to inflict pain.

"Greer," the demon said, stroking a finger along her jaw, "it's time to collect the Codex."

Her eyes were completely white, but a tear trickled down her cheek. *She was fighting it.*

"Your struggle is pointless," the demon went on. "I will have what I came for." He raised his hand and struck Greer across the cheek. Greer's head snapped to the side, the sound of the blow echoing through the library.

Movement pulled my gaze to the other side of the library, punctuated with a flash of silver. A dagger flew tip over tail across the expanse, faster than my eye could follow.

The metal shard imbedded into Greer's chest and her mouth gaped as a rush of black smoke poured out of her. A flash of white Light streaked across the room as an arondight blade arced towards the pulsating swirl that was the Infernal. The greater demon turned to block the blow and I sprung into action.

I brought my arondight blade to life, purple sparks

showering onto the carpet as I sprinted towards the danger zone.

"Hey, arsehole!" I exclaimed.

The demon spun and I ducked, swinging the blade towards his exposed stomach. The Infernal wailed as the other sword cut through it, a burst of hot air signalling it'd been sent back to Hell.

The greater demon smirked, his body phasing in and out of reality, and my blade passed right through him. I stumbled in shock and cried out as a fist slammed down onto the back of my neck. As I fell, my gaze met Wilder's.

I knew it, I thought. *He rushed in to save Greer.*

I moaned as a boot kicked me over and tensed as my gaze met the greater demon's. He stood over me, his shadow blotting out the portal. A pair of white eyes shimmered into green, and his mouth spread into a grin that revealed rows upon rows of razor-sharp teeth.

It was him.

"Ah," the Balan said, towering over me, "we meet again, Scarlett Ravenwood."

20

The Balan grinned down at me, triumphant and full of his own self-importance.

I was forced upright, my neck throbbing where I'd been hit. Kneeling before the greater demon, I scowled. There I went, rushing headfirst into danger yet again. It seemed I hadn't learned anything. I'd rushed in the night I'd first met Wilder, confronting a man I believed was a murderer instead of calling the cops. Staring at the Balan's feet, I wished I'd stayed in my box and waited for Aldrich.

Wilder was forced to his knees by a drooling lesser demon, its fingers digging into his shoulders. He landed with an *oomph*, his hair falling into his eyes. He was covered in dirt and soot, and blood trickled from his nose.

His eyes went to Greer, who was lying on the floor, the cold iron dagger protruding from her chest. He looked to her before he turned his attention on me, and I couldn't help the pang of jealousy from twisting my stupid heart. *So not the time.*

"Scarlett Ravenwood," the Balan declared with a smirk.

"That's my name, *don't wear it out.*"

"You've grown into such a lovely young woman," he went on, "ripe and ready to——"

"*Puke*," I declared. "I like my men with one set of teeth and only a slight murderous intent, thank you very much."

The Balan glanced at Wilder.

Wilder gritted his teeth. "Just get it over with."

"I'm not here for you, Natural," the Balan declared. "But you will make a perfect host."

Wilder tensed and attempted to rise, but the lesser demon forced him back down again.

"Watch him," the Balan commanded, turning his focus back on me. "I have work to do."

The lesser demons circled us as the Balan grasped me around the neck and lifted me like I weighed nothing at all. I felt the fight bleed from my limbs as his touch overwhelmed my senses. I just… There was nothing I could do to stop him as he bore into my mind.

"Scarlett!" I heard Wilder's voice, but it sounded so far away.

The lid of the box opened, and I cowered in the corner as the Balan appeared. He stood over me, a fake smile on his lips.

"Get out of my head!" I shouted.

"Here she is," he crooned. "C'mon, sweetheart." He

reached out and grasped me under my arms, then plucked me from my hiding place.

As I was lifted out of the box, I saw my parents lying on the ground. It was exactly as I remembered it. They were covered in blood, their eyes unseeing. Dead meant forever.

The Balan's hands dug painfully into my sides as he shook me. "Where is Arondight?"

I screamed in terror and thrashed, trying to break free. He was manipulating my mind, using my worst memories to torture answers out of me. Too bad I didn't know squat.

"*Tell me!*" he roared. "Don't make me hurt them, Scarlett. You love him. Do you want me to kill him like I killed your parents?"

"Eat shit, arsehole! You're all talk, you know that?"

"What do you know of Human Convergence?"

I gasped as hot pincers buried into my brain. "Nothing."

"*Lies.*"

"I can't tell you what I don't know," I cried. "How about you tell me what it is? Then we can compare notes."

The Balan roared and buried its hooks deeper. "*Human Convergence.* Tell me."

"Your Infernal buddy mutated my best friend." I kicked, and I felt my heel smashing against a pair of rotten demon balls. "Converge that, arsehole!" *That's for Jackson.*

The Balan cried out in anger, then lifted his fist.

As his knuckles collided with my face, I was pushed to the ground. I landed on my side, stars exploding through my vision.

This isn't real, Scarlett, I told myself. *He's in your head. Fight back!*

"I was there," the Balan murmured into my ear. "I know what happened to them. Your parents died at my feet. Do you want to know why?"

I tensed as he pushed another vision into my mind. *My parents lying on the ground, covered in blood, their eyes open and unblinking.* Shut up, you little shit.

"I can tell you everything you want to know," the Balan crooned. "All you have to do is give me Arondight."

"I don't know where Arondight is."

"Yes, you do. You've seen it, Scarlett. You've been touched by its flame."

"I don't remember," I muttered, tears welling in my eyes. "I don't…"

"That's okay. You will. I can help you." The Balan towered over me, his hand outstretched. "Just reach out and take my hand, Scarlett. That's all you have to do. Then you'll be at peace."

I stared at his fingers, almost expecting them to have clawed tips, but he was normal enough if he didn't open his mouth.

He knew what happened to them. He knew why they died. He knew all the answers I longed for. Everything I'd ever wanted was within my grasp, all I had to do was reach out and take the Balan's offer.

But…

If I didn't fight back, the Sanctum would fall and the Codex would be corrupted. Greer, Romy, Wilder, and the others would be possessed and mutated into super soldiers, enslaved to the very enemy they'd pledged to destroy.

But…

Let go of your past. Embrace your future…

"No," I said. "The price is too high."

The Balan roared and I was lifted into the air, his fingers tightening around my neck, choking the life from me. *The price was too high…*

I was wrenched to the side, my consciousness tearing away from the vision. The world splintered and the ruined library materialised.

I gasped as I focused on an arondight blade protruding through the Balan's chest. The demon let me go and my knees hit the ground, my flesh tearing on the rubble underfoot. The creature wailed, its jaws opening wide with a picture of fury and pain.

My arondight blade was lying within reach and I snatched it. The moment my hand curled around the hilt, it burst into life with a shower of purple sparks and I struck. The blade arced through the air and sliced through the Balan's neck, severing its head from its shoulders. The body fell to the ground with a thud and my gaze met Wilder's. It'd been his blade that'd severed the demon's connection. *He'd freed me.*

I stumbled back a step as a mass of inky black smoke oozed from the Balan's neck, and another tendril snaked from its head as it rolled across the floor, the open wound leaving smears of blood on the posh carpet.

The smoke rushed together, creating one giant mass, then surged upward and collided with what remained of the ceiling. The plaster cracked, then splintered as the Balan struck again, showering shards over the assembled Naturals, who were now conscious and witness to everything.

The smoke rolled across the ruined ceiling before spilling out into the night, the remains of the pillar sucking it up. A moment later, the light flickered, and then the portal vanished, plunging the library into silvery darkness.

Wilder grimaced, his hand slapping against his side. I dropped the arondight blade, the sword clicking back into the hilt as it clattered onto the rubble, and I caught him before he fell. Steadying his bulky frame, I was hardly aware of the assembled Naturals, or Greer, who was bundled in Aldrich's arms.

"Careful," I murmured, my palm landing over Wilder's heart. I could feel it thrumming, most likely from the adrenalin. *Yeah, Scarlett, it's the adrenalin. Pfft.*

I glanced at his side. "You've been stabbed…"

"Is that where all that red stuff is coming from?"

"*Wilder.*"

"You did good," he whispered, his voice strained.

"You're complimenting me? After I rushed in like that?"

"Yeah… But don't let it go to your head, Purples."

As the library erupted into chaos around us, we smiled at one another, hardly aware the other Naturals were circling us.

We'd won, but at what price? I guessed only time would tell.

21

———

The day after a disaster was the eeriest thing.

I walked through the Sanctum, stepping over piles of rubble, weaving around wet floor signs, and watching crews of tradesmen file into the building. The mammoth clean-up had commenced at first light, mere hours after the demon incursion was defeated.

The Naturals didn't mess around—talk about laser focus.

As I climbed the wrought iron stairs that led up to the conservatory, I was surprised to find it untouched by the chaos. The dome was intact and there wasn't a speck of dust on the crimson carpet. There must be some serious wards protecting this place.

I stopped at the top of the stairs as I spotted Greer standing within the glass encasing the Codex. She turned a page, the air shimmering as the paper leafed over. The vibration pulsed through the air and tickled the edges of my Light—the Light I was well and truly aware of now—pulling me towards the pedestal. This time, I listened to the call and approached.

Greer's head lifted and she smiled. "Do you want to see?" she asked, gesturing for me to come forward.

"Really?" My eyes widened. "I'm not sure—"

"Come."

I took a deep breath and rounded the glass, angling myself so I could see the open Codex. I didn't have the courage to enter the protective enclosure, but here was perfectly fine for now.

"This is all the Naturals know about Arondight," Greer said, looking back at the page before her.

It was a single leaf of images and text, an illuminated medieval understanding of the blade the Naturals lost. It was written in Latin, or something close to it, so I had no idea what I was looking at. I'd left my translated copy on the roof.

"Only one page?" I asked.

"Yes. You can understand why it pains us that it has been lost for so long."

"Oh."

"I wanted to thank you, Scarlett," she said, exiting the glass enclosure. "Wilder told me what you did last night."

"I did what I had to do," I replied uncomfortably, unsure of Greer's standing in all of this. I decided to test the waters. "The Balan asked me what I knew about Human Convergence."

Greer tensed. *Man, I really hoped there wasn't a twist coming.* The bad guys had been defeated—for now—and the good guys relax… then *POW!* They're cut down and there's an epic cliffhanger. Yeah, I really hoped this wasn't one of those moments.

"Now it is my turn to confess," Greer said, lowering her head. "A long time ago, I was part of Human Convergence."

I gasped. "Greer… *no.*"

"I was young, idealistic, and stupid. I believed it would make the Naturals stronger and tip the balance in our favour, but I was deceived. I was unknowingly aiding the enemy. When I found out the truth, that they were experimenting on Infernal demons, I did what I could to destroy the project. I thought I was successful and for years, I heard nothing… until you arrived with Jackson."

That was why she was so interested in him, I thought. *It was personal, but not romantic.*

"The Infernal who possessed Jackson," I began.

"Was likely a subject of the Human Convergence Project," Greer confirmed. "When it came into contact with your friend, it altered his DNA."

"So…" I didn't want to bring it up, but the thought was on my mind. If Jackson was a victim of Human Convergence, then it might mean his end.

"We have to bring him in," Greer said. "We have to understand what's happening."

"I know Jackson," I said, shaking my head. "I know he wouldn't willingly do any harm to anyone."

"Scarlett, Ramona stopped the mutation from spreading. If we can understand how his DNA was altered, we might be able to reverse it. In him and anyone else who the demons harm."

She had a point. I nodded, squirming over the inevitable grovelling at my best friend's feet I'd have to do.

"It seems whoever has resurrected the research has made advances beyond what the project originally achieved," she went on. "Someone who wants the demons to win. This new age of technology… It's a war like none we've ever known."

"And they need to neutralise Arondight to succeed," I added.

"It would seem so. They believe it's resurfaced. With it in our grasp, they would be powerless to stop Light from winning the war, even with their advances."

"So, what will you do now?"

"Every day I do what I must to atone," she murmured, placing her hand on the glass. "I've been entrusted to protect the Codex." She glanced at me, her eyes brimming with sadness. It took me a moment to realise she was asking for my forgiveness.

I shook my head. "If your intentions weren't pure, the Codex would have outed you. I know I'm still new here, and I've got a long way to go, but that's enough for me. The Codex already decided, and as a Natural, I will abide by its choice."

"Yes," she said, her lips curving into a smile, "you are a Natural."

I smiled, a surge of something that felt a lot like belonging pumped through my veins. This was home —the Sanctum, the people within it, the things we fought for… I belonged to them now. They were my burdens, too. Being a Natural was my calling.

"Will you explain something to me?" I asked, tucking my hair behind my ear.

Greer nodded.

"Where did the Balan go? I thought Infernals were the only kind of demon who were made of smoke."

"No, they're not the only kind," she explained. "The Balan can possess, but it can also construct its own body. Their kind is arrogant, so it's likely hiding someplace, reconstructing what you took from it, so we have time before it resurfaces."

"Reconstuct from what?"

"Corpses."

"That's kind of gross." I shuddered, regretting that I'd even asked.

Greer smiled. "Yes, it is."

The Balan didn't look like a mouldy corpse, so I assumed it used its version of Light to hold himself together. I didn't want to know more about Frankenstein, so I shoved away the repulsive image and focused on more lingering problems.

Glancing at the Codex, I asked, "Was it harmed?"

Greer shook her head. "No."

"Were you?"

"The Infernal didn't alter me," she confirmed. "If it had—"

"You wouldn't have been able to touch it."

"No." She glanced at me. "But you and I know the Codex wasn't their main target."

"The cat is out of the bag, I guess," I drawled. "I hate to break it to you, Greer, but I know less about my funky Light than you do."

"You've been touched by Arondight," she declared.

"You sound so sure about it."

"It's the only logical conclusion. Your parents died to protect you, and the whereabouts of the blade."

I sighed, the weight of all the revelations pressing down on my shoulders like a tonne of bricks. Where did it all end? Would it end? The Naturals had been fighting a war that was over a thousand years old. It was likely I'd never in my lifetime see its end. The thought was rather depressing, but if Wilder and Greer were right and I had come into contact with Arondight, then maybe I could help end the violence and banish demon-kind forever.

"What now?" I asked, glancing at Greer.

"We need to destroy the Human Convergence Project, find Arondight, then put an end to this war once and for all."

I made a face. "That's a tall order."

"Small steps, Scarlett," she said. "Wars aren't won in a day."

"No," I murmured, glancing at the Codex, "no, they aren't."

The Sanctum was a hive of activity as I made my way from the conservatory to the infirmary.

Naturals and tradesmen were busy cleaning up the mess—thankfully the demon corpses were removed before the builders came in with their crews—and repairs were slowly being made. I wasn't sure how letting in outside people worked, but I assumed Light had something to do with it. That alteration thing would be getting a hammering at the end of the workday, though.

The infirmary was buzzing when I walked in. The medical staff was a skeleton crew as it was, and they rushed back and forth, tending to everything from small lacerations and broken bones, to full-blown possession checks. It was a sight, that was for sure, and it didn't even include the Light-enhanced antibiotics for cuts that'd been infected with lesser demon gore.

All the Naturals who'd been present in the library were enduring scans and blood tests to make sure they hadn't been possessed, and everyone else had turned up to make sure they weren't infected, either. After Jackson's mutation, no one was taking any chances.

Ramona waved at me as I made my way down the row of beds.

"Scarlett," she said, "how are you?"

"Fine. Thank you for the…" I rubbed my neck, grateful the bruising from the Balan's choke hold had faded. "Whatever it was that you did."

She nodded and gestured to the end of the room where a blue curtain surrounded a bed. "He's still there. Or at least I think he is. He's got a terrible habit of defying doctor's orders."

"I think it's just orders in general," I said with a smile.

I made my way towards the back, surprised to find I was slightly nervous. After all we'd been through? Nerves were the last thing I should be feeling.

Peeking around the curtain, my gaze locked with Wilder's. He was lying on the bed, his shirt off and a thick white bandage wrapped around his middle.

"You can come in," he said with a rasp to his voice.

Sliding through the curtains, I stood beside his bed, staring at the bandages.

"I'll be fine," Wilder said. "Ramona stitched me up."

"How many?"

He shrugged. "Fifteen."

"Cool. Chicks dig scars."

His lips quirked.

"I see they washed you," I declared with a pout.

"I got a sponge bath," he retorted with a sly wink.

"I brought you a present," I declared, ignoring the reemergence of his sharp wit. "Ramona said you'll have to stay in bed a while, so I thought you might need some company."

Wilder narrowed his eyes as I tugged the toy out of my pocket. I set the troll doll down on the side table, angling it so its plastic smile was aimed right at Wilder's head, then smoothed the tuft of purple hair into a point.

"Seriously?" he asked.

"I've never been more serious about anything in my life."

He stared at the troll doll so long, I was beginning to wonder if he'd hit his head during the fight.

"Scarlett… I was wrong," he said haltingly. "I believed—"

"I know what you believed," I declared. He'd thought Greer and the others had sinister motives, but in the end, we were all on the same wavelength. "It doesn't matter anymore. We're all on the same side now. Or is it 'the same page of the Codex'?"

Wilder frowned. "You told them?"

"Greer and I had a little chat and worked a few things out. After my display in the library, I kind of had to, but it didn't seem to matter as much as I thought it would. Aldrich already seemed to know about my suspected contact with Arondight, and Brax… Well, Brax is just grumpy." I smiled, knowing I had Wilder genuinely lost for words for the first time since I'd met him. *And it only took me stepping up for it to happen.* "We've got a lot to do," I added. "Training, Balan hunting, Arondight clues to decipher, and a family tree to put together. And that's only the tip of the iceberg. Will you help me?"

He snorted. "Of course I will."

"FOMO?" I titled my head to the side.

"FO-what?"

"Fear of missing out." I laughed and shrugged. He was all anarchy and screw the establishment, but deep down, Wilder wanted to be part of it all. We had that in common. "Don't worry. Your secret is safe with me."

"What secret?" he asked with a scowl.

"*Shh.*" I waved him off. "It's in the vault."

We sat together for a while, the comings and goings of the infirmary bustling behind the curtain.

"Wilder?" I asked, breaking the silence. "What happened? After the Balan picked me up, it bore into my mind like a drill." I winced at the memory. "The next thing I remember…"

"Aldrich," Wilder replied. "He caused a diversion and I was able to attack."

I nodded. They must've cut down the lesser demons, freed the others, then Wilder stabbed the Balan, breaking its hold on my mind. It also meant Aldrich was a total bad-arse by cutting down that Colossus solo. I still had to figure out what one was exactly, but it sounded horrifying.

"Wilder? What's a Colossus?"

"A seven-foot-tall wall of muscle infused with electrified scrap metal, powered by a ball of Darkness woven by a powerful greater demon."

"Oh… is that all?" I shivered and was suddenly glad I missed out on tangling with it in the back halls of the Sanctum. It also elevated Aldrich to god-like status, knowing he'd taken it down on his own.

"When… What did you see?" Wilder asked.

"I…" I shook my head and studied the hem of my jumper. "It, *he*, showed me the night my parents died. He had all the answers, Wilder. I could've…"

He frowned, then reached out and grasped my

hand. His touch was almost alien, the gentle gesture uncharacteristic. Almost like that kiss…

"You turned him down," Wilder stated.

"*Let go of your past and embrace your future*," I whispered.

He stared at me, confusion clouding his eyes. I didn't know how to explain it to him. When those words appeared in my mind, I wasn't even sure they were my own, but without them, I would've submitted to the Balan and signed a deal damning everyone.

"Scarlett—"

"Thank you," I whispered, "for saving me."

"It's fine," he said. "Don't mention it." He grimaced as he stood, the gash in his side hindering his movements. "And if you think you're going to get out of training just because I got skewered, you've got another thing coming."

I laughed and shook my head, a little pang of unrequited something-or-other tugged on my heartstrings. Now I understood how Jackson felt and it sucked big time. Knowing how well things had gone between my best friend and I, I decided to let my burgeoning feelings for Wilder go. I didn't know when our relationship had changed, but he meant a great deal to me. After all, he was my mentor.

"Scarlett—"

"It's your turn to not mention it," I interrupted. "I've got to focus on becoming the best Natural I can be. There's a war going on, you know."

Wilder smiled, but it never reached his eyes. "Tomorrow," he said. "Today, we rest."

"Sounds like a plan, Grumps."

He raised his eyebrows.

"You call me *Purples*, it's only fair you get an annoying nickname, too."

"You could've thought of something better than *Grumps*."

I grinned. "I did, but it's far too rude to say out loud."

22

THE BIT AT THE END

Scuffing my toe through the rubble on the roof, I uncovered the corner of my copy of the Codex.

Above, a crane was lifting a new glass panel onto the reconstructed library dome, the crew of workmen shouting instructions at one another. The low drone of the crane's mechanism vibrated through the air as I bent over to pick up the book.

It was strange how rebuilding took an age, but destruction only took a few seconds. I don't know why humans are always so fixated on destroying one another when it took this much bother to repair the aftermath—bother and cold, hard cash. The Naturals must be loaded to bankroll these kinds of repairs.

Dusting off the leather cover, I held onto the Codex and glanced at the view beyond the rooftop. London stretched ever outward, a heaving beast full of life and progress. Cranes littered the riverside, building apartment blocks and commercial structures, and in the distance, the glittering skyscrapers of the financial district reached towards the sky, intermingling with older, more ancient parts of the urban sprawl.

I closed my eyes and listened to the sounds of the city. A familiar sensation wrapped itself around me and I turned. *The Codex.*

It was the same tug I'd felt the day of the attack when I'd stood before Greer and received my punishment for leaving the Sanctum. Frowning, I wondered if it did that to everyone. It seemed insistent, like a toddler tugging at my trouser leg trying to get my attention, and the more I attempted to block it out, the worse it got.

Fine, I thought, storming off the roof and back inside, *let's see what you want, Codex. What's one more indiscretion on the epic list that is my growing rap sheet.*

Stopping in the main foyer, I glanced at the halberds on the wall, noting the one I'd used to cut down that lesser demon had been replaced. Overhead, the elaborate domed skylight let in the morning light, filling the space with dreary gloom. I stood amongst the black veiny marble on my own and for the first time, was able to approach the small metal plaque screwed into the wall and read the words etched there. *Let there be Light amongst the Dark.*

"Hey." I turned at the sound of Romy's voice. "What's up?"

"I was on the roof." I held up the book and shrugged. "I left it up there the other night. Luckily for me, it was still there."

"It's a little battered," she said, her voice echoing off the marble.

"Symbolic, right?"

Romy laughed softly, glancing down the hall. "Listen, Scarlett, what you did... Well, it took real courage."

"Actually, it was stupid." I grimaced at the memory of rushing at the Balan like a fool. I had no chance, but I flung myself at him anyway.

"Maybe, but when you're in the middle of a real fight... Well, the rules fly out the window."

I nodded, knowing this time I'd gotten lucky. Without Wilder and Aldrich, I might be dead or worse—like stuck in a one-sided contract with the demon who may or may not have killed my parents.

"What are you up to now?" Romy asked, looking hopeful.

"I'm supposed to be training, but Wilder's still sulking in the infirmary."

"And you're up there picking through rubble?"

I winked. "What he doesn't know won't hurt him."

"You two are made for each other," she said with a sigh, causing me to pale. "Two rebels in a pod, or however the saying goes."

"It sounds like trouble if you ask me. If that's the case, then I don't know why Greer forced him to mentor me." I glanced down the hall, the tug from the Codex becoming more earnest the longer I lingered. "I'll see you later."

"Oh, okay." Romy offered me a little wave and we parted ways. "Hey, Scarlett?"

"Yeah?" I turned, surprised to see she was a little nervous. I wondered why that was? I should be the one grovelling at her feet.

"You want to get lunch later?"

I smiled, hugging the Codex against my chest. "Sure."

Romy grinned and bounced on the balls of her feet. "Great."

And with that, we were friends again. As I walked away, I hoped it was because I was a super cool person, not because I was the chick *supposedly* touched by Arondight. I was still hesitant to claim the title, no matter what Greer or Aldrich said.

The conservatory was empty when I arrived. Greer was likely someplace else, overseeing the repairs of the Sanctum. I crossed the room, my gaze locked onto the Codex, knowing I had time to figure out what was calling me here. I knew I should've just asked, but something about this felt personal.

I hesitated, throwing a look over my shoulder at the stairs. This was bad news. If I was caught in here, I'd be on probation for life. I tried to imagine being on permanent house arrest and I couldn't fathom never going to *TopShop* ever again. I mean, there was online shopping, but somehow, I didn't think the Sanctum had a post office box.

Circling the case, I couldn't see where the opening was. Like the bars in the vaults downstairs, there were no joins or latches. Placing my palm against the glass,

I wondered if I was supposed to know a secret password like *open sesame*.

Open, I thought. The glass rippled, then my hand passed straight through. I made a face, not believing the solution was so easy. Who would've thought the simple act of asking could work so well? I rolled my eyes at the irony.

The Codex shimmered as I stepped within, and I breathed deeply. The air tasted like popping candy. It was weird, but what wasn't around here? The more appropriate question was, what was normal when everything was strange?

Pure of heart, I thought. *Be pure of heart, Scarlett. It's called to you for a reason.*

It was hard to trust when everyone told you the magical book burned. I wondered what happened if someone unworthy tried to read the real thing? Greer said it was full of secrets only the worthy could read. Standing over it, I could feel the power that'd been woven through its pages for over a thousand years, but to me, it just looked like a fancy book in a museum.

"So, I'm here," I whispered, my voice echoing back and forth against the glass. "What do you want to tell me, Codex?"

Naturally, it didn't reply.

"So, it's going to be like that, huh?" I wove my fingers together and cracked my knuckles. "Touch the dangerous book that might burn me from the inside out and *don't* learn from my mistakes. Got it."

I raised my hand, my stomach twisting in anticipation. My fingers shook as the Codex's Light brushed against my skin, and it hummed, inviting me in.

This is what kidnappers do, I thought. *They lure kids into the back of their creepy vans with sweets, then murder them. Don't murder me, Codex.*

The very tips of my fingers brushed against the page, but that was all it took for the Codex to drag me out of the present and shove me headfirst into a spiral of colour and sound. I spun, my breath tearing from my body, and then I saw it—a sword hung in the air before me and I tensed.

"Lady Lake person?" I called out in a childlike voice. "Is that you?"

No one answered, which meant I was supposed to look at the sword. I mean, why show me it in the first place? Funky book calls out to me, lures me into the back of its van with its siren song, then shows me a pointy sword. *Why? Unless…*

The blade was long and silver, its form rippling as if it was underwater and something had disturbed the surface. I studied it closer, looking for clues. The hilt was pure silver, wrapped with Celtic knot work and long enough to be held aloft by two hands, and the cross guard was set with more elaborate designs, each end curving towards the blade and fashioned into sharp points. The pommel—the counterweight that balanced the sword—was a circular design, set with a clear, raw crystal.

As I focused my vision, the blade flared, revealing runes etched into the metal. My brow broke out into a cold sweat, the Codex piercing my mind. It was showing me Arondight. Not a copy or a symbol or a long-lost memory, but the real thing, as it was… *right now*.

"Where is it?" I whispered. "Where…?"

I reached out, desperate to pluck Arondight out of its watery safe-deposit box, but the moment my fingers brushed against the water, I was torn out of the vision and flung backwards.

A blur of light formed in front of me. I was vaguely aware I was lying on the floor, but my limbs weren't responding. The last time I'd fainted—after I'd been hit in the head by a discus at a high school sports day, and not counting the altercation I'd had when I'd first arrived at the Sanctum—I'd had a mean concussion and, most mortifyingly, I'd peed a little bit. *Oh man, I hoped I hadn't peed a little bit.*

"Scarlett?"

I screwed my face up and attempted to sit, recognising Greer's voice. I was in so much trouble.

"Greer," I whispered.

When my vision had cleared enough to make out her features, I saw she looked horrified, and rightly so. I'd done what I was forbidden to do, and what probably should've killed me.

"Scarlett… what have you done?"

"I-I saw it, Greer. *I saw Arondight.*"

Scarlett's adventure continues with DARK

ILLUSION, the second book in the thrilling Arondight Codex!

An ancient war with demons. A lost sword with the power to end it all. And a woman with purple hair is the world's only hope.

Keep reading to the end of this ebook for an exclusive peek at the next chapter...

OTHER BOOKS IN THE ARONDIGHT CODEX

by Nicole R. Taylor
series is complete!

Dark Descent #1
Dark Illusion #2
Dark Abandon #3
Dark Genesis #4
Dark Crucible #5

Continue the adventure in:
THE CAMELOT ARCHIVE

Demons, Druids, and buried secrets. The Camelot Archive is open for business.

Demon Bound #1
Demon Sworn #2
Demon Forged #3
Demon Eternal #4

ABOUT NICOLE

Nicole R. Taylor is an Australian Urban Fantasy author.

She lives in the western suburbs of Melbourne dreaming up nail biting stories featuring sassy witches, duplicitous vampires, hunky shapeshifters, and devious monsters.

She likes chocolate, cat memes, and video games.

When she's not writing, she likes to think of what she's writing next.

Follow Nicole Online:

Website: www.nicolertaylorwrites.com
Twitter: twitter.com/nicole_noir
Facebook: facebook.com/nrtaylorwrites
Newsletter: www.nicolertaylorwrites.com/newsletter
Email: nicole.this.is@gmail.com

DARK ILLUSION (THE ARONDIGHT CODEX - BOOK TWO)

A SNEAK PEEK…

The library was a ruin around me, the ombré portal swirling like an angry tornado through the shattered remains of the dome.

The scent of phantom smoke filled my nostrils and I scrambled across the floor, my hand curling around the hilt of my arondight blade. As soon as I had it in my grasp, the sword erupted into life, sparking with purple Light.

My throat was raw, and my knees were red with blood, but I pushed to my feet and swung my blade with my last ounce of strength. The demon roared with fury, the sound cutting off with a gurgle as I severed his head from his body.

I'm waiting for you, Scarlett.

I jumped as a book slammed down on the table in front of me, bringing my consciousness back to the present. I was in the kitchen at the London Sanctum eating lunch, not battling a greater demon who'd been trying to trick me into selling my soul.

"What's that?" I asked as Wilder slid into the chair opposite. Wilder was my Natural mentor, trainer, and an all-round pain in my arse. "Don't tell me there's bland reading involved."

"You had a lucky break," he said glowering at me, the light catching the subtle silver sheen in his eyes. "There's still a long way to go with your training."

Sighing, I pushed away my half-eaten lunch and dragged the book towards me. The hardcover—simply entitled *Demonology*—was a deep midnight blue with gold embellishments.

"Why didn't anyone think to give me this when I first got here?" I complained as I opened it.

"It's a kids' book," Wilder declared.

Ugh, he was right. As I flipped through the pages, I found illustrations of different demons and simplified explanations for each kind of manifestation.

I shot him a pouty look. "Are you trying to tell me something?"

"I'm trying to impart on you the wisdom of a fifteen-year education in as little time as possible," he drawled.

"Is there such a thing as a spell book? Or is it called a Light book?" I wondered. "That could be useful."

"Light doesn't come with an instruction manual," Wilder said with a disgusted look. "It's a personal experience, and different for everyone."

"So how does anyone learn to fully control it if it's unpredictable?"

"I can guide you, but the rest is up to you." He

gave me a pointed look and added, "I don't know why you're so worried. You did just fine in the incursion. I heard you blew off the doors in the gym."

"How do you know that was me?" I demanded. "I was the only one there."

Since the incursion, the Sanctum had been in high-alert. Naturals had been scouring the city for traces of the Balan demon who'd attempted to take over the building and steal the Codex, but so far, no traces had been found. At least we didn't have to worry about the Infernal who'd been trying to alter people's DNA—Wilder had taken it out after he'd excised it from Greer.

"Romy said there was an academy," I said, stroking my fingers over the book. "Where is it?"

"The Cotswolds." *Fancy*.

"Did you go?"

"Yes."

"And?" I prodded.

"And what?"

I rolled my eyes, not interested in prying information from Wilder so early in the day. "What's it like?"

"Like any boarding school that teaches you how to kill demons." He smirked and nodded at the book. "You better study that, Purples. The alert level isn't going to drop until we've found your buddy, the Balan demon."

My scowl deepened. "He's not my buddy. He killed my parents and tried to trick me into selling my soul."

"All the more reason to kick your training into overdrive."

Wilder was so infuriating. He had this thing where he liked to brush off people with his abrasive personality. He was my mentor, and most days he drove me to the brink of fire and brimstone, but I didn't know what I'd do without him. *I so wasn't telling him that.* Talk about complicated.

I was pulled in two directions. Four if I took my heart into account. North and south were the Human Convergence Project and the search for Arondight. East and west were Jackson and Wilder. Then they all had their own personal tug of wars, which just made the whole thing confusing as hell.

At the thought of Jackson, I groaned and lowered my head into my hands. My poor best friend, who'd been possessed by a genetically modified Infernal demon, had his DNA mutated, and was now a world champion e-sports bazillionaire. He was also my closest family, had hidden romantic feelings for me, and caught me kissing Wilder—something that would never happen again—in the hall outside my room. To say we'd parted on bad terms was an understatement.

"What now?" Wilder asked with a groan.

"At some point I have to go find Jackson."

He snorted and leaned back in his chair. "Good luck with that, Purples. You might have to flash a little boob to entice him back here."

"*Wilder!*"

"He's the weedy little demon-hybrid that's in unrequited love with you."

"He's also the guy who could help Ramona cure innocent people infected by DNA-altered Infernals," I fired back. "Human Convergence, remember?"

He rolled his eyes. "It's always something with you."

"He was the only person who cared," I murmured, snapping the demonology book closed. "After years of bouncing around foster homes, getting kicked out of school after school, and being the weirdo loner, he was the only one who stuck. And now he hates me."

"That's his problem, not yours."

I snorted, which caused Wilder to take away my unfinished lunch and slide it down the table out of reach. *He could've had the decency to ask if I was finished first.*

"C'mon. You can't do anything about him today. Let's get back to the gym." He rose to his feet and smoothed down his tight black T-shirt. The fabric left nothing to the imagination, and I tried not to stare at his defined muscles. "Don't forget your colouring book."

Smart-arse.

I rose to my feet, the bruises on my bruises shrieking at me. What I wouldn't give for a nice hot bath right about now, but *no*, Wilder wanted to humiliate me with more hand-to-hand combat training.

"Hey, there you are," Romy said behind us.

I turned, smiling at the Natural who'd fast become a good friend amongst the others who still looked at me with trepidation. Having purple Light wasn't exactly a normal thing around here.

Romy was tall, muscular, yet lithe, and her skin was a flawless ivory—apart from the black geometric tattoos that snaked up and down both arms and onto her neck. She said the designs didn't mean anything, but I wasn't entirely convinced.

"Greer has summoned you to the conservatory," she said, glancing warily at Wilder. Her black hair was in a loose braid today, which was different to her usual severe ponytail.

"We're going to the gym to train," he said, "it'll have to wait."

"She said she'd like to see Scarlett immediately."

Wilder narrowed his eyes, clearly annoyed it was a one-person invite, and I squashed down an irritating pang of jealousy.

"It must be important," I said. "I better go see what she wants. I'll come straight back to the gym, okay, boss?"

He grunted and stalked out of the kitchen, causing a group of younger Naturals to scatter in multiple directions like frightened mice.

"I swear he gets grumpier every time I see him," Romy said making a face. "How do you handle him?"

"He's not so bad," I replied with a shrug. "You just have to get to know him."

She raised her eyebrows.

"Okay, okay," I said, waving her off, "you have to impress him with your slashy-stab-stab sword skills first."

"If you say so." She laughed and nudged me towards the door. "You better not keep Greer waiting."

"Do you know what she wants?" The only time Greer summoned me was when I was in trouble…and I'd gotten into trouble a lot since I arrived. Not even killing the greater demon who'd tried to steal the Codex had lifted my probation.

"Like she'd tell me," Romy said with a huff. "Maybe you'll get lucky and they'll let you leave the Sanctum now."

"Cool. I was itching for a visit to Primark for some new pants."

She laughed and shooed me away. "Always a pleasure, Scarlett."

Dark Illusion is OUT NOW!

Want more novels just like this one? Check out Nicole's other series:

THE ARONDIGHT CODEX - An ancient war with demons. A lost sword with the power to end it all. And a woman with purple hair is the world's only hope.

THE CAMELOT ARCHIVE - Set in the same alternate Arthurian world seen in **The Arondight Codex**… Deadly secrets. Murder and revenge. The end of the world is nye and Camelot is the last bastion of hope.

THE WITCH HUNTER SAGA - Vampires and witches collide in this thrilling Urban Fantasy adventure. You've never met vampires quite like these…

THE CRESCENT WITCH CHRONICLES - Witches, shapeshifters, and ancient myth collide in this colourful Irish flavoured series! Come on an adventure fraught with danger and forbidden romance… and the ultimate battle to save magic before it's gone forever.

THE DARKLAND DRUIDS - A woman with no living relatives travels from Australia to the other side of the world to find out the truth of who she is…only to land in the middle of a prophecy of destruction.

Druids, witches, fae, and shapeshifters abound in this thrilling magical adventure!

Find out more at: NicoleRTaylorWrites.com

See what titles are FREE at: Nicole's Free Reads